To David, $1

THE GIRL WHO STOLE J.E.B. STUART

PAUL FERRANTE

Best Wishes,

Paul Ferrante

2021

D1213545

For more information on the author and his works, please see http://www.Paulferranteauthor.com.

Digital ISBN: 978-1-7324857-7-8
Print ISBN: 978-1-7324857-6-1

Dedication

To my colleague and mentor, the late Tom Parry,
who taught me the meaning of empathy.
And to all my students during the Mount Vernon years.
I thought I understood.

Acknowledgements

Special thanks for this project go out to Michael and Tanya Brown, Ryan and Danielle Engle, and Marlena Davis. Also, thanks to my advance readers Carrie McCabe, Barb Szepesi, Rev. David Spollett, Emily Sawyer, and Dan Woog.

Especially helpful in the research for the book were *Cavalryman of the Lost Cause* by Jeffry Wert, *Bold Dragoon* by Emory Thomas, and *Confederates in the Attic* by Tony Horwitz.

Finally, thanks to the curators and guides of all the museums mentioned in this book for their ongoing efforts to bring history to light, and the dedication of our national park rangers at all Civil War battlefields across the states.

Prologue

Yes, you heard it right. "The girl who stole J.E.B. Stuart." That's what they called me… on the news, anyway. And in the papers. You know, when it all hit the fan, as they say.

It got so crazy that I just wanted to go somewhere and disappear. But you can't do that in America. Its people want sensationalism. They want drama. They want heroes and villains. They want a *story*. What they ended up getting was me, Didi Diyoka. And, depending on who you are, I might be, or be involved in, any of the above. That's for you to figure out, I guess.

So what happened was, a writer came knocking on my door. He said he wanted the true story of what happened back then, with all the juicy details. I explained to him that I'd already told my side to a lot of people. But this reporter said he wanted to dig deeper and get to the story's *essence*. He seemed really serious when he said it was important, especially in light of what's going on in the country right now.

I told him, then, that he should also talk to the other people who were on the inside: my parents, my teachers, and my friends Heidi, Pierce, and Bad News. Especially Bad News. He promised he'd get everyone on board and provide an honest account of what happened. So I gave in and said okay.

I hope that when you read this, you'll see the situation for what it was, and have a true understanding of me, and what made me do what I did. That's all I can ask for.

Didi Diyoka, 2020

Chapter One

She'd never been so terrified.

The middle-age woman who sat across from her and her parents seemed pleasant enough and had a fairly innocuous name—Ms. Redwine—but that didn't ease the girl's anxiety one bit. However, she had learned over the years how to seem impassive and unaffected in the worst of situations, a talent that was invaluable in her homeland for people like her. Nevertheless, a droplet of sweat slowly snaked down her back, despite the frigid atmosphere in the office being generated by a humming window air conditioner.

Ms. Redwine, who had layered, shoulder-length salt-and-pepper hair and pink skin with wrinkles extending from the corners of her hazel eyes, was poring over the girl's transcript as the large electric clock behind her ticked, its sound amplified in the empty building. School would not begin for two weeks, and the only people there besides them were the occasional janitors passing in the hallways beyond the guidance offices as they got things ready for the beginning of the year.

Like her, they were black.

"Well," said Ms. Redwine finally, "I have to say that this is a first for us here."

Her comment was met with a respectful silence.

"So," she continued, "let's get off on the right foot. I'm Ellen Redwine, guidance counselor for the eleventh and twelfth grades. And you are…Di…you'll have to help me, dear."

"It's Dihya," said the girl softly, her voice betraying a French inflection.

"What a beautiful name," said Redwine, and she smiled broadly, trying to put the girl at ease. "I don't believe I've ever heard it before."

"It's a Congolese name," said her father, who was nattily attired in a suit and tie, in a rich baritone. "It means 'woman who advances.'"

"But my friends call me Didi," offered the girl, who managed a smile herself.

"Then Didi it is," said the counselor. She turned to the bespectacled man, whose short Afro was graying at the temples. "Dr. Diyoka, would you like to explain the circumstances that have brought you here? Just so we can know each other better."

"Of course," he said, in lightly accented English. "Both my wife and I were born and grew up in the Democratic Republic of the Congo, formerly the Belgian Congo. We met at the Université de Kinshasa Faculté de Medecine, where I was pursuing a medical degree and she was a secretary to the department chairman. We married when I was completing my internship at Monkole Hospital in Kinshasa, which is the largest city in the DRC, many times the size of your state capital.

"We were blessed when Dihya came along as I had just begun my practice at HJ Hospital in Kinshasa, one of the most respected medical institutions in all of Africa. Fortunately for my daughter, we have always lived in the center of the city, having access to many scarce amenities that might seem commonplace here in your beautiful country.

"Anyway, I was approached earlier this year by the head of my department, which is pediatric cardiology, about my possible participation in a one-year physician exchange with Providence Heart Hospital in Columbia. As it was explained to me, the American physician and I would live in each other's homes and basically trade places. Are you aware of a Dr. Joseph Buono?"

"Oh, of course!" said Redwine excitedly. "We had both of his daughters here at Stuart. I would imagine they're well into their college careers now. Wonderful family. Please continue."

"Well, the people at Providence Heart have been most gracious, arranging for a leased automobile for me to drive to work in Columbia, which as you know is only a half hour away. Fortunately, I owned a driver's license in the D.R.C., though never my own automobile, as it was unnecessary because I could bus to the hospital."

"And how are you finding our little old town of Magnolia so far?"

He answered, "Having only been here for two weeks, we are still becoming acclimated. But I must say, Ms. Redwine, compared to our cramped apartment in Kinshasa, Dr. Buono's home is palatial. The rooms are spacious, and I even have an office. Almost every room features appliances and electronics that are considered extreme luxuries in the D.R.C.—if the power has not been blacked out, that is. And there is a wonderfully serene backyard with a terrace where we can sit and read under shady trees. I'm afraid I have the better of the exchange where lodging is concerned. Furthermore, Gabrielle's secretarial position in town is only a short walk from our neighborhood."

"We love it here," said the petite woman, who seemed somewhat younger than her strapping husband, her ample dark hair pulled back into a bun. Slim like her daughter, she was wearing a colorful Congolese blouse with matching skirt. Also like her daughter, she seemed to Redwine as the retiring type, her voice barely above a whisper.

"The people at the hospital were able to help Gabrielle find what they call a 'temp' position in town with the law firm of Leber and Tunney," explained Dr. Diyoka. "They have a woman who will be going on maternity leave. So, you see, we will all be quite busy."

"No doubt," said Redwine. She turned to the girl. "So, Didi, tell me about yourself. What's there to know?"

After briefly glancing at her parents, the girl cleared her throat—politely—and began to speak. "Honestly, Ms. Redwine, my life has been pretty normal so far. As my father said, I was born in Kinshasa, at HJ Hospital, where he is on the staff. I have attended Lycee Francais René Descartes from Pre-K through high school, where I would be entering my final year."

"I see," said Redwine. "Tell me what the school is like."

"Well, there are around 900 students. We start at 7:30 in the morning and end at around 4:30 in the afternoon, with some time for lunch at midday. The classes are about an hour long. It's fairly strict and structured. Students are expected to dress appropriately and show respect for their classmates and adults. Things

6

like smoking and drugs are, of course, forbidden. You can't have a cell phone, either, and you must obtain a pass to travel anywhere on the grounds. The entire campus is under video surveillance, except for the lavatories, of course. We have Internet access, which is tightly monitored as well. But I've enjoyed it, really. I like the structure, and my teachers have been kind."

"If I may ask, what is the racial balance in the school, Didi?"

"Oh, I'd say it's pretty well divided between blacks and whites. But everyone gets along. With all the rules we have to follow, it's hard to act out."

Redwine shuffled the papers before her. "I see that your curriculum has been pretty broad, Didi. What are your favorite subjects?"

"I have always had an interest in the humanities, literature and philosophy," she replied. "I can't say I enjoy mathematics, but I seem to have a knack for numbers, so that's never been a problem. Oh, and I really like history, of any type. And as my foreign language I took English, because I was already fluent in French, the D.R.C.'s national language, as well as Lingala, which is our traditional Congolese language—well, one of them."

"Any outside interests? Clubs or sports?"

The girl thought for a moment. "I'm a member of our honor society," she began, "but I suppose that's academic. I also enjoy football—which you call soccer here. Then, of course, there's fashion, which my friends and I love talking about."

"I love your tops," said Redwine, taking in the multicolored patterns sported by mother and daughter. "And your hairstyle is terrific."

"Oh, it's just a fairly regular box braid," she replied, referring to the ringlets that fell from a middle part and curled inwards below her jaw line, framing her very dark, smooth skin and high cheekbones. "Many of the girls wear them. They're easy to maintain, especially in Kinshasa's heat."

Redwine nodded. "Back to academics for a moment," she said. "As you know, we sent you a variety of tests before you came over to the States, to try to determine where you fell academically as far as ability and such—"

"I'm sorry if the results were not satisfactory," broke in Dr. Diyoka. "There was a certain amount of anxiety in my daughter as she took the tests—"

Redwine put her hand up to stop him right there. "Dr. Diyoka," she said reassuringly, "there's no need for worry here. The fact is, your daughter scored so highly across the board that she should have no problem dealing with the curriculum here, especially for what will be her senior year, when most students take elective courses anyway."

At that, all three Diyokas seemed to sit back with relief, especially Didi, whose thudding heart had finally begun to slow down.

"And so, Didi," said the counselor, "what is it exactly you hope to gain from your senior year of American high school?"

"May I say something, Ms. Redwine?" interjected Gabrielle.

"Surely," the counselor replied.

"Forgive me if I seem a bit nervous," the woman began, "but this subject is quite important to me. In the country where my husband and I grew up, women are

8

not fully invested in society. We are brought up to be subservient and know our place. Fortunately, my husband, though he was surely expected to adhere to this philosophy, has chosen to be more enlightened."

She paused and continued. "While it is true that the chance for my husband to serve, if only briefly, at such an esteemed hospital as Providence Heart in the United States, is a once-in-a-lifetime opportunity, the main reason—for me, anyway—to be here is for my daughter to become acclimated to the culture and way of life in this country, so that she might gain acceptance to an American college, where she will have as equal a chance as any man to pursue whatever career she wants, and not be relegated—as I was—to a menial clerical position with no chance of advancement.

"Maurice and I have spoken about this, and agree that if Dihya is able to excel in her studies and attend university here, that she will be free to either return to the D.R.C. or remain in America to pursue a career in her chosen field."

With this revelation, the girl's eyes widened in amazement. The thought of such autonomy in her own life was stunning.

"That's right, Dihya," said Dr. Diyoka. "You are being given the opportunity to find your own way in this world. However, we will expect nothing but your best effort going forward, as your end of the bargain."

"Yes, Father," dutifully answered the girl.

Redwine, clearly taken back by what was going on in front of her, cleared her throat and asked, "So, Didi, as I put together a schedule for you for the first semester, are there any subjects I should concentrate on?"

"Well," she replied, barely repressing her excitement, "I would like to take some science, biology perhaps, but as much literature, writing, and history as possible."

The counselor scribbled down some notes. "Is there anything else?"

"Ms. Redwine, I just want to fit in," the girl said earnestly. "I want to learn about American culture more than what little I've seen on television in the D.R.C. I want to make friends and participate in social activities outside the classroom." She glanced at her father and added, "Provided they don't interfere with my studies, of course."

"Of course," said Redwine with a friendly wink. "Well, as you pulled into the parking lot you might have seen our football team hard at work on the back field. This fall there will be a game nearly every weekend into November, and pretty much the whole school, and the town of Magnolia, turns out to cheer our boys." She opened a lower desk drawer and rooted around for a few seconds before pulling out a couple of red T-shirts emblazoned with the figure of a uniformed man on horseback. "These are for you," she said proudly. "Official Stuart Cavalier gear. That's our school team's nickname—the Cavaliers."

When the Diyokas stared back at her blankly, Redwine said, "Oh, silly me. I should've known you'd have no idea about all this. Our school is named after a famous soldier. In fact, you passed a bronze bust of him when you entered the lobby."

"Oh, yes," said Didi, fingering the shirts like they were silken robes. "He had a hat with a plume as well."

"That's our Jeb," said Redwine, nodding. "I'll tell you what, I can sign you up for an elective course where you'll learn all about him. You said you liked history, right?"

"Yes!" the girl gushed.

"Well, there you go. That's one class penciled in already."

It was then that Maurice Diyoka felt compelled to restore the atmosphere to a more serious tone. "Ms. Redwine," he said formally, "you have been so kind to us and our daughter, opening the building during your vacation time to meet with us and try to smooth Dihya's transition. And I do want her to 'fit in' and be happy. But make no mistake. I have seen elements of American culture, especially regarding the behavior of both young whites and blacks, on television, and have listened to what they consider music, and I consider some of it demeaning and vulgar. That was not the way my daughter has been brought up, and I am asking you, as her guidance counselor, to please advise her so that she will remain true to her goal here in America—to acquire a first-class education and go on to great things in whatever field she chooses. Am I clear?"

"Totally," rasped the woman, who looked like she'd just been hit by a truck.

Chapter Two

Didi stood by herself at the bus stop at the end of her block, clutching her backpack for dear life. Even at this early hour, the temperature hovered around 90°, the air still and soupy. But the weather was the least of her concerns, as it was always hot in Kinshasa.

She had hoped to see another black face among the handful of children awaiting the school bus that would make a daily run to Hampton Elementary School, Shelby Middle School and Stuart High, but it was not to be. In fact, her walks and bike rides (one of the Buono girls had apparently left hers behind) around the leafy neighborhood had failed to reveal anyone of African descent. She gawked at the comfortable mix of ranch and colonial-styled structures, all featuring finely manicured lawns and wide sidewalks, and made it a point to wave at any residents she passed along the way. Most waved back, or acknowledged her with a nod.

Some did not.

However, her next door neighbor, Mrs. Stanton, had come by with a lovely pecan pie to welcome the Diyokas to the neighborhood. She explained that Dr. Buono's wife and herself were close friends, and that she'd been alerted as to the arrival of her temporary neighbors. But although Mrs. Stanton had smiled a lot and said all the right things, Didi could detect an undercurrent of apprehension—probably because, as Didi was finding out, this was a white neighborhood, and Mrs. Stanton was most likely not used to such interaction.

Overall, though, this section of Magnolia was lovely, quiet, and apparently very safe. In fact, Mrs. Stanton had told her mother that many people on their street didn't even choose to lock their doors—something unthinkable in Kinshasa, where travel beyond the modern urban center quickly transitioned to large tracts of sprawling, dangerous shantytowns where the roads had yet to be paved. Yes, the Diyokas were fortunate to live where they did because of her father's occupation, but even the best accommodations in the capital of the D.R.C. paled in comparison to a small town like Magnolia, South Carolina—at least this part of it.

Suddenly, someone behind her was clearing his throat. She turned to find a pleasant-looking blonde boy of medium build outfitted in a golf shirt, khaki shorts and sandals. "Hi," he said cheerfully. "Are you going to Stuart High, by any chance?"

"Why, yes," she replied.

"Hard not to tell," he drawled, "bein' that you've got that Jeb shirt on. It looks good with your jeans."

"Thank you," she said. "I bought them at a wonderful store called Old Navy."

"Did you, now?" he grinned mischievously. "Well, my name's Pierce Farnsworth, and I live on the next street. And I'm guessing you're not from around here."

She wanted to die. Was it *that* obvious? "My name is Didi," she said, extending her hand and hoping he'd take it. "Didi Diyoka. And you're right, Pierce. I'm not from around here. I'm from the Democratic Republic of the Congo, in Africa."

The boy lightly shook her hand and let out a low whistle. "The Congo, huh? Man, I've never met a person from Africa. What you doing here? I mean, what brings you to South Carolina?"

"My father is a doctor, and he and the doctor who usually lives in the house I'm staying in are trading places for a year. Do you know Dr. Buono?"

"Oh, yeah," said the boy. "I delivered newspapers my first couple years of high school, and he was on my route. He's a good guy. What year are you in?"

"Well, it's 2013, isn't it?"

The boy laughed. "No, I mean, what year of high school are you going into?"

"Oh," she said, embarrassed. "I'm actually a senior."

"Me too," he said as the yellow bus pulled up and opened its folding door. "I'll bet we're in the same homeroom because our last names are so close. Tell you what, follow me once we get there and I'll help you find your way to wherever you're supposed to be. Sound like a plan?"

"Yes, thank you," she said, infinitely relieved.

But when they boarded the bus, she noticed Pierce gravitate towards some other white teens in the rear, leaving her to a seat by herself near the front. Still, it could have been worse, her fear of being alone the reason why she had tossed and turned all night, finally dragging herself downstairs to where her mother was enjoying a cup of coffee after seeing her husband off to work.

It had been Didi's idea to forego her traditional clothing and instead wear her new school's colors. And though her mother wasn't in love with her daughter wearing jeans and sneakers, she realized that the wardrobe choice was a means of calming the girl down somewhat. Didi had only picked at her breakfast of cold cereal and fruit, and her mother, sensing the girl's nervousness, hadn't forced her to eat. However, she had packed for her a healthy lunch of fruit, cheese and African fufu bread, which she had baked herself the previous night. Her daughter would have to buy her own drink in the cafeteria, hopefully milk.

With everyone aboard, the bus pulled away from the curb, its interior a cacophony of excited voices—kids getting reacquainted after the summer break, comparing class schedules, or good-naturedly bantering about their outfits and whatnot.

Didi, who was always extremely observant, noticed how the neighborhoods and houses varied as they went from stop to stop. As more kids boarded in areas further removed from hers in relation to the school, the surroundings looked a little rougher, though surely not as bad as anything one encountered in Kinshasa. And, to her relief, more black kids got on the bus—though they did give her some looks that were a bit disquieting. In fact, when it came down to the empty seat next to her being the last one, a rather large black girl with bronze colored hair extensions and a tank top, and incessantly snapping her gum, unceremoniously plopped herself down next to Didi, who scooted over to give her space. Not a word was exchanged, and Didi was treated to the girl's staccato gum snapping for the rest of the ride in. They were not a block away from Stuart High when the girl noticed Didi observing her. "You got a problem, Miss Thing?" she snarled while shooting her a sideways glance.

"No, not at all," Didi managed, before melting back into the sticky plastic seat.

* * *

Happy to be freed from the confines of the bus, Didi stepped onto the pavement and took in the sight of her new school. The two-story, red brick building seemed huge, its front entrance featuring a wide concrete stairway and painted white columns. The surrounding grass and shrubs were neatly trimmed, and stone sitting benches were positioned here and there.

Hundreds of kids were milling about, exchanging hugs, high-fives, and screeching hellos. Didi was fighting off her momentary urge to turn right around and get back on the bus when she spotted Ms. Redwine, who was posted on the front steps and waving her over. She picked her way through the clumps of students to where the counselor waited. "Well, you made it!" the woman said above the surrounding din. "Any problems with the bus?"

"No, ma'am," replied the girl, putting aside thoughts of her intimidating seat-mate. "It was fine."

"Hey, Ms. Redwine," said Pierce, who had materialized at Didi's side. "Y'all know our new student here?"

"Indeed I do, Pierce," said the woman. "I take it you two are on the same bus?"

"Yup. I figured I'd show her to homeroom."

"That's so sweet, Pierce. Thank you." She turned to Didi. "Okay, you're in good hands. Now, if anything comes up during the day, you remember where my office is, right?"

"Yes ma'am," she said.

"Okay, then, you two git while I make sure nobody's killing each other out here."

Didi followed the boy through the huge double-door entrance. As the hordes of students were milking every last second of freedom before going inside to start the school year, it was still cool in the hallway, and the rotunda-like foyer—highlighted by the bronze bust of J.E.B Stuart, which was perched on a formidable marble pedestal—was spotless. Narrow six-foot high gray lockers contrasted with the painted red walls and blue-and-white patterned linoleum floor. The whole place smelled of antiseptic and floor polish.

"This anything like your old school, Didi?" asked Pierce as they clipped along.

"No, not at all," she replied. "It was made up of smaller buildings with one or two classrooms apiece, with outside walkways connecting them."

"Oh. Well, this is a big place," said the boy. "We're all in one big ol' building, 'cept for the attached fieldhouse where we have phys-ed and all the indoor sports teams practice. You'll find your way around before you know it."

"I'm sure I will," she replied hopefully.

Suddenly, he stopped at a room with a black #121 plaque on the door. A roster of students' names was taped underneath the plaque. "Yep, just as I thought," he announced. "We're in the same homeroom. Let's go."

They entered the classroom, which featured the same linoleum patterned floors, worn but buffed to a moderate shine. There were twenty desks, set in rows of five, with both a traditional blackboard and a permanently attached whiteboard at the front, as well as a wooden teacher's desk. A young white woman stood beside it, her lustrous brown hair in ringlets. "Welcome!" she cried. "Pierce, I know. But who's this beautiful girl with you?"

"Miss Martin, this is Didi—from Africa!"

"Oh yes," said the woman, extending her hand. "Ms. Redwine told me to expect you. Welcome to Stuart High." They shook hands, and Martin riffled through a sheaf of papers. "Ah, here it is. This is your schedule," she said, handing it over. "Maybe Pierce can help you figure it out."

"Sure thing, Miss Martin," said the boy after being handed his own schedule. "Didi, let's sit down and take a look."

"Everyone seems to know you, Pierce," observed the girl.

"Well, they should. I'm the senior class president. We had the election end of last year."

"Oh."

"Tell you the truth, Didi, it's mostly a popularity contest. But hey, I just try to be nice to everybody, and it kind of works for me."

Didi nodded, as other students began to file in, greeted warmly by the personable Miss Martin. It was an odd mix of people, with about a 60/40 split of white and black. All of them said hi to Pierce, who was obviously, as he had mentioned, very popular. In turn, he introduced Didi, who offered a shy hello. Her classmates varied in their greetings, from friendly "Heys" to more reserved nods.

"Okay, let's see who's here," said Miss Martin, and she called the roll. Everyone was present, except one. "Oh dear," she said, "we seem to be missing—"

As if on cue, the door banged open, and the strangest looking girl Didi had ever laid eyes on blew in. Her black hair was short and choppy, and her pasty white skin was accentuated by black eyeliner and purple eyeshadow. She appeared rather shapeless, with a black sleeveless T-shirt featuring some kind of emblem, black jeans, and workboots. A metal chain that was clipped to her studded leather belt disappeared into her jean pocket.

"—Heidi Dorsch," Miss Martin finished.

The girl sauntered over to a desk, flung a tattered backpack on its tabletop, sank into the seat and yawned loudly.

"Mornin', Heidi," said Pierce.

She just looked back at him.

"Well," said Miss Martin in a perky tone, "glad to have y'all back for your last go-round. As you know, homeroom will be from eight sharp to eight-ten, including announcements on the PA and the pledge."

The students nodded wearily; they'd heard the same spiel for the past three years, which was as long as Miss Martin had been at the school.

"And here's Mr. Hufnagel now!" she chirped as the PA speaker above the blackboard crackled to life.

"Gooooood mornin' Stuart High!" boomed the principal as the Room #121 seniors rolled their eyes. "Welcome back to our upperclassmen, and greetings to the class of 2017 on your first day. Would everyone please rise for the Pledge of Allegiance." With a few sighs and muffled groans, the students rose from their seats (even Heidi); most then placed their right hand over their heart. Didi, totally confused, followed suit as the majority of the students parroted Mr. Hufnagel's words before dropping back into their seats.

"Do you do this every morning?" Didi whispered to Pierce.

"Oh, yeah. Some of us are more into it than others. Miss Martin's only request is that we stand. After that, it's up to you."

"What do you suggest?"

"I'm happy to do it, is all I can tell you."

After a few opening-day announcements about lunch periods and keeping the building clean, Hufnagel ended with, "Have a good day and... Go Cavs!"

A bell sounded, signaling the end of homeroom. "Okay," said Pierce, "your first class is American Lit, room 142. That's just down the hall. You'll find it easy."

"Thanks."

"Oh, and your locker's right outside the room here, #1015. Let me show you real quick how to work the combo lock." They left the classroom and stopped in front of the locker. "It's a three-number lock. First, you spin the dial to clear it. Then, to find the first number you go left. The second number you spin to the right, and then back to the left for the third one. What's the combo on your sked sheet?"

"Uh, 16-30-12."

The boy deftly turned the black dial with white numerals and in seconds had the locker open. "See? Easy as pie," he said. "Gotta go. Good luck. I'll

20

probably see you at lunch." With that, he jogged in the other direction, greeting everyone in his path.

"There goes the Mayor," said Heidi, shutting her own locker with a clank. "Where are you off to?"

"Room 142," said Didi.

"That's near mine. C'mon."

Unlike Pierce, Heidi said hello to no one, and barely acknowledged those who addressed her. As they walked along, Didi noted the attire of the other students. A few, like Pierce, wore casually neat outfits. Most sported T-shirts, tattered jeans, or worn shorts, with work boots or sneakers. A few wore Stuart High shirts like hers, but most T-shirts she saw featured the names of music bands, sports teams, and finally, a strange-looking flag with a diagonally oriented blue X filled with white stars, set against a red background. As if reading her mind, Heidi said, "Wondering what that symbol is? Honey, that's the Confederate battle flag. Real popular down here."

"Oh. Well, I like your shirt."

"Really? Not too many Megavenom fans in this place. They're a rock band."

"I see."

"Did someone give you your shirt, or did you buy it?"

"I got it from Ms. Redwine."

"Figures."

Didi entered the classroom, found a seat, and settled in. Her first day as an American high school student was underway.

By lunchtime her head was spinning with names and information. Mr. O'Toole, her American Lit instructor, seemed rather dry. Conversely, Mrs.

Webster, her physical education teacher who was also the girls' lacrosse and softball coach, was a dynamo of energy who stressed the importance of her students maintaining a healthy lifestyle that included a balanced diet and exercise, which she promised would begin in earnest with their next meeting. Didi, who loved to be active, made a mental note to bring exercise clothes to class. And Advanced Biology with Dr. Zavorskas promised to be interesting, especially with the news that they'd be "dissecting a lot of neat stuff."

She was starving by the time lunch period rolled around. The fairly spacious cafeteria featured both round tables of eight with attached stools, and rectangular tables of twelve; large gray garbage pails were stationed throughout. As Didi purchased a small carton of ice cold milk she viewed the school's menu offerings, which included sandwiches, salads, and a "hot feature" of the day, which in this case was fried chicken, mashed potatoes, and carrots. One or two teachers circulated amongst the tables, chitchatting with students and reminding them to clean up after themselves. But what really caught her eye was the mural which began some six feet from the floor and continued to the twelve-foot ceiling on all four walls. It depicted some kind of battle scene, with soldiers in blue and gray locked in conflict amid yellow bursts of cannon fire. But the centerpiece, over the main entrance door, featured the same character displayed on her T-shirt, charging astride a black stallion, waving his plumed hat as he led his men into the fray. The whole thing was dramatic, if a bit over the top. Still, it gave her something to look at because, unfortunately, senior lunch period found the new girl sitting by herself. Didi observed that the kids tended to sit at racially segregated tables, except for a bunch of especially large, noisy boys who wore red jerseys with black numbers and gray piping, and the word CAVALIERS above the front number.

She had opened her brown lunch bag and was unwrapping her fruit when Heidi Dorsch plunked herself down across the table from her. "Are we having fun yet?" she asked, while unwrapping a Snickers bar.

"There's a lot to take in," Didi replied.

Heidi popped open a Red Bull and washed down her first bite of the Snickers. "Yeah, well, you'll get used to it. So, besides your probable bore-a-thon in American Lit, where else have you been this morning?"

She told her, and Heidi chewed thoughtfully. "Coach Webster is okay, though she's too gung-ho with the exercise thing. I drive the phys-ed teachers nuts because I don't like working out."

"Why not?"

"'Cause I *don't*," she snapped. "Who wants to get all sweaty and go back to class? Yuck. And the kids really like Dr. Z 'cause he likes to do a lot of gross stuff." She looked over her shoulder at the table of boys in their red jerseys. "Jeez, day one and the jocks are already in rare form," she grunted.

"Pardon?"

"Okay, honey, lesson number one," said Heidi. "Those guys—the football team—own the school. They get whatever they want, from whomever they want, and breeze through here taking easy classes and fighting off all the girls who throw themselves at them—and I don't just mean the cheerleaders. They're definitely the B.M.O.C.'s."

"Excuse me?"

"Big men on campus. But you'll see what I mean on Friday at the pep rally."

"What is that?"

"Just the biggest deal at Stuart High. See, the first game is Saturday afternoon, so Friday night they'll have this huge bonfire and the marching band and like a gazillion people there to get everyone revved up for the game. It's actually pretty cool, 'cause I like fires. Oh, and then Jeb shows up."

"Jeb?"

"Stuart. You'll see what I mean. Anyway, if you really want to understand what this school's about, you've gotta check it out."

"Thanks for telling me."

"Yeah, well, that's my good deed for the day. Ta-ta." She abruptly stood up, tossed her Snickers wrapper wide of the trash can, and clomped off, leaving Didi to finish her lunch alone. When she was done, she threw out Heidi's Red Bull can with her own garbage.

The afternoon's classes were also a mixed bag. Didi started with art, and featured her only black teacher, Ms. Woodard, a plump woman with a close-cropped Afro and large hoop earrings, who seemed to have all kinds of interesting projects planned for the semester. Then there was study hall in the library, during which Didi plucked a few novels from the shelves while the other students whispered, goofed around, or slept.

By two o'clock she was ready to call it a day, but her last class, Civil War Studies, was jarring, on a few counts. First, there was Mr. Stephen Pennington, the teacher, a man with a Southern accent so thick she could barely understand him. Pennington was tall and rail-thin, with a thick goatee and longish brown hair that he combed straight back, so that it fell below his collar. He promised that they would, in this elective class, learn "the truth" about what he called "the War Between the States" and "the War of Southern Independence," and seemed pretty excited about it.

The second reason Didi was taken aback was that none other than Heidi was also in the class. When Didi asked later what made her choose the elective, the Goth girl said, "Because I like to bust chops, and Pennington is supposedly a dyed-in-the-wool Rebel apologist. He even does reenactments."

"What are reenactments?"

"You'll find out."

But the most notable image that Didi took from the class was that of the boy-man who lumbered in and sat down with a *whomp* in the desk next to her. He was black, though not as dark as her, with shoulder-length dreadlocks and a frame so massive that the one-piece chair desk barely contained him. She estimated his weight at over 250 pounds and determined most of it was muscle; in fact, he seemed to have no neck at all. He was also wearing one of those red numbered jerseys she'd seen in the lunchroom. According to the roll call, his name was Travis, and he was perhaps the most threatening-looking human being she'd ever laid eyes on. Even Heidi seemed to cut him a wide berth.

"Who was *that*?" Didi asked her after the final bell had sounded, ending the school day.

"It's more like a *what*," she replied. "That's 'Bad News' Braxton, and he's probably the best football player in the county, or one of 'em. Rumor is he's gonna go to Clemson or the University of South Carolina on a full scholarship. That's real big-time football, by the way. I'm kinda surprised he's taking this elective, to tell the truth. Figured he'd go for something more simple, like basket weaving."

"The school offers a class in basket weaving?"

"It's a figure of speech," said Heidi with exasperation. "Oh well, one down, 179 to go. See you tomorrow."

"Okay, thanks for helping me out today."

"Whatever," said the girl as she walked off, her belt chain rattling.

Didi climbed aboard the bus exhausted, but at the same time exhilarated. If the first day in an American school was any indication, this was going to be an exciting year. Thankfully, Pierce bounded onto the bus, and this time sat next to her. "So, how did it go?" he asked.

"It was fine," she replied. "But I couldn't find you at lunch."

"Oh, that. It seems we had a student council meeting I'd forgotten about. Did you meet any people?"

"Well, I did sit with Heidi for a bit."

Pierce shook his head. "She's a rough one," he said. "Really negative. You might not want to get mixed up with her. Doesn't really have any friends, and she seems to like it that way."

"Oh, I don't know," said Didi. "I'd like to believe she's not all bad."

"Suit yourself," he said with a shrug.

"And then, in my last class, there was this boy called 'Bad News'?"

"Braxton? Yikes. What class was this?"

"Civil War Studies, with Mr. Pennington."

"Oh, yeah. Mr. P. loves football players. That's an easy A for Bad News."

"Are you two friendly?"

"Heck no. I mean, he spent most of our freshman year stuffing me into lockers."

"But those lockers are so narrow!"

"Tell me about it. Of course, I was a little smaller then. Anyway, we've reached an understanding over the years. I kiss his butt, and he doesn't beat on me. Just don't get him mad...not if you want to live, anyway."

* * *

That night at dinner, Didi breathlessly related her first day's adventures to her parents, who listened patiently while enjoying an African chicken and rice dish her mother had managed to find the ingredients for at the local supermarket. "Are you sure these courses you're taking are challenging enough?" asked her father.

"Oh, I'm confident they'll be fine," she replied. "And who knows? Perhaps if I really enjoy biology, I'll pursue medicine in college. Wouldn't you like that, Father?"

"Yes, it would make me happy," he said. "But medicine is a tough course of study, no matter what college you attend. It's a real commitment, Diyha."

"Maurice, it's only the first day," chided his wife. "Let her give it time."

"Of course," he said. "Did you make any new friends?"

"Well, there's Pierce, who rides the bus with me and is the president of the senior class. He lives on the next street. And a girl named Heidi who's a bit awkward, but seems okay."

"I take it they're white?" asked her mother.

"Yes, but there are many black students in the school whom I'm sure I'll get to know." She didn't mention the gum-snapping girl on the bus, or the boy they called Bad News. There was only so much one shared with Dr. and Mrs. Diyoka, she had learned. Didi knew her parents loved her dearly, but could be somewhat overprotective. Even in Kinshasa, her television viewing was restricted, and she was never allowed out on the streets after eight o'clock. Which was why she didn't even bring up the thing called a "pep rally." This was something she'd have to work on for Friday night, which was only three days away.

Chapter Three

It didn't take long for word to get around the student body that their new classmate was an honest-to-God African. Thus, Didi found herself confronted by a half-dozen black girls at her locker before homeroom. And though their presence was at first a welcome sight, it quickly became apparent that they were anything but welcoming. All had a kind of toughness about them and wore skin-tight jeans to accentuate their backsides, some of which were quite ample. "So let me get this straight," said one girl who didn't even bother introducing herself. "You're like, from Africa? For real?"

"Yes," said Didi as affably as possible. "The Congo, actually."

"The *Congo*," she bleated. "Like, in the jungle? With lions and elephants and stuff?"

"Well, not where I lived. I was in a pretty modern city called Kinshasa."

But the clique of girls wasn't hearing her. "Ongo-bongo, we got a sister from the Congo!" crowed one with dyed blonde hair extensions, and the group went merrily on their way, laughing uproariously and high-fiving.

Didi exhaled embarrassedly and returned to the task of getting her locker open. Pierce had made it seem so simple the day before, but try as she might, she couldn't get the latch to disengage. Attempting once more to work the tumblers while staring intently at the dial, the girl was startled when a meaty fist whizzed by her head and slammed into the locker, popping it open. She turned in terror to find Bad News Braxton, his other arm around an attractive, mocha-skinned girl with straightened, shoulder-length hair. "The lockers open easy if you know where to hit 'em," he grunted, and the couple moved along, the girl suspiciously looking back over her shoulder.

"Thanks," said Didi, her voice trailing off.

Outside of its inauspicious beginning, the day went fairly well, with the new girl falling into the routine of school. She noticed that today Pierce wasn't on the bus or in homeroom, but heard him on the PA after Mr. Hufnagel was done. As class president, apparently, it was his duty to handle the day-to-day announcements following the Pledge of Allegiance. Of course, Pierce performed his duties with aplomb, mentioning the day's lunch special (pulled pork sandwiches and fries) and reminding the students—as if they needed it—about the upcoming pep rally and football game. Also, like Hufnagel, he concluded his monologue with "Go Cavs!" which elicited an "Oh, brother" from Heidi.

Day Two of American Lit saw Mr. O'Toole launch into a discussion of Edgar Allan Poe, who seemed to Didi to be an interesting character, and she was pleased to have the opportunity to run around a bit in phys-ed, as the girls engaged in the rudiments of soccer, her favorite sport. Most of their efforts were half-hearted, but it was still fun.

However, it was Civil War Studies that most intrigued her, with Mr. Pennington "setting the stage," as he called it, for the course. They started by watching fifteen minutes or so of a documentary by a man named Burns, introduced by a melancholy violin tune. Over the music, Pennington explained that this extremely long production had held the entire country in its thrall when it first came out on public television around twenty-five years previously.

The documentary began with various learned people stating their opinion on the magnitude of the war as a part of American history. Accompanied by the narration were aged black and white photos of soldiers, both posed studio portraits and candid shots in the field, interspersed with stark images of dead, decomposing bodies lying in farmers' pastures. In those few minutes Didi learned that over three million Americans had fought in the war, and that over 600,000 had died of wounds or disease. She heard snippets of information about men named Ulysses Grant, Stonewall Jackson and Robert E. Lee, as well as a man she had heard about in Africa, Abraham Lincoln, whom she remembered as being regarded as perhaps the greatest president in United States history. She learned that before the war, the United States had been a mostly agrarian society, meaning that the majority of the country's population lived and worked on farms. A white commentator with a Southern accent told the audience that the Civil War "defined us as what we are, good and bad," while a black female historian remarked that the war "was not about weapons or soldiers, but about something higher: human dignity and freedom."

It was at this point that the image of an African slave from an American plantation appeared on the screen, and Didi's breath caught in her throat. She was both appalled and fascinated; thus, she was taken back when her teacher abruptly shut off the white board screen and told his students, "Now, this is what those people in the North—who were the creators of this series—would have y'all believe. But I'm here today to tell you that this course will present the *truth* about the War of Southern Independence that occurred from the years 1861-1865, why its outcome is yet unresolved in our society, and why, as South Carolinians, you must understand your state's role in the ongoing conflict."

Heidi raised her hand.

"Yes?"

"But Mr. Pennington," she said, "didn't the war end when the South surrendered?"

"Miss Dorsch," he said coolly, "I thank you for that question. Before I answer, though, I'm curious as to where you might originally hail from?"

"Jersey City, New Jersey," she responded.

"Jer-sey City," he drawled, stretching out the words and letting them bounce off the classroom walls. "Again, I'm glad for your question, and equally as glad you're taking the course. I think you'll find it enlightening."

Someone in the back of the room muttered, "Damn right," but if Heidi heard the remark, she gave no indication.

"The fact of the matter is," Pennington continued, "this conflict is, to this day, much misunderstood, and hopefully we will be able to provide an answer for you by the time all is said and done."

"I'm looking forward to it," she responded, her eyes steely.

It was at that moment Didi realized that, besides Bad News—who seemed to have been dozing—hers was the only black face in the room. She looked at the clock; ten long minutes remained in the period. Fortunately, this time was consumed with the teacher instructing them on how to set up their notebook, and distributing the course outline—which, she noticed, included a couple field trips. "This could change as we go along," he cautioned, "but we'll pretty much follow the plan. There's no exam at the end, but there will be a research paper that will count for fifty per cent of your grade. The rest will be class participation and engagement."

Mercifully, the bell sounded, and the class got up and left, including Bad News, who seemed refreshed and ready to go for football practice after his snooze.

"I'm sorry about what happened in there," said Didi to Heidi, struggling to find comforting words.

"*Sorry*? For what?" the girl retorted. "Hell, I *welcome* the challenge to deal with this guy's redneck BS. I'm going to enjoy messing with his head. Hey, it's only an elective anyway." She stopped short and looked Didi in the eye. "You might not realize this, or even care, but I've got like a 3.8 GPA over my first three years at Stuart, and this one'll be a breeze. Just so you know, a 4.0 is the highest you can get. And, I scored a 1200 on my college board exams, which is really high. Long story short, I'm going to have my pick of colleges."

"Do you have a particular school in mind?" asked Didi.

For the first time, Heidi Dorsch ruefully smiled. "Somewhere as far away from this godforsaken town as I can get," she said.

* * *

That night after dinner, Didi sat down at the computer in her father's office and Googled the Civil War documentary they had been watching in class. She was hoping to be able to see more of it than Pennington had provided; fortunately, the entire first installment of ninety minutes was available on a site called YouTube. After locating it, she scrolled through the segment they had already covered and then hit PLAY.

Where they'd left off began with the rendition of a mournful spiritual, presumably sung by slaves, as it was juxtaposed with grainy images of black workers in ragged shirts and dresses, the women with bandannas or turbans on their heads, toiling in open fields. The narrator calmly explained how the institution of American slavery worked, and what it was like. Blacks were bought and sold like horses or other farm animals on the auction block, sometimes to be re-sold multiple times, preventing the establishment of the family unit. They worked from sunrise to dark, and of course had no rights in American society. They were punished severely or killed for failing to obey their masters.

Apparently, the invention of a machine called the cotton gin around 1800 caused the institution of slavery to explode in the United States, especially in the South, where there was an immediate need for cheap labor. Thus, by the time the war began in 1861 there were some four million slaves in America. Didi was heartened to see that by this time some people—especially in the Northern states, which had earlier embraced slavery—began speaking out against it. They called themselves abolitionists and campaigned for an end to this practice.

However, the legitimacy of slavery had been written into the very Constitution of the United States, and the Southern states—including South Carolina, who seemed to be quite vocal—argued that each state should be able to set its own laws. Thus began a conflict that reached its boiling point in 1861 when thirteen Southern states, who renamed themselves the Confederate States of America, tried to secede, or break away, from the United States. They formed their own government, with a man named Alexander Stevens, the vice-president, declaring, "Our new government is founded upon the great truth that the Negro is not equal to the white man."

At this point in the video, Didi had to hit PAUSE and take a break, as tears were streaming down her cheeks. "Not again, not *here*," she whispered. Indeed, the girl had been informed about the harsh realities of apartheid in her homeland and its implementation in the Belgian Congo. Her ancestors on both sides had been mired in the depths of poverty and deprivation for many years, and though her parents tried to keep the nastiest bits from her, she had come to understand how tough it had been for them to rise above their prescribed "station" in society and become successful, especially her father.

After blowing her nose, Didi returned to the documentary, which described the initial conflicts of the war: the shelling of Fort Sumter in Charleston, South Carolina; and a battle called Bull Run or First Manassas. And she saw the carnage both had wrought as the United States began to tear itself apart.

At the video's conclusion she was left with a couple of images that would haunt her dreams that night: a photo of a male slave, his back a grid of welts caused by a leather whip; and a petite black woman in a dark dress with a white collar, her hair pulled back in a bun, her face dark and serious. The woman's name was Harriet Tubman, and Didi was struck by how much she was reminded of herself.

Chapter Four

"Sorry I missed you yesterday," said Pierce at the bus stop. "Seniors are allowed to drive to school and park on campus, and my mom lets me use the second car once or twice a week. It's just the plain ol' Honda Accord, but it's a set of wheels, so I can't complain."

Didi nodded, and wondered if the boy would ever invite her to ride in his "plain ol'" car. Changing the subject as they waited, she said, "Hey, did you ever have Mr. Pennington as an instructor?"

"Mr. P.? Oh, yeah. Great guy. I took his Civil War elective last year. It was pretty cool, and there's field trips and all. Why, are you taking the class?"

"Yes," she said, thinking back to the previous day's session and her home research that night. "There's so much to learn."

"That's for sure," said the boy. "But if you live in South Carolina, heck, we're the state that started the whole thing, so it's good to learn about your history, you know?"

"Yes, I'm sure," she replied.

"And listen," he continued, "if you need help with any of the assignments and stuff, just let me know. I might even have my class notes from last year laying around somewhere."

"Thanks. That would be nice."

The bus pulled up and the kids boarded; but again, "the Mayor" sat with his pals in the back. And again, poor Didi was stuck with her gum-snapping partner. This time she simply buried her nose in a book.

* * *

She was at her locker before homeroom with Heidi when Bad News sauntered by, his meaty arm slung around the same girl's shoulders. "'Sup," he said to them, not waiting for an answer as the couple moved along.

"Who's the girl with Travis?" Didi asked casually.

"Oh," said Heidi, crinkling her eyes, "you haven't met his main squeeze yet? That, honey, is Tanya 'don't speak to me unless spoken to' Mims. Besides being one of only three black girls to crack the cheerleading squad lineup, she's secured the rights to our friend Bad News and would probably destroy you, one way or the other, if you tried to invade her territory."

"The word 'destroy' seems a little extreme," observed Didi.

"Not really," replied the Goth girl as they walked down the crowded hallway. "Look at it this way. Bad News is one of the two main stars of the football team, the other being our resident pretty-boy heartthrob, Troy Winchester. Anyway, here's how Tanya probably sees it: girl snags football player; player gets scholarship to big time college program, which leads to mucho dollars from a pro team down the line; girl marries high school sweetheart and lives happily ever after."

"Don't you think that's a bit simplistic?"

"Not around here. Bad News might not be a scholar or a gentleman, but he sure can crush people. Come to the game Saturday and you'll see. And you'll also get to observe Tanya and all her phony beauty queen friends cheering their hearts out for good old Stuart High. They'll be front and center at the pep rally too, don't you worry."

"I was thinking about the pep rally, and what you said yesterday," said Didi cautiously, "and I think I really would like to go...I just don't know if my parents would approve, or if they would take me there."

"That's not a problem," said Heidi after they entered homeroom. "Tell them it's an important school activity, and that a friend of yours will be driving you there and home."

"And who is that?"

"*Me*, dummy. I've had my license for over a year now. My dad always lets me use our SUV on weekends, or whenever he thinks I'm attempting to socialize and act normal."

Didi was anxious to find out more about what that meant, but Mr. Hufnagel came on the PA to lead them in the pledge.

* * *

Once again, she had the experience of "dining" with Heidi at lunchtime; today the girl had chosen a pack of cherry Twizzlers to accompany her Red Bull. "Do you always eat candy for lunch?" Didi asked innocently.

"Not always," replied Heidi, tearing off a stalk. "Sometimes I do a bag of Doritos. I like the Cool Ranch ones the best."

"Oh," said Didi, making a mental note to research Doritos.

"What about you? Do your parents make you eat fruit and cheese every day?"

"I actually like it," she replied defensively. "And here the fruit is always so fresh."

"Whatever. Want to try a Twizzler?"

Didi smiled. "Yes, actually."

Heidi peeled one off and handed it over. "Here, live a little," she said.

"Thanks." Didi bit into the gooey confection and smiled. "Tasty," she managed, prying her teeth apart with her tongue.

"Yeah, they're the best. So, are you ready for some more Civil War stuff this afternoon?"

"Yes. And I did a little research last night on my own."

"Really? Like what?"

"I watched the entire first episode of that Civil War documentary on YouTube."

"And?"

"What I saw was horrible. It was mostly about slavery."

"Yeah, that's pretty grim stuff," Heidi agreed, biting off the end of another Twizzler. "Of course, Pennington's gonna play it down, you watch. He's gonna tell you the war was all about 'states rights' and the unjustness of the nasty Northern people trying to impose their way of life on the poor people of the South. Boo-hoo."

Didi managed to smile at Heidi's biting sarcasm. She said, "Well, on a positive note, I was talking to Pierce this morning, and he told me he's already taken the course and could even help me with it."

"Pierce? He told you that?"

"Why, yes," said Didi. "Is there something wrong?"

"Well," replied the girl, stuffing the rest of the Twizzler into her mouth, "that's a story for another time, but not now. Let's get into the class a little more, first."

"Sure. Thanks for the Twizzler."

"No problemo. You've gotta start eating like a normal kid."

* * *

That afternoon, Didi was surprised when Mrs. Woodard stopped her on the way out of art class and asked what she was doing the next period. When the girl told her about the study hall, Woodard pulled out her pack of hall passes and signed one. "Why don't we meet here and chat," she said. "I have a free period, and I'm sure you don't have anything major planned for study hall this early in the semester."

"That would be fine," said Didi brightly.

"Okay, present this to the monitor, and I'll see you back here in a few minutes."

She returned to find that Woodard had put two desks together, and was spreading her lunch out on hers. "Sorry," she said, biting into a sandwich, "I haven't eaten yet. Would you like some?"

"No, thanks, I've already had lunch," said the girl.

41

Paul Ferrante

"Well, I figured I'd ask. The reason I wanted to talk to you is that there are only three art teachers in the building, so by the time kids are seniors I've had them all as students at least once. But you, I know nothing about. I mean, I did get a heads-up from Ellen Redwine, but I still felt the need to know you better. So tell me, how's it going so far?" Her almond-shaped eyes were bright and friendly, and Didi immediately felt comfortable with her.

"So far, it's going well," Didi replied. "I'm still learning about the workings of the school, and the culture."

"Well, don't get frustrated if it takes a while," said the teacher. "This place can be tough to navigate at times. There are a lot of factions that don't always blend well."

"I can see that. Except for the sports team members, it seems there is a division between whites and blacks."

"Unfortunately, yes. It's better than in the past, but it's still there. Just more subtle."

"Did you grow up here, Mrs. Woodard?"

"Not exactly. My family is originally from Georgia. I moved here in 2000 with my husband when he found a job in Columbia. It just so happened that Stuart High had an opening in art, so it all worked out. We have a four year-old who goes to pre-k, so it's kind of a juggling act. But we get by. Of course, my ancestors were slaves in Georgia. They came from Senegal. I thought it important to trace my family back as far as I could. I wish more of our black students would as well, but they don't seem interested, which I consider tragic. Tell me about your life in the Congo, Didi."

"Not much to tell. I grew up in the center of Kinshasa, which used to be called Leopoldville, after the King of Belgium. It's a large city, but I only knew the small area in which we lived. The outskirts of the city are squalid, but I was fortunate to attend a good school and live in a fairly modern apartment. And the home we're staying in here, Dr. Buono's, is fantastic."

"That's because your address is in one of the more affluent parts of town," said Woodard. "You'll see that, like Kinshasa, the farther you travel outward the more rural and underprivileged it becomes. Many of your classmates' families require financial assistance from the state, and jobs are hard to come by in a small town like this. And I'm not just talking about the black students. There are white kids who live in some pretty sketchy areas as well, or out in the woods."

Didi sighed. "I just don't understand why no other black students have tried to make friends with me," she said. "A group of girls came over this morning, but only ended up making fun of me because I was African."

"It's fear, Didi," said the teacher. "Fear of the unknown. They just don't know what to make of you yet. It's kind of their defense mechanism. They see that you're reserved and well-mannered and might interpret this as you being standoffish, which I don't get it all. Don't worry, I'll help spread the word that you're great kid. What about the boys?"

Didi chuckled. "They're quite different from the boys in Kinshasa, at least the ones in the city center," she said. "Over there they are called 'Sapeurs'—guys who are really into fashion and good manners. When they are out and about they wear three-piece suits and shiny shoes. When you consider the poverty in the D.R.C., in parts of Kinshasa and the outlying areas, it seems a bit silly. But still, I find it preferable to the clothes and behavior of some of the boys here. They walk around in dirty, torn jeans or army-style pants with sleeveless T-shirts. And once outside the school, a lot of them smoke or spit—I think it's tobacco.

"Of course, some of the students are smartly dressed and well-behaved. In fact, I ride the bus with Pierce, the class president. Do you know him?"

"Didi, everybody knows Pierce," Woodard laughed. "He's quite a character."

"Heidi Dorsch calls him 'the Mayor.'"

"Ah, yes, Heidi," said Woodard. "Another interesting personality. I take it you two have become friends?"

"Somewhat. She's hard to get to know. I actually found out that she's one of the smartest students in the school."

"That she is. I think her whole 'Goth' persona is another defense mechanism, to tell the truth. She probably gravitated to you because, like herself, she considers you an outsider. But be careful these first few weeks, Didi, and don't put too much stock in initial impressions. You might find that people here, both kids and adults, may not be what they first appear."

Didi nodded. "I'm thinking about attending the pep rally this Friday," she said. "Do you think that's a good idea? Heidi said that if I want to get a true idea of the school, it's a must."

"I agree," said the art teacher. "If you've never been to anything like it before, it's a real eye-opener." She shook her head.

"Didi, there are two things that are truly important at Stuart High. The first is the football program. Coach Kurtt is a pretty tough guy, but to his credit, he gets most of his players to graduate, and finds athletic scholarships or financial aid for many of the boys who want to go on to college. That being said, we pump more money into that program than all of the arts programs combined. You see, the football team is a showcase for the town of Magnolia, a source of civic pride. You'll see 'Go Cavs!' signs in all the storefronts in town. For home games, whether it's Saturday afternoons or Friday nights, the town empties out and fills the stands to cheer the boys. Being a team member and wearing your jersey around school is a big deal. Same for the cheerleaders. They all 'buddy up' with a senior player for the season and wear their jersey around school on Fridays, make lawn signs for their houses, bake them cookies, etc. It's kind of ridiculous, but it's tradition here. And one thing they don't do at Stuart is break tradition."

"I take a class with Travis Braxton. He seems to be quite popular."

"Bad News? Yes, he's a piece of work. But again, perhaps not all he appears to be. Personally, I hope he does get a football college scholarship, because if he doesn't, he'll be stacking cans at the Winn-Dixie. That's the big problem with us being a football factory. Academics take a backseat with a lot of the boys. So, if the college scholarship doesn't pan out, they're out of luck. You'll see some thirty year-old men around town still wearing their Stuart varsity letter jackets. It's kind of sad."

"I was told that some teachers aren't too

demanding of the players because of their status. Is that part of the problem?"

"You might be right, though it would be unprofessional of me to name names. All I can do is uphold my standards in this room, but let's face it, art class isn't a killer. You really have to work at it to fail." She looked up at the clock, nestled between two colorful modern art posters. "Well, the time's really flown here. Where are you off to?"

"Civil War Studies, with Mr. Pennington."

"Ugh. What made you take *that* course?"

"Well, I think it's my own fault. I mentioned to Ms. Redwine that I love history, and she signed me up."

"And what do you think, so far?"

"It's a bit confusing."

"I'm sure it is, if what I've heard about Pennington's take on the war is true. If you *really* want your eyes opened, research the percentage of American slaves who got shipped over here from the Congo. But, proceed with caution in that class. I would imagine you're outnumbered in the room."

"Eighteen-to-two. The other one's Bad News."

"If he's awake, that is."

Didi laughed. "You *know* that he sleeps in that class?"

"Why wouldn't he?" said the art teacher. "He slept in mine. But before you go, back to what I was telling you about the two most important things in the school. Like I said, football is number one. But the other is our connection to the past, namely the Confederacy. We are, after all, named after one of its hallowed heroes. He greets you every day when you walk into the rotunda, and he's splashed across everything from the cafeteria walls to our official school gear. Again, watch yourself in this area. Old traditions die hard down here, and anyone who bucks them is asking for a load of trouble. I just want you to have a happy, rewarding senior year."

"I do, too."

"Well, fine then. And you just drop in any time you want to talk, because I imagine that there will be a few of them."

"Thanks, Mrs. Woodard," said Didi, rising from her desk. "My parents have so much on their minds that the things we've discussed here would make them question their decision to ever come to this place."

"They still might, when all is said and done. But I'll help when I can. Good luck."

Chapter Five

The next morning dawned, as sunny and languidly humid as the one before. As had become her custom, Didi awoke and went to her bedroom window, which looked out on the patio and expansive backyard. She was constantly amazed at the precise nature in which the shrubs and plants were trimmed and maintained, and how green the grass was, right up to its edge. A couple of spreading oaks dripping with Spanish moss served as sentinels at the rear property line, with birds chirping on their branches. After the noisy, smelly clamor of downtown Kinshasa, this quiet neighborhood in Magnolia, South Carolina seemed like the Garden of Eden.

She smiled at the recollection of the previous night's conversation at dinner, and how her parents had acquiesced to her request to attend the pep rally. "Oh, yes," her mother had said. "It's all anyone at the office is talking about, and how well the football team will do this year. All of the storefronts I walked by were displaying red and black banners."

"I'm a little wary of how you are getting there, though," said Maurice. "Are you sure that the girl who is bringing you there is responsible?"

"Heidi? Oh, yes, Father. She has been driving for over a year now," Didi answered nervously.

"That's not what I mean, Diyha. I know all about how the young people over here have wild parties and drink and drive. I just want to make sure you're safe."

"I will be, Father. And I'm sure that we will come right back after the pep rally is over. I just wish you and Mother could attend as well."

Her father sighed. "I'm afraid that's impossible," he said. "I have paperwork to do and your mother has had a long week of work. Our agreement is that we will forego the pep rally and attend tomorrow's football game with you, all right?"

"That will be fine."

"Although I'll have no idea what I'll be watching. This American football mystifies me."

"And me as well. But, by all indications, it seems to be quite exciting. I even have one of the team's players in my class."

"Oh," said Gabrielle. "Is he a nice boy?"

"I can't tell," said Didi. "The others call him 'Bad News,' but I think that's because he's supposedly a big problem for his opponents."

"I see. And will we get to speak with the girl who is driving you tomorrow?"

Didi thought of the impression Heidi might make on her parents and inwardly shuddered. "I guess so," she finally answered.

* * *

Friday brought a whirlwind of activity to Stuart High. The hallways were festooned with school-colored streamers, and the varsity players paraded around in shirts and ties, overlapped with their red home jerseys. The cheerleaders wore the white "road" jerseys of their assigned player; some of the girls had applied streaks of red and black face paint to their cheeks or their hair. Didi couldn't help but make a comparison to the facial decorations of some of the tribes in the more remote areas of the Congo. During morning announcements both Mr. Hufnagel and Pierce issued their daily reminder to the student body to attend the pep rally.

It was on the way to American Lit, which Didi was quite enjoying despite Mr. O'Toole's dryness, that she first laid eyes on the school's glamour boy. Troy Winchester breezed through the halls of Stuart High like he owned the place—which was true, to some degree. With his longish black hair, blue eyes and chiseled features, he looked like an American movie star. It was no coincidence, then, that he was literally surrounded by fawning girls, as well as a few of his teammates, wherever he went. And when he shot Didi a wink in passing, she could actually feel her heart skip a beat.

Heidi, who was observing the circus, described this as the "Winchester effect," and told Didi that, unlike Bad News, the affable Mr. Winchester preferred to "keep his options open," thus giving the horde of females who stalked him equal opportunity to gain his favor—for the current week, anyway.

Didi was also impressed with the tremendous pile of scrap wood and used pallets that was being assembled in a space beyond the far end zone of the football field in preparation for the upcoming pep rally bonfire. Temporary metal bleacher stands had already been placed nearby, as well as a speaker's podium. As she circled the adjacent running track with her fellow phys-ed classmates, Didi took note of how meticulously the maintenance grounds crew were putting down white lines on the football field for the game. (The huge Jeb Stuart logo found on her T-shirt had been crafted at midfield earlier in the week and roped off.)

Her classes that day had been rather bland, with the teachers trying to keep their students' high spirits under control. True to form, Mr. Pennington had chosen to strictly adhere to his lesson plan, which was day two of an explanation of how the American slave trade came to be. After assigning most of the blame to the Portuguese, with an assist from the stronger African tribes whom he said "sold out" the weaker ones, Pennington proceeded to rationalize the thinking of the Southern plantation owners who brought in the slaves to work the land, and how it was a fight for economic survival.

Most, if not all, of Didi's classmates' minds were elsewhere. Bad News, who was uncharacteristically awake, was nervously tapping his right heel on the ground the whole time, his knee bouncing up and down as he watched the clock and awaited the evening's festivities.

But Didi was hanging on Pennington's every word and taking notes, because she was intent on looking up his "facts" over the weekend. And then she wondered if it was his intention all along to skim over this part of the historical narrative on a day when his students' thoughts would be elsewhere. She'd have to ask Heidi about that later.

* * *

At dinner, Didi was so excited she could hardly touch her food, and when Heidi pulled up a little late in a black SUV at the curb outside her house, she practically jumped out of her chair. Predictably, Dr. Diyoka walked her out to the car to meet the girl. Pleasantries were exchanged through the driver's side window as Didi buckled herself into the passenger seat; and though her father was clearly taken back a bit by the girl's appearance, he never let on to his daughter, only reminding her to come home after the pep rally's conclusion.

"Yes, Father," she obediently replied.

"Wow," said Heidi as she pulled away from the curb, "your dad's wound pretty tight."

"He is a bit conservative," agreed Didi.

"*A bit conservative*? Oh well, at least he let you out tonight," said the Goth girl. "I see you have your official Stuart High T-shirt on again."

"I figured this was appropriate," Didi responded innocently.

"Oh, it is," chided Heidi. "You'll fit right in, believe me." She turned on the SUV's radio to a heavy metal station, and Didi could feel the vehicle's doors vibrating. "We're gonna go through town first," Heidi shouted over the din. "You've just gotta see this."

Since they had moved in, Didi had only been "to town" a handful of times. Many of the larger stores, including the Old Navy and Walmart where she'd purchased her clothes, were located closer to the highway and could only be accessed by automobile. But the original town of Magnolia and its Main Street seemed to come from an earlier era. Many of the storefronts were fashioned from brick or stone and were no higher than one story, though a few had second story apartments overhead. There were quaint antique shops, cafés and offices such as the one her mother worked in, as well as a small grocery market, a laundromat, and the post office and library. But though there was still daylight left, they were buttoned up tight. Magnolia, South Carolina was a ghost town. "If you ever want to rob the bank," said Heidi, pointing to a stately granite building, "come on a Friday night during the football game. Nobody will notice."

They approached the Stuart High campus, passing Hampton Elementary and Shelby Middle School. "You realize, of course, that all the schools are named after Confederates, specifically cavalry guys," said Heidi. "They had to stay with the theme, I guess." She squinted through her purple eyeshadow. "Okay, start looking for a parking space. This is gonna be a challenge."

The girl was right; vehicles were parked haphazardly all along the feeder roads and embankments. The vast school parking lot was full as well, even in the rear. And across the street, in a huge vacant lot, SUVs, pickup trucks and minivans were surrounded by people tending to outdoor barbecue grills, their smoke wafting through the air, carrying the scent of pork and beef. "Oh, yeah," said Heidi. "This is called 'tailgating.' They do this before every home game, day or night, and of course the pep rally. You can bet a good deal of the adults are knocking back a few cold ones to get psyched for the rally, too."

"Cold ones?"

"Drinking, honey. Like beer or serious alcohol. As long as they're not on school grounds, the local police let them get away with it. Not the greatest example to set for us impressionable youngsters, don't you agree? And speaking of examples, do you notice how many of those pickup trucks are sporting flagpoles with the Stars and Bars?"

"Quite a few," observed Didi.

"Uh-huh. Football really brings out the rednecks. For a lot of 'em it's just an excuse to get sloshed and yell."

"I see."

"Hey, there's a spot!" Heidi quickly reversed into a space between a large rock and a motorcycle on the school's front lawn. "We're lucky. Now we only have to walk around to the back. Come on!"

They hopped out of the SUV and made their way to the football field, part of a streaming mass that came from all directions. The people were of all ages, dressed in school regalia, camouflage outfits, or bib overalls with T-shirts underneath. Some of the adults—and more than a few kids she'd seen around school—appeared to be inebriated, loudly addressing each other and calling attention to themselves.

Nearing the football field, they passed a tent, under which members of the student council—led by Pierce, of course—were selling Stuart T-shirts, hats, sweatshirts, seat cushions, and just about anything else with the Cavalier logo on it. Pierce waved to Didi and her friend as they speed-walked by. "Heidi, can I interest you in a shirt?" the student council president joked. Heidi smiled and gave him the finger.

"What does that mean?" asked Didi.

"That he's number one in my book," she replied tartly.

Within the throng Didi also spotted most of her teachers, and even waved to Mrs. Woodard, who was there with her husband and child. She wondered if the teachers felt any pressure to attend the gathering.

"Show's about to begin," said Heidi, as they settled onto the grass near the temporary bleachers. Many others had brought lawn chairs or staked out patches of real estate with blankets and coolers. Didi wondered what was in the coolers.

Suddenly, there came forth the sound of a marching band, the drums beating furiously. They emerged from around the side of the school in rows of six, the drum major out front and wielding a huge baton. Didi thought the musicians' uniforms closely resembled the photos of Confederate soldiers that Mr. Pennington had posted in their classroom, gray tunics trimmed in gold with brass buttons in a double row down the front, and matching gray pants accentuated by a gold stripe down the side. Their military-looking peaked hats were red with black trim, a large black and red S above the visor. Methodically, they trooped across the green space to the athletic field, the brass section complimenting the booming drums.

Behind the band skipped the cheerleaders, clad in a clingy white tops and short skirts, with the familiar black and red S on their chests, and shaking gray and red pom-poms. They were followed by other girls in Stuart High T-shirts and black pants whom Heidi explained were the pep squad. "Those that didn't make the cut as cheerleaders," she snidely pointed out.

The pep squad was finally followed by the varsity

team athletes and their coaches. First came cross country, then field hockey and soccer. They marched in rows of two, in uniform, waving to the cheering crowd, before taking their seats by team beginning with the bottom bench of the portable bleachers. Finally, the football squad emerged from the building, led by co-captains Winchester and Braxton, wearing their jerseys over khaki trousers. The place went wild, and the band launched into a jaunty tune Didi had heard before. "That song was in the Civil War documentary," she said to Heidi.

"No duh. That's 'Dixie,' honey, the Confederate theme song, which just happens to be our school's fight song as well."

The rebel anthem took the crowd's fever pitch up another notch, and many of the adults—the white ones, anyway—sang along. *Oh, I wish I was in the land of cotton...*

Once all the athletes were seated, Mr. Hufnagel—a portly white man with sandy hair and dressed in a red Stuart golf shirt—quieted the crowd, and then offered a quick welcome before turning the introductions over to a Mr. Ketler, a reed-thin, balding man who identified himself as the athletic director. He thanked everyone for coming out on "this beautiful South Carolina evening" and emphasized how hard the athletes had been working for the opening of their seasons. The crowd cheered. Then, one by one, the teams were introduced by their coaches to polite applause from the parents and the students.

"Okay, that's out of the way," said Heidi, swatting a mosquito. "Now the fun starts."

Indeed, when Bryan Kurtt, the square-jawed,

crewcut head football coach strode to the podium, he was met with whooping and hollering that he drank in for a good thirty seconds before raising his muscular arms for quiet. "Good evenin', Stuart High!" he called, touching off another round of cheers and whistles. "I just want to say how proud I am of this group of young men who will be representing Stuart High and the town of Magnolia this season. I'll tell you what, we won't be happy until we bring y'all home the district championship trophy!"

Again, the crowd erupted.

"And I am proud to introduce to you the members of your 2013 Stuart High Cavaliers!" One by one, he read the names of each player, who stood up to bask in the glory of the moment. Finally, he called his co-captains down to the podium to say a few words.

Troy Winchester and Travis Braxton approached the microphone and let the adulation of the crowd wash over them, waving and laughing. They met with Kurtt, who shook their hands and stepped aside. Winchester, the golden boy, played to the crowd, winking and pointing to a few (probably female) members of the crowd before promising, "If y'all come out tomorrow and support us, I guarantee you we'll play our hearts out!"

Then it was Braxton's turn, and the crowd chanted "Bad News! Bad News! Bad News!" until he raised a hand to quiet them. Didi couldn't help feeling that this must be the high point of the young man's life, which for some reason gave her a twinge of sadness. "Hope to see y'all tomorrow," he said in a pleasant baritone Didi had never heard. "Gonna be a great game." He turned to his co-captain. "But, uh, aren't we missing something?"

"I think we are!" Winchester cried dramatically.

At that moment, the crowd began to chant, "We want Jeb! We want Jeb!"

As if summoned, a dark-bearded horseman appeared over the rise in a nearby field that was bordered by a low, split rail fence. He sat tall in the saddle, his garish gray and gold uniform finished off with knee-high black boots complete with shining spurs, and a gray slouch hat with an enormous plume. A saber hung at his side, and a black cape with red lining flapped in the breeze as his ebony stallion picked up speed. In one white-gauntleted hand he carried aloft a blazing torch. The crowd held its breath as the steed accelerated toward the fence, then cleared it with a magnificent leap. "Jeb" galloped ahead toward the enormous pile of wood, and with a throaty yell, flung the torch into the gasoline-soaked structure, which ignited with a *whoosh*. Then he pulled back on the horse's reins, causing it to rear dramatically in front of the conflagration. The gathering nearly lost its mind, and even Heidi grinned. "I love fires," she said, the blaze reflected in her eyes.

Finally, with a flourish, the rider removed his hat, windmilling it around before replacing it and bolting from the scene, again clearing the fence with ease and disappearing over the ridge.

The crowd whooped and screamed (Heidi described it as "the rebel yell") and for some minutes watched the bonfire with pure rapture as the athletes dismounted the bleachers and mingled with their parents and friends. It appeared the party would go on for quite some time, though by Didi's watch, it was already nine p.m.

"Okay, I've seen what I wanted to see," said Heidi abruptly. "Want to go for a burger?"

"Where?" asked Didi, remembering her promise to return home after the rally. "The whole town is shut down."

"Yeah, but there's a Mickey D's out by the highway. Don't worry, I'll have you home by 10:30, max."

"What's Mickey D's?"

"Something you need to experience," she said, and grabbed her wrist. "C'mon, we've gotta beat the crowd out of here."

* * *

If the small town of Magnolia could be interpreted as "Old South," the shopping mall out by the exit for State Highway 26 could be termed "anywhere America." Contained in its boundaries were not only a McDonald's, Wendy's and Pizza Hut, but a Starbucks, Home Depot, Super Walmart, Old Navy, and a bank. Because of the hour and the pep rally nearby, it was fairly quiet, which was great, as far as Heidi was concerned. "You've been shopping here, I take it?" she said as they turned into the huge parking lot.

"Oh, yes," replied Didi. "It seems there isn't anything you can't find here. My father takes my mother to the Super Walmart for groceries because the selection in the Magnolia market is so small."

"Uh-huh." She pulled the car around to the drive-up display. "So, what do you want?" she asked. "I'm buying."

"I really don't know what to order," confessed Didi. "What is their specialty?"

Heidi rolled her eyes. "Let me handle it," she said, and put in an order for two quarter pounders with cheese, two large fries, and two vanilla shakes. When the speaker squawked back with the price, Didi's eyes widened. As if reading her mind, the Goth girl said, "Don't worry, I got it." She pulled up to the pickup window, peeled off a twenty dollar bill, and brought back an aromatic brown bag. "We'll eat in the car," she said, drifting over to a parking space near the edge of the McDonald's lot. "That way we can keep the AC on and not get eaten alive by the bugs." She put the SUV in PARK and opened the bag. "Now, let's see what we've got here," she said eagerly.

Didi hadn't had much to eat at dinner, mostly due to her excitement over the pep rally, and it took the aroma of a hot burger and fries to remind herself that she was famished. Heidi placed their shakes in the console cupholders, jammed in plastic straws, and then handed over Didi's boxed quarter pounder and container of fries. "I don't know if I can finish all of this," Didi said.

"I'll bet you can, once you get started," Heidi replied while squirting ketchup from a packet onto her burger. "Someday I'm going to start eating healthy," she said, replacing the bun top. "But today isn't it." With that, she tore into her quarter pounder with cheese.

They ate in silence, and Didi was captivated by the strange tastes rolling around inside her mouth. The gritty texture of the meat, the vinegary tang of the pickles, the gooey cheese—it was almost too much. And the fries! Crunchy, salty, cooked to perfection.

Following Heidi's lead, she stopped occasionally for a sip from her thick and creamy shake, which coated the food as it slid down her throat. "This is so delicious," she finally said.

"No doubt. It can kill ya, but it's pretty darn good."

Didi took another pull on her shake straw. "Are you going to the game tomorrow?" she asked.

"Nah. I'm not into football, though I'm sure the team will win. Spring Valley won't know what hit them. Like I said, I go to the pep rally 'cause I like fires."

"Jeb Stuart was quite impressive. Who is he, exactly?"

"As far as I know, a local Civil War enthusiast who's a Stuart maniac. He does reenactments and all."

"What exactly *are* reenactments?"

"Oh, you don't know? Well, it's an excuse for grown men—and some women, if you can believe it—to dress up and play soldier. These guys suit up in Union and Confederate uniforms, with horses and cannons and rifles—the whole nine yards—and reenact battles for other crazies who show up to watch it all. They also have campouts on farmers' fields and march in parades on Memorial Day and whatever. It's a real big deal down here."

"Don't they get hurt? With the guns and all?"

"No," chuckled Heidi, popping a French fry into her mouth. "They're just shooting blanks. It *sounds* real, though."

"But what's the purpose?"

"Good question. They say they're preserving history, but like I said, it's just a chance for them to run around and shoot guns. Would you want to check out one of these deals?"

"A reenactment? Sure, I think it would be interesting," said Didi. "Do you know of any that are coming up?"

"Not off the top of my head, but we can ask Pennington on Monday. He's one of those nut cases who do it."

"Speaking of Pennington, what did you think of the lesson today? I felt that he was glossing over the slavery issue."

"Of course he was. And, I'm sure you noticed, he picked a day when everybody in the class would be out to lunch mentally. You see, in his curriculum, slavery is just a nagging detail in the epic story of the South's struggle for independence. I doubt if he will spend much more time on it."

"Well, I think we should. You know, after school today I did some research on the role of my region—the Congo—in the slave trade. Do you realize that roughly three million slaves came from my region of Africa? Almost forty per cent of all the slaves transported?"

Heidi took a long pull on her straw. "Yeah, okay, but so what?" she said. "Are you gonna call him on it in class, or just sit there all pissed off?"

"I'm not sure."

Heidi gathered their garbage, stuffed it back into the McDonald's bag, and disposed of it in a nearby trash can as Didi watched a swarm of moths circling a parking lot light above the SUV. "You can moan about it all you want," she said, returning to the vehicle and starting the car, "but unless you speak up, he'll just keep spewing his crap. Just remember, honey, if you *do* speak up, you're in enemy territory. What you've got to say might ruffle some feathers."

They left the shopping mall lot and headed for Magnolia, the moon shining brightly above. "Thanks for the Mickey D's," said Didi. "It was fabulous."

"No problem," said Heidi, accelerating to the speed limit.

"I just have one question," said Didi. "When Mr. Pennington dresses up for his reenactments, what uniform does he wear?"

"You've got to be kidding," said Heidi.

Chapter Six

It had rained sporadically during the late-night hours, but the inclement weather provided no relief from the next day's humidity level. Didi was awakened by the sound of a truck entering her driveway, followed by the banging of its doors opening and machinery being offloaded. A trip to her bedroom window revealed the presence of the Tomlin Landscaping Company, whose rather large flatbed truck held a riding mower and various trimming and pruning tools and equipment.

Among the workers hopping out of the truck's cab was Seth Tomlin, one of the boys from her Civil War Studies class, who today was outfitted in work boots, camouflage pants and a long-sleeved green pullover shirt with *Tomlin's* emblazoned across the back in gaudy gold script. In school, Seth seemed to be one of a group of boys that Heidi referred to as "rednecks" or "crackers"; he spoke with a pronounced drawl and always appeared to move in slow motion. This morning was no exception, as the man in charge, whom Didi presumed to be his father, started barking orders as soon as the boy's work boots hit the driveway surface. These directives were met with a languid "yessir" or "uh-huh" as the lanky teen took down a gas-powered edge trimmer from a side rack on the truck's flatbed.

Didi quickly showered, changed into jeans and her Stuart High T-shirt for the football game that afternoon, and went downstairs, where her parents were having breakfast as her father read the paper.

"How was the pep rally, Dihya?" asked her mother as she placed a bowl of homemade fruit salad before the girl.

"Very exciting," she replied. "It seemed like the entire school was there, and many other people as well. There's certainly a lot of support for the athletic teams, especially football. Everybody was looking forward to the game today."

"I was less than impressed with the young lady who drove you to the rally last night," said Dr. Diyoka. "Does she dress like that every day?"

"That's just her style, Father," she answered, sipping her orange juice. "I think Heidi is actually a good person underneath. And I must admit, she's shown a true interest in making me feel more comfortable here, whereas most of the students are rather indifferent."

Her father turned the page with a snap. "If you say so. I'm just hoping your circle of friends gradually widens."

"I'm sure it will." She decided to change the subject. "Did you know these workers were coming this morning?" she asked.

"Oh, yes," said Maurice. "Dr. Buono told me they will be attending to the yard every week or two while they're away." As if on cue, the gas trimmer and riding mower fired up outside.

"I think one of the workers is in my class at school," said Didi. "I'm going to go say hello." She finished her fruit salad, kissed her father on the forehead, and left through the rear entrance to the patio. Crossing to the grass, she came upon Seth, who was diligently edging around Dr. Buono's flower bed. She wondered if he had even noticed her in class, or if he'd recognize her. That he did became obvious when his eyes widened upon her approach.

"What're *you* doin' here?" he asked, shutting off the trimmer, whose blades had deposited wet grass on his lower pant legs.

"I live here," she replied. "My family is staying in Dr. Buono's house for the year because my father's working at Providence Heart Hospital in Columbia. You're Seth, right?"

"Uh-huh," he replied. The boy seemed incredulous that Didi's family was occupying such a stately residence.

Didi sensed his discomfort and tried to make conversation. "Are you going to the game today?" she asked.

"Gotta work," he replied. "My dad over there let me try out for football as a freshman, but I got cut, so that was that. After that, I kind of lost interest. 'Sides, this is gonna be my business someday, so I might as well learn all about it."

"I see," she said. "So, ah, how are you enjoying our Civil War Studies class?"

"It's okay, I guess," he replied. "A lot of it I know already, but Pennington's an okay guy, and a pretty easy marker. I just wanna graduate and get on with my life, you know? One thing confuses me, though."

"What's that?"

"Why on earth would *you* want to take that course? What are you gonna get out of it?"

"I'm just trying to learn about America, I guess," she replied.

"Suit y'self," he said. "Listen, I've gotta get back to work. My old man's giving me the eye already." He pulled on the starting cord and the trimmer's motor howled to life, abruptly ending their conversation.

"See you Monday," she said, but Seth had already resumed his task, his head down. She waved to the man in charge, who nodded in her direction, and went back inside.

* * *

As was the case the previous evening, the school's parking lot and adjoining grounds were packed with cars. It also seemed that some of the vehicles located in the tailgating lot had simply stayed overnight to do it all over again this afternoon. (According to the schedule posted at school, this was to be the only home game not played on a Friday night). Again, many patrons were grilling, eating, and drinking beer.

The Diyokas seemed impressed at the outpouring of town spirit being exhibited, and Didi tried to explain the few football-related traditions she'd learned about so far. She did, however, notice her father staring at the Confederate flags that flew in the tailgate lot, and her mother nervously clutching her husband's hand as he took in the sight.

Nevertheless, they stopped at the student government tent, where Didi introduced her parents to

Pierce, who made it a point to come around the table so he could shake hands with them both. "We're so pleased to have y'all staying with us here in Magnolia," he said sincerely. "And I'm real happy to have Didi in my home room."

"Why, thank you," said Mrs. Diyoka. "My daughter speaks highly of you as well." They each ended up purchasing a Stuart Cavaliers pennant, and a big box of popcorn to munch on during the game.

"That boy is a real politician," said Maurice, echoing Heidi's words.

They found a seat in the bleachers and settled in as the visiting team from Spring Valley went through their pregame drills. The stands on both sides were full, and Didi estimated they held upwards of 5,000 people. "Where is the Stuart team?" asked Dr. Diyoka.

"They already went through their pregame stuff," said a man wedged in alongside him. "Now they're inside the locker room gettin' psyched up. They'll be out shortly, don't you worry."

Didi noticed that down below in the stands, the band occupied their own section, with their director atop an elevated platform facing them. An enticing aroma of grilling meat drifted over from the concession area beyond one of the end zones. A minute or so later, the cheerleaders and pep squad moved to the end zone closest to the school and formed a chute, with the two girls on the end unfurling and then gripping the edges of a large red paper banner with the inscription *GO CAVS 2013* in black. This flurry of activity got the crowd buzzing in anticipation.

"They're comin', son!" announced Dr. Diyoka's neighbor excitedly.

And then, the doors to the field house up the hill burst open and the Stuart Cavaliers emerged, with captains Winchester and Braxton out front, their helmets buckled on. Purposefully they strode down the hill to the end zone, and the band broke into "Dixie" as the home crowd stood and roared in what Heidi had termed as the "rebel yell."

Once the team reached the end zone, they took off in a sprint through the lane of cheerleaders and pep squaders with upraised pom-poms and burst through the paper banner, evoking howls from the crowd. They came together on the sideline in one large mass, jumping up and down and chanting; Didi couldn't help but compare what she was seeing to some tribal rituals in the Congo. Then, Mr. Hufnagel, who doubled as the football team's home announcer, asked everyone to please rise and remove their hats for the playing of the national anthem by the Stuart band. And although she noticed that practically everyone complied with the standing part (with the Stuart and Spring Valley football players standing at attention along the sidelines, their helmets held in the crook of their left arm) a lot of fans failed to bare their heads. Some of the hats on those heads bore the Confederate flag.

Once the pageantry was done, the game began, and even to those like the Diyokas who knew nothing about American football, it quickly became apparent that the team from Spring Valley was overmatched. When Stuart had the ball they methodically marched down the field, with Troy Winchester flinging the ball all over the place. Every time they scored, the band burst into "Dixie" and Mr. Hufnagel, who appeared so controlled during morning announcements, seemed to ratchet up his fervor with every score, practically screaming through the stadium's PA system. The cheerleaders celebrated each touchdown by going through a gyrating dance routine that Didi (and her parents, though they didn't come out and say it) considered somewhat suggestive. Of course, her focus went to Tanya Mims, who pranced and preened, totally in her glory.

But Didi was most interested in the play of her classmate Travis, and he didn't disappoint, throwing blockers aside like rag dolls and chasing down whoever had the ball before thumping them to the ground. The crowd rang cowbells and chanted "Bad News! Bad News!" every time he made a tackle, and he acknowledged their cheers by popping up and beating his chest three times with his right fist, his dreadlocks trailing from the back of his helmet to his shoulder pads.

"Your friend is quite an athlete," observed Dr. Diyoka.

"I hope he's not hurting anyone," added Gabrielle, who winced with each audible *pop* on the field below.

By halftime the Cavaliers were ahead 28-0, and the home crowd was euphoric as they left the bleachers for the concession stands which sold hot dogs, hamburgers, chips, and soda pop. It was at the concession stand that the Diyokas ran into Ms. Redwine, who seemed pretty charged up by the team's performance. "So, what do y'all think of our boys?" she asked, swigging an RC Cola from a can.

"They're performing beautifully," said Dr. Dioka, "though I'm still mystified by the rules of the game."

"Oh, you'll get it eventually," she replied jovially. "It isn't rocket science. Just keep scoring touchdowns, and stop the other team from doing it, too!"

"I suppose," he said. Then he lowered his voice an octave, and Didi became worried—he only did that when he was distressed about something. "Ms. Redwine," he said, "I've been reading in the papers how there's a serious controversy in Columbia about the flying of the Confederate flag on the grounds of the State Capital Building. Are you aware of this?"

The woman blushed. "Why, yes, Dr. Diyoka, of course I'm aware. It's been a big story for some months now," she said.

"Then can you please tell me why this acknowledged symbol of oppression is permitted on school grounds? I see flags and apparel with it everywhere, displayed by young and old alike. Is this an image that Stuart High is promoting?"

"Well, no, not actually," she spluttered, and Didi was dying of embarrassment watching her struggle. "It's just a part of our football—"

"Tradition? Is that the word? Because I would hardly think that a team so focused on winning would draw upon a losing cause for inspiration."

"Maurice, please," whispered his wife, who also sensed the guidance counselor's distress.

Meanwhile, the band had run through their halftime repertoire and was returning to the bleachers for the second half. Didi asked her father if she could please have a hot dog, and both she and her mother gently steered him away from Ms. Redwine, who stared after them. "Father, would you like to go home?" Didi asked as he handed some bills to one of the booster club parent volunteers that ran the concession stand.

"No, no need for that," he said quietly. "We paid for a ticket to a full game, and that is what we'll see." So they returned to the stands and found a spot, and while Didi was somewhat distracted by the pleasant experience of her first grilled hot dog with mustard, deep inside she wished she could be somewhere else.

The second half of the game followed the same pattern as the first, with Stuart piling on points and their fans becoming more and more rowdy, especially with "Dixie" being played what seemed like every two minutes. Finally, in the fourth quarter, Coach Kurtt pulled his starters and gave the substitutes some playing time. The final score was 47-14, but it wasn't that close, as Spring Valley only scored against the Cavaliers' second teamers.

The game mercifully ended with Mr. Hufnagel blaring, "And the final score is your Stuart Cavaliers 47, Spring Valley High...14! Y'all have a safe trip home, and we'll see you next week at our Friday night game over at Calhoun. Our bus caravan will leave from here at five p.m., so come on out and support your Cavs!"

The Diyokas walked to their car in silence. Once again, Didi spotted some of her teachers and waved, though there was no way she was going to stop and chat—not after the debacle with Ms. Redwine. But alas, a clean exit from the grounds of Stuart High was not to be.

In the row of cars before theirs two men—one in a Stuart hat and the other in Spring Valley green and gold colors, were yelling at each other about a scratch on the Stuart man's pickup truck. "Y'all hit my car!" the beefy Stuart fan, red-faced and apparently somewhat inebriated, shouted at his nemesis, who was a good six inches shorter.

"That's bull!" the other man retorted. "You're a damn liar!"

People returning to their cars cut this escalating altercation a wide berth, looking the other way, but Didi was mortified to see her father actually slow down.

"You're just cryin' 'cause we beat your ass, boy!" the Stuart fan taunted. "Maybe I should beat yours too, all the way back to Spring Valley!"

"Yeah? Go on and try it!"

The Stuart man started pulling back his fist, but the smaller—and less drunk—man from Spring Valley was too quick, slugging him in his ample belly and dropping him like a sack of potatoes. As he writhed on the ground the Spring Valley fan and his wife climbed into their car and took off, their rear tires throwing up patches of grass.

The stricken man was clearly having trouble breathing, with his wife, a wiry woman with shoulder length bleached blonde hair and tattooed forearms, desperately trying to roll him onto his back. It was then that Dr. Diyoka approached her to offer assistance. But instead of welcoming his help, her eyes bulged and she screamed, "Get away from him! Don't you touch him!"

"Madame," he said, "I'm a doctor—"

"I don't care *what* you are! You get away from us!"

Dr. Diyoka took a deep breath, then let it out and walked to his car, with Didi and her mother in tow.

Calmly, he buckled his seatbelt, pushed the ignition button, and checked his rearview mirror before putting the car in DRIVE and falling into the long line of vehicles leaving the parking lot. Didi felt like she was going to melt. "I'm sorry, Father," she said finally, tears rolling down her face. "I'll never go to another football game, I promise."

"Dihya," he said, his voice wavering ever so slightly, "this today was about more than a football game. The fact is, I'm wondering if I have failed you."

"*Failed* me? But how?"

"By bringing you to this place. I...I don't know if we belong here."

Didi was beside herself with panic. "Please, Father," she begged, "this position at Providence Heart can be so important for your career. And I do want to go to college here in America. It's your dream!"

Finally, her mother spoke. "Maurice," she said, "you made a commitment, both to the hospital and to your daughter. We have to see this through. Don't let one experience cloud your reasoning. There is so much more at stake."

Dr. Diyoka sighed. "We shall see," was all he said.

Chapter Seven

"So, how was the football game?" asked Heidi as the girls removed the morning's materials from their lockers.

"The game itself was fine," replied Didi. "It was quite exciting, actually. And Travis played very well. The crowd kept chanting his name."

"Yeah, I heard they put a real beat-down on Spring Valley. Everybody's patting them on the back this morning." Indeed, none of the team's players could venture down a hallway without some kind of acknowledgment—usually a high-five—from their classmates and teachers.

But Heidi could sense there was something more to the story and said, "What else, then? Did your parents like it?"

"Not exactly." She then proceeded to relate the various events that had occurred involving her father.

"Wow," said the Goth girl. "He really got in Redwine's face about the flag thing? I bet she wanted to die."

"So did I," said Didi.

"And why's that? It's not your problem, it's theirs for allowing it. Your dad was just calling them on it. I kinda think I like him." She paused. "And what did he think of me?"

"Truthfully? He isn't sure what to make of you."

"Perfect. Let's get to homeroom so we can hear Hufnagel's happy recap of the game."

Sure enough, after the pledge their principal lauded the gridiron exploits of the Cavaliers while also commending the spirit and "exemplary behavior" of the student body at both the pep rally and the game. "Now if only the adults could do the same thing," quipped Heidi, and Didi couldn't help but chuckle. Then Pierce came on and offered his two cents on the rout, before inviting his fellow students to join the car caravan to Calhoun on Friday night. "In the paper they said the team might go undefeated this year," remarked Heidi as they left homeroom. "I don't even want to think what that would be like. Those guys will be insufferable."

* * *

It was becoming obvious with each passing day that Didi was an academic all-star. She traded insights with Mr. O'Toole on the protagonist's motivation in Poe's "The Cask of Amontillado" and delicately led her team in a frog dissection that had Dr. Zavorskas calling her a "future surgeon." And, of course, art and phys-ed were easy and fun.

But then came Civil War Studies, where she clearly felt overmatched. Today Mr. Pennington started talking about the early battles of the war and showed clips from a History Channel program called *Civil War Journal* about a battle named Antietam, where over 20,000 men had fallen in a matter of hours. A moral victory for the Confederates, who fought an overconfident Union force to a standoff, Antietam was in Pennington's words "an indication that the war would not be an open-and-shut affair," and that "the fighting spirit of the Southern man" had been grossly underestimated by the people in the North.

He also rattled off the names of battles fought in South Carolina: Secessionville, Simmons Bluff, Rivers Bridge, Aiken and Honey Hill. Didi furiously took notes, but couldn't keep pace with the information being thrown at her.

"Don't feel bad," said Heidi after class was dismissed, "this guy's a walking encyclopedia on battle strategy and casualties and military minutia. Just keep saying to yourself, 'The good guys won.'"

"That's not enough," Didi countered. "If I'm ever going to dispute his claims, as you said I should, I have to know more. Look what I got in the library during study hall."

Heidi's eyes widened as Didi pulled from her backpack the entire Ken Burns documentary DVD set and its accompanying text, which had to be three inches thick. "You're gonna go through all that?" she asked incredulously.

"I'll use it as we move along," she replied.

"Have fun."

But Didi wasn't finished. On the bus ride home she made it a point to ask Pierce for his class notes on the course.

"Funny you asked," he said. "I actually came across them the other day and put them aside for you. Would you like me to bring them to school tomorrow?"

"Actually, I wanted to get a look at them before I do my homework tonight," she replied. "Is it okay if I stop by today after school and pick them up? I'm only a short distance away."

"Don't see why that should be a problem," he said. "The address is 55 Harmony Street."

"Great," she said. "I'll be over in about an hour."

* * *

After unpacking and enjoying a healthy snack (her mom strongly opposed American junk food such as chips and candy), Didi strolled over to Harmony Street. It was a glorious afternoon, with a cooling breeze that provided a welcome respite from the ever-present humidity.

Pierce's home, located on a cul-de-sac, was impressive, a three-story Greek revival structure with two huge Doric columns framing the front door. It made Dr. Buono's house look relatively small, and the lawn and shrubbery bordering the slate front walk were carefully manicured.

Didi climbed the short staircase to the front porch and depressed the doorbell; a stately chiming sound rang within and seemed to echo. Seconds later a woman who looked like a female version of Pierce answered the door, wearing a tennis outfit and sneakers and holding a drink in a tall glass. She had wrapped the glass's bottom with a napkin and secured it with a rubber band. Didi wondered what could be in the glass, as it was of an amber hue with a mint leaf as a garnish.

"Can I help you?" said the woman brightly, the tanned skin at the corners of her eyes creasing.

"Hello, ma'am," she answered. "I'm Didi Diyoka,

Pierce's friend. He said to come over so I could borrow some materials for school."

The woman seemed taken aback, but never lost her smile. "Oh," she said, "of course. I asked Pierce to run into town to pick up some groceries for dinner, so I'm afraid you've missed him. But he did tell me you might be coming, so he left the school stuff inside. Please come in, and I'll fetch it for you."

Didi entered a hardwood-floored foyer with a sweeping double staircase that led to the second level. A crystal chandelier hung from above. "Your home is very pretty," she said with admiration.

"Why, thank you. Please wait in the living room and I'll be right with you," said Mrs. Farnsworth with a sweep of her unoccupied hand.

Once inside, Didi was met with a sight that she never expected. The spacious room - furnished with antique sofas and wing chairs, with Persian area rugs atop the polished hardwoods - though extravagant, were not what caught her eye. Instead, it was the decorative accessories that dominated, for Confederate-themed memorabilia seemed to be everywhere. End tables featured statuettes of Robert E. Lee, Stonewall Jackson and Jeb Stuart, and the side walls were adorned with portraits, in gilded gold frames, of Lee and Jefferson Davis.

But the huge framed piece over the white fireplace mantel was a show-stopper: entitled *The Last Meeting*, as indicated by a brass plaque built into the frame, it depicted Lee and Jackson conferring, presumably before a battle. Didi was reading the plaque as Mrs. Farnsworth crept up behind her, so she almost jumped when the woman said, "That's a print of a famous painting. It captures the parting of the generals before Stonewall was killed at the battle of Chancellorsville. Some believe his death turned the tide of the war."

Didi turned to find the woman with a sheaf of papers in one hand, and an obviously refreshed drink in the other. "Uh, it's very well done," she managed. She pointed to a jar of round and oblong metal objects that sat on the mantle. "What are those?"

"Oh, those are spent bullets, minié balls and such, from various battlefields in the war," Mrs. Farnsworth said nonchalantly.

"I see."

The woman smiled. "I'll bet you're wondering about our choice of decor. Well, I wouldn't blame you—it's somewhat eccentric. But you might want to know that one of Pierce's ancestors was an officer in the 7th Carolina infantry regiment during the war. He lost a leg in the Battle of the Wilderness and died later of complications brought on by infection. This is just our way of memorializing his heroism."

Didi dumbly nodded.

"Colonel Dunham, that was his name, is buried in the Confederate Cemetery in Richmond, which as you might know was the capital of the Confederacy for most of the war. But he was actually from this very area."

"Oh," said Didi. "Was he wealthy?"

"Oh my, yes," said the woman. "He had a huge tobacco plantation, which was ravaged, and then confiscated, by the Yankees." She seemed to spit out the last few words, and Didi wondered if perhaps it was the alcohol talking. "So," said Mrs. Farnsworth, "if I may inquire, what made you decide to take the Civil War course?"

She shrugged. It was the second time in a matter of days she'd been asked this question. "I just like history, I guess," she replied. "But I had no idea Pierce had a family connection to the war."

"Well, he tries not to brag about it," she sniffed, "but that doesn't mean—"

At that moment Pierce, who seemed out of breath, burst through the door, clutching a brown bag of groceries to his chest. "Oh, Didi, you're here," he said as calmly as possible.

"Yes," said his mother. "And we were having a wonderful chat. Please bring the groceries into the kitchen, Pierce," she said, and led him through a swinging door, leaving the girl alone again.

Didi felt extremely uncomfortable, but what happened next made it even worse. The voices of mother and son—obviously heated—were muffled by the door, but still discernible. "You didn't tell me the girl was *black*," said the woman. "What were you thinking?"

"Mom, I didn't feel it should matter," replied the boy. "I was only trying to be helpful—"

"*Helpful?* That girl is probably in there laughing at you—at *us*. I want her gone. Do you hear me?"

"Yes, ma'am. Right away."

He pushed through the door, and Didi could spy the woman taking another gulp from her drink in the background. But if Pierce was out of sorts, he managed to conceal it behind his usual dazzling smile. "Sorry I was late," he said, guiding her to the front entrance. "Everything you should need is in that packet. Let me know if you have any questions at school tomorrow. I'll see you." And he gently closed the door, leaving her alone on the porch, her heart sick.

* * *

That night Didi, who was becoming more comfortable with the Internet, googled Pierce's ancestor, Colonel Ramsey Dunham, of the 7th South Carolina infantry. A black-and-white portrait image came up showing a man of medium build, with a neatly trimmed beard and slicked-down, side-parted hair. He was pictured in military dress, his hat on his lap, with a gray uniform that seemed less ornate then that of her school's namesake.

Upon further examination Didi found that Colonel Dunham did, indeed, own one of the larger plantations in Calhoun County; his tobacco fields had encompassed 300 acres and registered a working force of 125 slaves. Didi gawked at the number. Not only was Pierce's relative a Confederate war hero—he was a major slave owner! She sat back in her chair, stunned. No wonder the boy's home was a shrine to the Confederacy.

But the question remained as to whether Pierce shared the obvious pride his mother had exhibited during her visit…or if his cheerfully abrupt dismissal of her from the house belied a sense of shame about his heritage. She was curious to find the truth.

Chapter Eight

"Wait a minute," said Heidi during lunch the next day, "you eat *bugs* in Africa?" They had been discussing dietary traditions in the Congo, and Didi had included this nugget of information while describing a trip to the Grand Market of Mossendjo, where such delicacies as crushed, boiled or fried insects—especially caterpillars, her favorite—could be found.

"They're quite nutritious, actually," she said while peeling a banana. "And tasty, if you can believe it."

"I'll stick to Starbursts, thank you," said the Goth girl. "Want one?"

"Sure," said Didi. After popping it into her mouth and wincing at the assault on her taste buds, she recounted her visit to the Farnsworth residence the previous day as Heidi listened raptly.

"Wow," she said. "Yeah, Pierce's mom is all over town—the Women's League, the country club, all kinds of stuff. And, the rumor is she likes to have a drink or three. So, their house is Johnny Reb headquarters, huh? Pretty freaky. But it makes sense, on a few levels. First, of course, is the fact that Pierce's great-great whatever was a Confederate officer. And a slave owner on top of it. Then there's the D.O.C. thing."

"D.O.C.? What's that?"

"Those initials, honey, stand for the Daughters of the Confederacy. Ever heard of 'em?"

"No."

"Well, you wouldn't, being over in Africa. So, I'll tell you what there is to know." She pulled out her cell phone and placed it on her lap, away from the prying eyes of teachers, as phone usage was frowned upon on school grounds. After a few seconds she said, "All right, got it. Here are the highlights. It was established in 1894 in Nashville, Tennessee, and has been labeled as neo-Confederate by a national organization that monitors hate groups and extremists. Now, the D.O.C. *claims* to be there merely to commemorate the valor of Confederate soldiers and fund memorials to them, but they've been tied to everything from promoting Confederate traditions and white supremacy, to supporting the KKK."

"What's that?"

"A major white supremacist hate group that was formed after the South's defeat to more or less harass blacks, Jews, and whoever else they determined to be 'un-American,' or at least keep them in their place. They sometimes get decked out in white robes and cone-shaped hoods and generally conduct mayhem."

"Can anybody join?" asked Didi.

"The D.O.C.? Nope. To get in, you have to be able to trace your lineage back to a Confederate soldier. Members consider it a proud birthright thing. Which brings us to our friend, Mrs. Farnsworth. As you learned, her ancestor was a fairly prominent soldier in the war. And that is why she is reportedly one of the top mucky-mucks in the local chapter of the D.O.C. And why, if one can extend the thinking here, Pierce is probably a proud member of the D.O.C.'s auxiliary organization, the Children of the Confederacy."

Didi felt as if she'd been punched in the stomach. "Pierce?" she said. "I find that hard to believe."

"Oh, really? Want to find out for sure?"

"How can we do that?"

"Simple. The Daughters of the Confederacy has a monthly evening meeting in the basement rooms of the Masonic Hall here in Magnolia. Hell, it's advertised in the local paper! If you're feeling adventurous, we can probably spy on them. I bet they leave the lower windows open to keep the place ventilated, so it shouldn't be too challenging...if you're not too scared."

"But how would we get there?"

"Again, no big deal. You tell your parents you're going to the library to study, I pick you up, and boom—there we are." She stealthily returned the cell phone to her backpack. "Think about it," she said. "It could be veddy interesting."

* * *

It seemed that something about America or her school surprised Didi every day or so, and this Wednesday provided a double event. The first occurred before homeroom when Heidi, polishing off her first Red Bull of the day, said, "Are you aware that you're starting to get looks from some of these boys?"

She was both flattered and concerned. "What kind of looks?" she whispered.

"Good ones, I would think," said the Goth girl, who then swallowed a belch. "Of course, it's the black guys. We are in South Carolina, don't forget."

"Of course. But why do you think this is?"

"Really? Duh. First of all, you're exotic to them. You've got that little accent thing going, and the conservative stuff you wear every day has them intrigued. You're like the mystery babe from the Motherland. Of course, it has kinda the opposite effect on your American 'sistas'. They probably think you're stuck-up or something."

Didi was horrified. "Why would they think that? I try to be kind to everyone!"

"I know, I know," she said. "But, see, unlike a lot of them you're not going out of your way to get attention, and the guys *still* notice you. I guess in a way it's intimidating to those girls."

"Great," she muttered.

"Hey, it's not your fault," Heidi shrugged. "You're just being yourself and not a phony, like for example, our friend Tanya Mims."

"Well, Travis seems to like her."

"I think he more than 'likes' her, if you know what I mean. But right now, she's just an ornament he can show off for his Neanderthal football buddies. It won't last."

"Maybe so." She paused and then said, "How about you, Heidi? I've never heard you mention a boy you might like."

"In *this* place? Please. Either you've got the Joe Jocks who only lust after cheerleaders, the rednecks who'd rather chew tobacco and shoot guns than kiss a girl, or the preppies like Pierce who go around brown-nosing the adults. I'd rather wait till college, thank you."

Didi nodded, but at the same time she wondered if this was all a defensive front for her friend. She also wondered what Heidi would look like if she dropped the Goth look and wore more mainstream clothing.

"Speaking of old Pierce," said Heidi, "there's a D.O.C. meeting tomorrow night. It's listed in the *Magnolia Town Crier's* community calendar. Want to check it out?"

She considered the library ruse Heidi had previously proposed. "I'd like that," she said.

* * *

At lunchtime Didi started to think her friend was a prophet, because she had barely sat down to unpack her bag lunch when a light-skinned boy with close-cropped hair asked if the seat across the table from her was taken. When she indicated it was open, he placed his food tray on the table and settled in. "Hi," he said. "I'm Jonathan Harris. We're in the same art class."

"Oh…yes," she said with a smile. "I'm Didi."

"I know. You're one of Mrs. Woodard's favorite students. She's a great teacher."

"I think so, too."

Jonathan twisted open his bottled water and looked down at his tray. "Ugh, Meatloaf Day," he sighed. "At least it comes with mac and cheese. You like the food here?"

"I wouldn't know," she replied. "My mother insists on packing my lunch. Mostly healthy stuff."

"Hey, nothing wrong with that," he said. "So, uh, the word is you're from Africa. I've never really met anyone from outside the U.S., but *Africa?* Wow. What's it like?"

She was opening her mouth to tell him when she

spied Heidi approaching the table from behind the boy. A part of her hoped the girl would take a seat with them, but instead she mouthed *I told you!* and veered off to another table.

And so, the two chatted cautiously, getting to know each other. She learned that Jonathan really liked art, and was also in the marching band as a trumpeter. He and his family, which included a younger brother and sister, lived fairly close to the school. For her part, Didi gave the boy an overview of her life in Kinshasa, for which he seemed really interested, especially about what constituted her social life, or lack thereof. He was quite impressed her father was so well thought of that he'd been chosen to partake in the physician exchange with Dr. Buono. "Of course," she said, "he works long hours and always seems to be on call. We're lucky if we see each other for dinner. But my mother, who works for a lawyer in town, manages to keep us together."

"Sounds like you have a great family," said the boy. "Hey, uh, Didi…would you want to, uh, go to the movies or something sometime? Weekends are tough for me because I'm in the band and we play at all the football games, but I think, if you want, we could find a day." The boy was clearly uncomfortable, and Didi found his vulnerability charming.

"I'd like that," she said. "Of course, you would have to meet my parents first."

The boy's eyes narrowed a bit. "Oh, yeah, of course," he said. "Well, okay then. I'll see you in class later. Bye."

Didi gave him a little wave as he gathered up his tray and moved off, then immediately picked up on the dirty looks she was getting from the group of girls who'd made fun of her the previous week. But that was a small price to pay. The fact that a boy had actually spoken to her and seemed to like her was worth whatever female cattiness would come her way.

She glided into Civil War Studies on a high, but a seemingly harmless question on her part created a stir. Mr. Pennington was talking about the class's upcoming day trip to Charleston, about an hour and a half away, and handing out permission slips to the students. After outlining the day, what time they would have to be at school and when they were returning, etc., he told them the cost per student, $30, would cover the school bus rental and admission to the attractions the class would be visiting. "Any of y'all who are on the lunch plan and might need some financial assistance, please see Ms. Redwine and she'll get you set up," he said. "Now, if there are no further questions—"

Didi put her hand up.

"Yes, Miss Diyoka?"

"Mr. Pennington," she said, "I'm reading the list of places we'll be visiting in Charleston, and I'm sure they'll be great...but aren't we going to visit any sites associated with the slave trade? Charleston was, after all, an important point of entry for slaves being brought in during the antebellum period."

The room went silent; Heidi's eyes widened, sensing some drama; and even Travis, detecting a break from the normal buzz of the class, woke up.

"Well," said the teacher, "as you can see, we've got just about every minute of the day accounted for—"

"Which I understand," pressed the girl, "but seeing as how the region of my ancestors provided the vast majority of the slaves forced into captivity, I thought it appropriate for at least a short stop along the way."

"And I appreciate that," he countered, "but again, the itinerary is fairly well set, though you are always free to visit the city with your parents—"

"Or go back to Africa," came a whisper from amongst some boys in the back of the room.

Didi felt the blood drain from her face; but before she or Heidi or even Mr. Pennington could respond, Bad News Braxton slowly turned in his seat and stared down the boys—one of whom was her gardener, Seth Tomlin—and said, "Yo, man." That was it. Two words. But the message got across, loud and clear, as the boys appeared terrified. Then, just as slowly, the football player turned back around.

Mr. Pennington never looked more relieved to hear the dismissal bell.

* * *

"Whoa," said Heidi as they returned to their lockers. "First that cute Jonathan guy, and then Bad News. Look at you."

"Both were quite unexpected."

"Not by me. I told you guys were watching. But keep an eye out for Tanya. If word gets back to her that her boyfriend stuck up for you, it might get nasty in a hurry."

"Heidi, it was completely innocent."

"That's how you and I see it. The marvelous Ms.

Mims, on the other hand…" She shrugged. "Anyway, talk to your parents about tomorrow night. Like I told you, just say we're going to study together at the library or something. If they think it's school-related, I bet they'll say yes."

Didi nodded, but the realization that she was becoming adept at deceiving her parents was starting to worry her.

* * *

"I told you they'd buy the library thing," said Heidi the next evening as Didi climbed into the passenger seat. "We're lucky this is the only night of the week they stay open late." She eyed Didi's backpack. "I see you brought some 'study' materials. Nice touch."

"I don't know about this," she replied. "I don't like misleading them."

"You're right," said Heidi. "Why don't you march right back inside and say, 'Hey folks, gotta be honest, I'm going to check out tonight's Daughters of the Confederacy meeting in town. Is that okay?' I'm sure they'll be all for it."

Didi frowned. "All right, I get your point," she said. "Can we just go?"

Heidi smiled and started the engine.

* * *

The Magnolia Masonic Hall was a fairly nondescript building somewhat removed from the downtown commercial area; in fact, it fit in seamlessly with the residential section in which it sat. Luckily, it was surrounded by trees on three sides, and the grounds were rather dark. Heidi brought the SUV to a stop across the street from the fairly full parking lot and killed her headlights. "We'll have to wait a few minutes so they all have a chance to go inside and get settled. It's just as I thought—the basement windows are open. See how they've been tipped back?"

"Yes," said Didi, her heart beginning to race.

"Okay. So when we get out, just follow me. We'll figure out what room they're in and check it out. You scared?"

"A little bit."

"Good. That's what makes it exciting. I'm glad you wore some dark stuff. We'll blend right into the shadows." She checked the time on her phone, and then turned it off. "Showtime. Let's go!"

They scurried across the deserted street and began to prowl the building's foundation. It was near the back that they heard voices emanating from below. Heidi dropped to her hands and knees like a commando and crawled towards the window. After a few seconds she waved her friend over, and Didi took a position on the other edge of the window frame.

The room they looked down upon was spacious and utilitarian, with wood-paneled walls. A large Confederate flag had been affixed to the wall at the front of the room, which also featured a speaker's podium, two six-foot folding tables with gray plastic covers, and around fifty or so folding chairs that faced the front of the room. Slim books bound in brown leather were laid out on the tables. Parents and children, all white and well-dressed, milled about, greeting each other with hugs and handshakes. Didi immediately located Pierce, who on this evening wore a blue blazer, a light blue shirt with red tie, khakis and loafers. As per usual, he was glad-handing everyone in sight. She also recognized a few other boys and girls from the halls at school, but there were many other children there, some quite young.

After a few minutes of chitchat, Pierce's mother approached the podium. "Well, good evening, y'all," she said brightly. "What a wonderful turnout for tonight's meeting! It makes me proud to see so many of our young people here. After all, you are our future. Would everyone please stand and raise your voices in song." Every single person in the room snapped to attention, and together rendered a heartfelt rendition of "Dixie." Didi looked over at Heidi, who rolled her eyes.

Once the song was completed, Mrs. Farnsworth asked everyone to remain standing for the pledge. Didi was expecting the Pledge of Allegiance that began homeroom every day, but this one was totally foreign to her:

We pledge ourselves to preserve pure ideals; to honor the meaning of our beloved veterans; to study and teach the truths of history; and always to act in a manner that will reflect honor upon our noble and patriotic ancestors.

This being completed, Mrs. Farnsworth invited everyone to take their seats. "That was wonderful, y'all," she gushed. "Now, a few announcements. First, on Sunday we will hold our quarterly trip to the Confederate Cemetery in Columbia to do some raking and fertilizing of the graves, and to lay flowers at the various monuments. We are looking for parents to volunteer with the driving, and a sign-up sheet will be placed on the refreshments table at the back of the room. We'll need at least ten vehicles for passengers and equipment, and a couple of pickup trucks would be a big help. After we're done we'll have a late lunch at the *Country Corner* restaurant in Columbia, which I heard y'all were raving about last time. It's definitely the best all-you-can-eat deal in this part of the state. Of course, dress for the day is casual but neat. No barnyard clothes, y'all!"

This joke drew some chuckles, but then the woman turned serious. "What I'm going to discuss now, my friends, is not so funny," she said.

"There are people in this state who are pushing for the removal of the Confederate battle flag from the grounds of the State Capital Building in Columbia," she began. "As I'm sure you are aware, it had previously flown from the capital dome since 1961, the 100th anniversary of the start of the War of Rebellion. But our state legislators showed their weakness and disregard for their heritage by passing what was ironically called the Heritage Act, a compromise bill that saw the flag moved to a pole next to the Soldiers' Monument on the capital grounds.

"But even this capitulation to our so-called leaders in Washington doesn't seem to be enough. Now there are those liberals clamoring for our flag's removal altogether!"

Grumblings resonated throughout the room, and one man raised his hand so Mrs. Farnsworth could acknowledge him. "But Peggy," he whined, "what can we do? The politicians have it in for us! They'd sell their souls to get elected!"

"Not all of 'em," she snapped back. "We have supporters out there. What's important is that we make our voices *heard*!" This statement drew raucous applause, and the woman had to raise her hands to restore quiet.

"I've prepared a list of all our local and state representatives," she continued, "with their office phone numbers and email addresses. What we've got to do is bombard these people as thoroughly as our boys bombarded Fort Sumter. Make them remember who butters their bread. And if we do, I guarantee they'll surrender just like the Yankees did in 1861!"

This exhortation brought the crowd to their feet. Didi found herself frightened, though Heidi seemed utterly fascinated with the display.

Again, the woman raised her arms to restore order; this time there were sweat rings under her arms from the heat that was being generated in the room. "All right, then," she said, dropping into a calmer tone. "I'd like the adults to come with me to the adjoining room so we can discuss some strategies. Please take a cold glass of punch with you from the refreshment table. The children have some business of their own to conduct." At that, she nodded at her son, who started passing out the slim leather books to the younger kids while the adults filed out of the room. For the first time there came to Didi the realization that if there was a Mr. Farnsworth, he was not present at the meeting; nor had Pierce ever mentioned him.

Once the children were alone, Pierce took the podium and asked the youngsters to move to the front rows. Three of the older boys and girls of high school age sat at the long tables facing the youthful audience, with pens and note paper before them. "Okay, everybody," said Pierce, "y'all have a copy of the catechism. I hope you've been studyin' at home, because tonight we're going to have a little catechism quiz. The one who answers the most questions right gets a prize: this very cool Jeb Stuart figurine!" He held aloft a porcelain statuette of the cavalryman, which drew oohs and ahhs from the children. "The senior pages and aides at these tables will help tally the results. So, if y'all are ready, let's get after it!"

From there it was an intense Q & A competition, far more passionate than anything Didi had witnessed at school. Pierce spat out questions about the war, though they were not really centered on facts and figures and strategies. These were more of an ideological nature, and the answers were all slanted towards the Southern viewpoint. And whenever the crowd was stumped, Pierce or one of his cohorts said, "Check your books!" and the kids started riffling like mad through the pages of their catechisms until one would vigorously wave his or her hand in the air.

Didi was gripped by the fervor of these youngsters and looked over at Heidi, who just kept shaking her head; whether it was in disgust or amazement, she couldn't tell.

Finally, it came down to a tie between a red-haired, freckled boy and a girl with a big ponytail and braces. Both looked to be around ten years old.

"All right, folks, for the Jeb Stuart statue," said Pierce. "Here's the question: What was the feeling of Southern slaves towards their masters?"

"I know, I know!" bleated the girl, springing to her feet. "They were faithful and devoted to their masters, who fed and clothed them. So, they were happy to serve them!"

Heidi gave Didi a "Is she *serious*?" look; but incredibly, Pierce cried, "Correct!" and awarded her the prize, as the senior judges provided high-fives.

Just then, a man exited the side door of the building, not ten yards away from Heidi and Didi, and lit a cigarette. He stood there, looking at the stars and blowing smoke rings, as the girls flattened themselves against the brick wall and held their breath. After a few agonizing minutes, the man ground the cigarette under his shoe and reentered the building, whistling "Dixie."

"Time to go," Heidi whispered. They're gonna let out soon. You seen enough?"

"Plenty," said Didi.

Chapter Nine

The second Friday of the football season was pretty much like the previous one. Once again, the hallways of Stuart High were draped with banners and streamers, and the major topic among the students was the arrangement of transportation to that night's away game at Calhoun. Today the boys wore their road game white jerseys, trimmed in red and black.

Having decided not to attend the game, Didi had pretty much assumed the role of casual bystander. That is, until none other than Tanya Mims approached her while she and Heidi were at their lockers. Upon Tanya's face was a bemused expression that Didi didn't quite know how to read, but Heidi had been correct: it hadn't taken long for word of Bad News's gallant intervention in class to get around.

"Hi," she said to Didi, "I'm Tanya."

"We know," said Heidi as she removed some empty Red Bull cans for the trash bin.

"Zip it, Dorsch," she snapped. "I'm here to talk to your friend."

"My name is Didi," calmly said the girl. "Didi Diyoka."

"I know," the cheerleader replied airily. "Our visitor from the *Dark* Continent." Her emphasis of the

98

word, Didi felt, was a dig at her complexion. "Listen, girl. The other day, Travis was just bein' a gentleman to you with those crackers in your class. Don't you be reading any more into it than that."

"I didn't, and I don't," replied Didi. "I was grateful that he stood up for me, though. You're lucky to have him as a boyfriend."

That remark totally disarmed Tanya, who seemed to have been seeking some kind of public confrontation. Recovering nicely, she said, "Well, I'm just making sure it stays that way. Don't be getting any ideas."

"I wouldn't think of it," said Didi, with a benign smile.

Again, Tanya was thrown off. "Well, good," she said, and marched off.

"You should've told her where to stick it," said Heidi.

"Stick what?"

"Forget it."

* * *

That afternoon Mr. Pennington announced that his reenacting regiment, the 1st Carolina Volunteers, would be staging a "living history" encampment in a nearby farmer's pasture the next day. Apparently, they held these events multiple times each year, and they were quite popular. "We'll be doing some drilling as well, and perhaps some target practice with live rounds," he added for the gun enthusiasts in the room. "There's nothing like firing a black powder rifle to get the true feel of those old battles," he said. "Maybe some of y'all will come out. We usually draw a good crowd."

"Would you consider attending the encampment?" asked Didi as she and Heidi left the room at the final bell.

"Uh, I think I have to give my dog a bath tomorrow," she replied.

"You have a dog?"

"It's a figure of speech," said the Goth girl with exasperation. "Actually, it's the last thing I'd want to do with my time. Why on earth do you want to go?"

"Oh, I don't know," said Didi. "I'm rather curious to see what this whole reenacting thing is about. I'd also like to see Mr. Pennington play soldier."

Heidi stopped and smirked. "You know, it might be entertaining at that. I'll pick you up tomorrow morning around ten."

* * *

After explaining to her parents—who readily approved—the relevance to her studies of visiting the military encampment, Didi was anxiously waiting when Heidi rolled up outside her house. The morning was comfortably cool, and though Didi had considered wearing a light jacket, she knew it would warm up eventually. Of course, her friend was predictably attired in her black jeans and boots, topped off today with a purple Rolling Stones T-shirt.

The farmer's property where the encampment was to take place was only about fifteen minutes away, but it felt like more. A glance in any direction revealed acres of crops interrupted only by clumps of woods and picket fences. In fact, it didn't seem that different from the 1860s photos in Didi's Civil War books.

After following a winding, unlined paved road, they came upon a staked sign on the shoulder that read *Civil War Encampment Parking*, with an arrow pointing the way. By the time they arrived there were a good hundred cars in the makeshift lot; whether they belonged to the reenactors or visitors like themselves was anyone's guess. The girls hopped out and followed another sign that directed them to a dirt path that cut through a thicket of trees. "I smell a wood fire burning," said Heidi. "And something cooking. Could be bacon." They followed the fragrant trail to the other side of the trees, emerging at an open space of cleared land. What lay before them was a window to the past.

The first thing that caught the girls' attention were the three neat rows of four triangular-shaped white canvas tents, bracketed by two larger, squared-off affairs with their flaps held open. In front of the tent area, two formidable cooking fires were going, each encircled by large stones, with a wrought iron tripod from which a large black kettle was suspended. Between the fire pits were groups of musket rifles with bayonets attached, stacked against each other to form a pyramid. On the other side of the cooking fires was a very large rectangular tent with a sign that read *Sutler's Row*.

Scattered about were clusters of soldiers in full dress who sat on wooden camp chairs or small, overturned barrels, smoking corncob pipes, chatting, or playing music on banjos or fiddles. Women in uncomfortable-looking hoop skirt dresses floated between the groups of men, some daintily cooling themselves with folding, hand-held fans. Finally, modern-day visitors of all ages meandered through the camp, checking out the accommodations and mingling with the reenactors.

"Welcome to the Civil War," said Heidi to her stunned partner.

"It's so…realistic," said Didi.

"Well, that's the whole idea," Heidi replied. "Let's check out the sutlers' area."

"What are sutlers?"

"That's the old-time term for merchants," she said. "Back in Civil War days, they followed the armies around, selling everyday goods the soldiers might need." They approached a series of long covered tables laid end-to-end for what must've been fifty yards. Different vendors, some in period dress and some not, offered everything from 1860s snacks such as beef jerky, rock-hard biscuits called hardtack and homemade candy, to reproduction leather shoes, flannel shirts and canvas pants, canteens, uniform buttons and French kepi-style hats for the reenactors. There were also patterns for 1860s women's dresses, homemade soaps and candles, and even playing cards and dice. For the modern youngsters who were roaming around the campsite the sutlers put out miniature Confederate flags, plastic swords, and cheaply made felt cavalry-style hats.

Heidi purchased a paper bag of jerky and offered Didi a piece, but the girl was quickly turned off by the toughness. "It's rather tasty, but chewing this isn't easy," she said.

"That's because they smoked all the juice out of it," explained Heidi, tearing off a hunk with her teeth. "It had to last them a long time in the field."

"Oh," she replied, impressed with her friend's knowledge.

They kept on walking past the sutlers to another tent where a sweating blacksmith was pounding on a red-hot horseshoe as the surrounding crowd looked on and asked questions. Beyond his tent a small split rail corral had been assembled, enclosing a nickering trio of brown horses that placidly cropped the grass. "Let's go chat up one of the soldiers," suggested Heidi. "I think you'll get a kick out of it."

They approached a gangly twenty-something guy with a sparse chin beard and scraggly hair who sat atop a camp chair next to a blanket, which had been laid out to display the various components of a Confederate uniform. Seeing that he was about to be addressed, he awkwardly rose to his feet. "Good day, ma'am," he said to Heidi, and then nodded to Didi, who wondered why she had not been personally addressed as well. "Would you like me to explain to y'all the typical Confederate soldier's uniform?"

"Please do," said Heidi.

"All right then. My name is Private William Cuthbert of the 1st Carolina Regiment, and you're visiting a typical camp circa 1862. Before you are the basic elements of my uniform." One by one, he pointed to the different articles and accoutrements and described them. "First is my gray shell jacket made of wool. This one has brass buttons, but late in the war they might have been made of bone or wood. Under that I would wear a checkered woolen shirt with bone buttons. You'll notice it has patches, as does the shirt I have on. That's because we Confederate soldiers would have to repair our own clothes, supplies being so hard to come by. In

103

contrast, the Union troops had more of a uniform look, because they were well-supplied. By the end of the war our troops wore whatever they could get their hands on. Of course, the officers, who generally came from more wealthy families, were able to have their uniforms tailored, and looked pretty sharp."

"Of course," said Heidi. "Please continue, Private."

He smiled, enjoying the opportunity to show off. "Next you see a pair of heavy woolen socks, which were quite a luxury, as many Confederate soldiers were barefoot by the end of the war, and cotton drawers for underneath. The trousers are of a heavy material with a button fly; I'm wearing a similar pair right now, although the gray has mostly faded out. On my head is a black felt slouch hat, but on the blanket here is a gray kepi with a black leather brim, which is government issue."

"Those shoes don't look too comfortable," observed Heidi, pointing to his feet.

"They're called brogans, actually," he corrected, "and they wouldn't be, since there was no distinction between a right and left shoe. You just kinda had to break 'em in."

"Hmmm."

"And then, finally, there's my wooden canteen with a cork top, a black leather belt with cartridge box and cap pouch for my ammunition, and a Bowie knife I brought from back home."

"Impressive."

"May I ask you a question?" said Didi.

Private Cuthbert nodded.

"Are you allowed to tell us what you do in the Twenty-First Century?"

The soldier thought about it for a moment, glanced to his left and right, and then whispered, "I'm a grad student at the University of South Carolina."

"Majoring in history, I bet," said Heidi.

"How did you guess?"

The Goth girl rolled her eyes. "Uh, Private Cuthbert, do you know where we can find our teacher, Mr. Pennington?"

"You mean *Captain* Pennington," he said reverently, and pointed to one of the larger military tents. "That's his quarters over there."

"Thanks," she said, "we'll put in a good word for you with the captain."

"Much appreciated, ma'am," he replied with a courtly bow.

They moved off and Heidi chuckled. "What a dork," she said with a sigh.

"Did you notice that he didn't ever formally address me?" asked Didi.

"I wouldn't make too much of that," Heidi replied. "You see, if the guy is 'staying in character' as these reenactors call it, he wouldn't feel obligated to speak to a black person. I'm sure that's what it was."

Didi nodded, but this reasoning didn't make her feel any better.

The girls wove their way through the growing crowd of visitors before reaching Pennington's tent. They found him sitting inside at a collapsible wooden table, poring over a military map of some sort. His officer's jacket hung from a peg on one of the wooden posts that held up the tent, and his gray hat with a wide brim and gold braid sat atop a rudimentary cot that was covered with a patchwork quilt. Pennington's linen shirt sleeves were rolled up to the elbow, with gray breeches tucked into black riding boots.

"Knock, knock," said Heidi playfully.

Pennington looked up and smiled. "Why, ladies, it's a pleasant surprise to see the two of you here. What do you think of my humble abode?"

"It seems more comfortable than that of the regular soldiers," observed Didi.

"Correct, Miss Diyoka. As an officer I would be entitled to a larger tent, a cot, a table, and some kind of trunk to store my equipment."

"But, how would you lug all that stuff around?" asked Heidi.

"Well, many officers had an adjutant to administer to them. Some even brought their servants from back home."

"Like, slaves?"

"Well, yes, in some cases. But of course, I don't have one here. Authenticity can only go so far, you know."

"Uh-huh. Speaking of authenticity, Mr. Pennington, I'm wondering…just what is it that makes people want to do all this?"

"That's a fair question, and I'll try to answer it. There are a few reasons why people get into reenacting. Some had ancestors who actually participated in the War and do it as an homage to them. Then, there are some—men, primarily—who served in the modern military and miss the regimentation, so this is an outlet for them."

"What about the women?" Didi asked. "I saw some ladies in knitting groups and the like around the camp."

He replied, "Believe it or not, modern-day

reenacting is quite a family event. It's a way to camp out and connect with other like-minded folks for the parents, and even their children.

"And finally, there are those like myself whose love of history leads them to seek what we call 'total immersion,' where one is actually able to transport himself to the past. It's hard to describe, to tell you the truth."

"It looks like you're doing some planning," said Didi, filling an awkward lapse in the conversation. "Is it for some kind of battle?"

Pennington motioned to the map, which was held down by an inkwell and a brass candle holder. "Oh, this? No, there's no battle today, although the regiment is scheduled to do some drilling and shooting in a few minutes. In fact—"

"Excuse me, Captain Pennington?"

The girls turned to see none other than their classmate Pierce Farnsworth, fully attired in a light gray uniform, with a marching drum on his hip suspended by a leather shoulder strap. For a few seconds, all three of the teens stood in place, wide-eyed, before Heidi managed a sarcastic, "Well, hello there, Johnny Reb."

"Uh, hi, Heidi...hi, Didi," he replied sheepishly. Then, remembering he was supposed to be in character, he straightened up, saluted Pennington, and told him the troops were ready to drill.

"Thank you, Private Farnsworth," replied the officer, reaching for his jacket. "If you'll kindly tell the men to assemble near the horse corral, we will begin shortly."

"Yes, sir," said the boy, and with a nod to the girls, slinked out of the tent.

"If you'll excuse me, ladies?" said Pennington.

"Sure, *Captain*," said Heidi. "Do you want us to put the tent flap down on our way out?"

Pennington, coloring, said, "That won't be necessary, thank you," and started rolling down his sleeves.

Once outside, Heidi let out a low whistle. "So, our boy Pierce isn't just a card-carrying child of the Confederacy... he's also a play soldier."

"He seemed a bit embarrassed to see us," observed Didi.

"Yeah, well, it wasn't *our* idea for him to parade around in that ridiculous outfit. But now I'm curious to check out this drill they're talking about. Want to hang out a few more minutes?"

"Sure."

They again picked their way through the visitors and soldiers who were extinguishing the campfires (breakfast had consisted of salt pork, beans, and hard tack, the girls learned), and reaching for their weapons. This flurry of activity got the crowd excited, and some of the modern mini-rebels even started dueling with their plastic swords.

Suddenly, Didi found herself walking alone and turned back to see Heidi, her fists ground into her hips, confronting a blocky, bearded soldier with a musket slung over his shoulder. "*What* did you just say?" she asked angrily.

"'Scuse me?" he replied innocently.

"I heard you singing right behind us," she said, her voice rising. "Don't tell me you weren't!"

Didi crept forward and could see her normally blasé friend trembling. A crowd began to gather.

"It's a free country," spluttered the man, who had bits of bacon grease in his woolly beard. "It's just, you know, you had the Stones shirt on and all—"

"Forgive me if my grasp of history is faulty," pressed the girl, "but you're supposed to be 'in character,' right? Well, I could be wrong, but Mick and the band didn't exist in the 1860s, correct?"

"What...was he singing?" asked Didi, totally confused.

"It's a song called 'Brown Sugar,'" she snapped back. "About a slave owner who abused the females on his plantation. And this goober was right behind us when he was singing it."

"Now, listen—" the soldier began, as onlookers started murmuring.

"No, *you* listen," she shot back. "I want you to apologize to my friend. *Now.*"

At that moment Mr. Pennington, in full battle dress, entered the scene. "Here, here, now," he began, inserting himself between the combatants. Struggling to stay in character, he asked, "Corporal Sturgis, what is the meaning of this?"

"I'll tell you what the meaning of this is," huffed Heidi. "This fine soldier here insulted one of *your* students—who happens to be the only person of African descent on the grounds, I might add—and tried to play it off!"

Pennington closed his eyes for a moment, took a deep breath, and said, "Corporal, I think it appropriate that you offer your apologies to this young lady—"

But that was as far as Pennington got, because Sturgis flew into a rage. "Apologize? For what? I can say anything I damn well please. Just 'cause you outrank me here don't mean *nothin'*! I make *twice* as much is you in the real world, so don't you go tellin' me what to do! She don't even belong here. Whose side are you on, anyway?" At that, he swiped his kepi hat from his head, threw it at Pennington's well-polished boots, barked, "I hereby resign from the 1st Carolina Regiment—sir!" and stormed off. The other soldiers, including Pierce, stood pie-eyed at the exchange.

For a few seconds, there was relative silence, save for some snickers from the visitors. "What just happened?" asked one youngster in a Confederate hat.

"History repeating itself," snapped Heidi, which drew some "oohs" from the bystanders.

And then the crowd parted and an older man in full officer regalia solemnly made his way to the center of the throng. He had snow white hair and a lush beard that was going gray. From all of the gold braid that adorned the forearms of his uniform, it appeared he was obviously of a higher rank than even Pennington. "Captain," he said calmly, "please apprise me as to the nature of this disturbance."

"Colonel Paige, one of the men was disrespectful to this young lady here," said the teacher, nodding towards Didi. "He decided to desert the regiment rather than apologize."

"I see," said the man. "Well, Captain, then I think it falls to you to make sure your men conduct themselves with proper decorum. What happened here is totally unacceptable, and is an extreme disappointment to me. Do you agree?"

"Yes, sir," said Pennington, his face flushed.

Colonel Paige turned to the girls. "I'm sorry for your troubles, ladies," he said with a courtly touch to his hat brim. "I personally invite you to stay for our unit drill."

"No, that's okay," said Heidi. "We saw all we needed to see." She fixed Pennington with an icy stare, and then clomped off. Didi, realizing she was about to be left behind, gave a little wave to her teacher and then followed.

It was not until they were in the SUV with the doors closed that Didi broke the silence. "I guess it's still not over," she whispered.

"What?"

"The War."

"Yeah, well, that's what I've been trying to tell you," she said, starting up the car. The Goth girl managed a sardonic smile, though Didi sensed she was on the verge of tears. "Guess we just lost our A in the course."

Chapter Ten

After the regrettable incident at the reenactment campsite, things quieted down for a while. Everything was status quo at Stuart High, including the football team racking up two more wins against River Bluff and Westwood. Their record now stood at 4-0, and both Bad News and his teammate Troy Winchester were reportedly drawing scholarship interest from big schools across the country.

On the academic front, Stuart held its annual Open House Night for parents, and of course Dr. and Mrs. Diyoka were eager to attend so they could meet their daughter's teachers. They even dressed up for the event, though once they arrived they noticed other parents attired in everything from casual jeans and golf shirts to camo fatigues and hunting hats.

As per their expectations, all of Didi's teachers praised her (even Mr. Pennington, who termed her "unquestionably inquisitive") and pronounced the African transfer student a wonderful addition to the class of 2014. Mrs. Woodard even made it a point to pull the Diyokas aside and assure them that she was keeping a special eye on their girl.

An especially curious moment occurred when the Diyokas met Heidi's parents during homeroom.

Probably expecting a liberal, bohemian couple, they were astounded to find the Dorschs as buttoned-down and conservative as they were, though somewhat older. "We're so glad our Heidi has made friends with your daughter," said Mrs. Dorsch, her styled brown hair graying at the temples. "She seems like such a well-adjusted, respectful girl from everything Heidi tells us."

"What my wife is saying is, she hopes some of it will rub off on our daughter," quipped Mr. Dorsch.

Didi had fallen into a routine of having lunch once a week with Mrs. Woodard, whom she regarded as a mentor of sorts, and who seemed wise beyond her years; in return, the girl provided her inquisitive art teacher with information about all things African. Jonathan had also made it a habit of stopping by her lunch table once or twice a week, sometimes sharing the space with Heidi, who was actually civil to him most of the time. To her relief, he didn't press Didi on the dating thing, though she was trying to formulate a strategy for persuading her father to let her go if Jonathan formally asked her out.

She feared, though, that Dr. Diyoka was working himself too hard. The hours at Providence Heart were arduous, but he dare not complain, lest he give his superiors the impression that he was not equal to the task. And when he was home, he stayed on the computer late into the night, trying to learn as much as he could about his field.

As always, her mother was the stabilizing influence in the household, heating up a home-cooked meal for her husband no matter what time he returned from Columbia, and keeping tabs on Didi's doings at school. However, the girl couldn't help but feel that her mother was lonely here in America. After all, she was the only person of color at the law firm, and outside of their neighbor Mrs. Stanton, who occasionally dropped by with a coffee cake, there wasn't much socializing going on with the people in their neighborhood.

Because of all these factors, Didi was careful to not reveal the negative experiences she encountered in school or elsewhere. The last thing she wanted was her father to repeat what he'd said after the football game a few weeks back about having made a mistake in coming to the United States.

As far as Mr. Pennington, he acted as if the reenactment incident had never occurred. Didi liked to think that it was because he was feeling incredibly guilty, but Heidi surmised that he was simply embarrassed. As for the 1st Carolina's drummer boy, Pierce could barely look Didi in the face, only mumbling quick hellos when they shared a bus ride in the morning. And though Heidi referred to him as "a Southern-fried phony," Didi sensed something needy inside the boy that prevented her from shunning him. Again, she wondered just what was going on in that Confederate shrine he called his home.

Thus, Didi went along, earning good grades and becoming more comfortable with her classmates, but always with the feeling that something unsettling lay around the next bend in the road.

* * *

One day she was looking for a book in the library when someone tapped her on the shoulder. Startled, she whipped around to find none other than Bad News Braxton, wearing a nervous grin.

"Did I scare you?" he whispered.

"No," she said, "I was just surprised—"

"About what? That I'm in the library?"

"Oh, no, no," she said, "it's not that—"

Then he smiled. "I'm just playing. Listen, uh, I have to ask you a favor," he said, his eyes darting everywhere.

"Is that why you followed me here? Because we're out of sight?"

"Yeah, kind of. You see—"

"Your girlfriend wouldn't approve."

"Uh-huh."

"So, what is it you want, Travis?"

The boy seemed genuinely taken back that someone would call him by his given name. "Listen," he said, "week after next we got a research paper due, and I…might need a little help."

"Well," she said, "Mr. Pennington said we could select any topic, as long as it's Civil War-related. What have you chosen to do?"

"That's just it," he said nervously. "I haven't really given it much thought yet."

"Oh."

"I just want to make sure, you know, that I go with a topic I can handle."

"And that's it?"

"Well, and maybe with some of the writing stuff. I make a lot of mistakes."

"Why are you asking me?" she said. "There are others taking the course."

"'Cause you're the smartest kid in the class," he replied. "Except, of course, for Heidi. But she's not the friendliest person. Besides, you, uh, probably might be closer to my point of view on all this Civil War stuff."

"Because I'm black?"

"Well, yeah," he said, as a bead of sweat rolled down his temple. "I just don't want to sound stupid in my paper."

"You're not stupid, Travis," she replied. "You're just preoccupied with other things in your life."

"Like football?"

"Of course. But if I do decide to give you some help, you have to understand that I will not simply write the paper for you. You're going to have to put in some time and effort. I suggest you don't give me an answer at this moment. Think about it, and then let me know tomorrow if you want to do the work. Either way, it's fine with me." She turned to go, but stopped when he whispered her name.

"I don't have to think about it," he said. "I'll do anything you need me to do. Just help me. Please."

"Fair enough," she said. "But how, and when, will this work get done?"

"I have an idea," he said.

* * *

That Saturday afternoon Didi got her research materials together, filled her backpack, and wedged it into the large basket attached to her bike's handlebars. She had gone on a website called MapQuest to find the directions for the address Bad News had supplied. Fortunately, it was less than a five-mile ride from her house, and the day, though cloudy, was free of rain. She had told her parents she'd be studying with a friend, which was true; of course, she'd left out the fact that it was a boy, and that the location would be his house, and not the public library. These transgressions caused her tremendous guilt, but Didi felt this was something she needed to do—though she couldn't put her finger on exactly *why*.

At school she had confided—with some trepidation—in Heidi, who told her she was crazy. "What's in it for you?" she'd cried. "If that witch Tanya finds out, she'll be your worst nightmare. On top of that, he's probably gonna want you to do all the work."

"He assured me I would only be there in a support role," Didi had replied defensively.

"Yeah, right. And besides, why should you trust him enough to be alone with him? You think he's some kind of choirboy?"

"I don't know if he is or isn't," she said, "but I've always tried to believe that people are basically good. There's something about him that made me willing to take the gamble. To tell you the truth, I think his whole 'Bad News' persona is a façade."

"Well, I guess you're gonna find out," said Heidi.

"I guess I will."

"But listen," said the Goth girl seriously, "if things at any point don't seem right, get the hell out of there."

"I promise I will," said Didi. "Thanks for your concern."

"Yeah, that's me, Mother Teresa."

"Who?"

* * *

Didi's ride took her farther and farther away from her neighborhood, to an area that was obviously depressed. The dwellings were a combination of tarpaper shacks with corrugated tin roofs, and the kind of trailer-type homes she had seen in American movies. The yards—if one could call them that— which surrounded the homes were for the most part unkempt, with children's toys, appliances, bicycles, and automobiles—some up on blocks—scattered about, as none of the homes had garages.

Unattended children were dashing here and there playing tag or tossing a football, while some adults— both men and women—sat on front porches or steps and drank from beer cans or bottles sheathed in paper bags. They all viewed her suspiciously, though they were all black.

Finally, on the third pass down a gravel street called Peachtree, she came upon Bad News's trailer house, which looked to be about sixteen by twenty feet in size. Its surrounding grounds were noticeably less cluttered than the neighbors', and there were even plastic planters with blooming flowers on either side of the wooden front steps. Additionally, the grass around the trailer seemed to have been recently mowed, and the lone tree on the property featured a collection of colored bottles suspended from its lower branches. For some reason, it made her smile.

Didi searched for a doorbell on the white aluminum structure and found none, so she simply knocked on the flimsy door. After a few seconds went by, she began to fear she'd come to the wrong address. But then she sensed the trailer-shaking vibration of someone rather heavy making their way to the door. With a yank, it screeched open, leaving Bad News to fill the entrance. He was wearing sweatpants and a

Stuart Athletics T-shirt that threatened to burst across his muscled biceps. There was also a dripping ice pack that was held in place atop his left shoulder by yards of pink stretch bandage.

"Hey," he said in greeting. "How'd you get here?"

Didi turned and pointed to her bike, which was propped up by its kickstand in the front yard.

"Nice bike," he said. "You got a lock for that?"

"No," she replied. "I—"

He brushed past her and went to the bike, popped up the kickstand, and carried it to the trailer. "Go inside," he said. "I'll follow you with the bike."

"Okay, thanks," she said.

The interior of the trailer was claustrophobic. The front door opened onto a kitchen area with a chipped, two-person formica table and dinette chairs, and the yellow linoleum floor was worn. But the trailer was spotless. There were no dirty dishes in the small sink, and the place smelled of pine disinfectant. On a nearby wall was a cross, bookended by artist renderings of Jesus and the slain American Civil Rights leader Martin Luther King, Jr., whom Didi had heard about back in Africa.

Bad News set the bike down in the narrow hallway, which extended out in each direction from the kitchen. He noticed Didi looking around. "You ever been in a single-wide?" he asked.

"I can't say that I have," she replied. "It's nice."

"No it isn't, but thanks," he said. "Let me get my laptop from my room. They gave me one to use at home. You can unpack your stuff here. We'll work in the kitchen."

"All right."

He lumbered off down the hallway to his room, passing the doorway that she suspected was the bathroom. She hoped she wouldn't have to use it while she was there. By the time he returned she'd laid all her materials on the table. He took the seat opposite her, opting not to sit alongside.

"What happened to your shoulder?" she asked, as the condensation from the ice pack was seeping further down his T-shirt.

"Got a stinger in my neck, where it meets the shoulder," he explained. "Ridge View's quarterback was runnin' all over the place last night. One time I was chasin' him down and a lineman from their team blindsided me. But I still ended up catching him," he added proudly. "Had six tackles and three sacks."

"I don't know what that means, but it sounds good," she said. "Did we win the game?"

"Oh yeah, 36-10, and it wasn't even that close. We're on track for the sectionals, for sure."

"Will you be able to play? With the injury and all?"

"This?" he said, pointing to the sweating icepack. "It ain't no big thing. The last thing college scouts want to see is a player sittin' out with a little ding."

"I see. And which colleges are showing interest?"

"You name it. I got letters from as far away as Oregon and everywhere in between: Ohio State, Oklahoma, Wisconsin, Florida State. But I'd really like to get a full ride to Clemson. They're crazy good and kind of close to home."

"So you like it around here?"

"I didn't say that. It's a matter of—"

"Travis!" cried a wavering voice from the other

end of the trailer. "Could you bring me my walker, honey?"

"Be right back," he said, and ducked into a small side room off the kitchen before emerging with a collapsible aluminum walker with tennis balls attached to its feet. Snapping it open, he entered the far room and was greeted with, "Oh, thank you, sweetie. Close the door behind you on the way out, hear? I'm gonna watch my soap opera."

The defensive lineman returned to the table, a sheepish grin creasing his manly face. "That's my gramma," he explained. "She lives here with me. Or I live with her."

"Oh."

"In case you're wondering," he continued, "my daddy died when I was ten, and my mom never recovered from it. Got into all kinds of bad stuff and finally just up and left me with Gramma, who's her mother. She's all I've got."

"I see."

"We live off her Social Security, which ain't much. But I get free breakfast and lunch at school, which helps. Coach Kurtt also got me a job at the local furniture factory in the off-season. It's heavy work, but it helps keep me in shape."

"So that's why an athletic scholarship is so important to you."

"Yeah. Gramma's actually in pretty good health, but she took a fall about a month ago and her hip's all screwed up. She probably should get a replacement, but her insurance won't cover it. That's why she needs the walker."

"And you."

"Yeah, I guess." He peered at her through the dreadlocks that hung in his eyes; Didi tried to picture what he must've looked like as a little boy but it was hard, for he seemed much older than his years.

"Let's get the work," she said. "What topic did you want to do?"

"Well, you know how Pennington's always talking about how the weapons they were developing during the war were too advanced for the old-time battle tactics they were still using? I'd like to research a couple of those weapons. You know, like repeating rifles or submarines. Do you think that's a good idea?"

"That sounds interesting," she said, impressed that the boy had actually been listening in class. "You could divide your paper in half—land weapons and nautical weapons."

Bad News smiled. "That's what I was thinking. Now I just have to find the info."

"That shouldn't be hard," she assured. "Mr. Pennington said he wants us to use a minimum of four research sources. Between the books in our school and town library and the Internet, you'll find everything you need. It's just a question of picking the right passages to help illustrate your points."

"Could you help me with that? You know, check over what I come up with and make sure it's the right stuff?"

"That's not a problem. Why don't we look online at our school library's catalog and the catalog at the Magnolia Public Library and see if there are any books specific to Civil War weaponry?"

"Sounds like a plan." They opened his laptop and began their search, but after a few minutes it became clear that the process would be more efficient if they sat side-by-side. So, Didi instructed him to slide his chair over. It didn't take long for them to find at least a couple volumes that looked promising.

"What's your topic?" the boy finally asked.

"I'm going to research something that Mr. Pennington mentioned in class, the idea that some slaves willingly ended up joining their masters and fighting for the Southern cause. I find that hard to believe, and wonder whatever would make them want to defend the very institution that was keeping them in bondage."

"Dang," said Bad News. "Are you sure Pennington's gonna approve of that topic?"

"I'm not concerned with whether he approves of it or not," she countered. "Like everything else, I want to see if what we're being told in class is the truth."

"Oh. Well, okay. But you'd better be careful, Didi. What you find might not be pretty."

* * *

They had been at work for about an hour when the door at the far end of the hallway opened and Bad News's grandmother emerged. She was a small woman, in relation to her grandson, anyway. Like the boy, she was dark-skinned, though nowhere as dark as Didi. Her iron-gray hair was pulled back in a severe bun, and her face was smooth, save for a few creases on her forehead. A faded yellow house dress hung on her frame, and Didi couldn't determine if her shuffling gait was caused by the bad hip or the enormous tangerine-colored slippers she wore.

"Well, Travis, who do we have here?" said the woman in a pronounced drawl. "This ain't your so-called girlfriend."

"Uh, Gramma, this is Didi. She's a classmate. She's helping me out with an assignment I gotta finish."

"Do tell," said the woman with a mischievous smile that immediately put the girl at ease. "What kind of name is Didi?"

"That's not my given name, ma'am," she replied. "It's really Dihya. Dihya Diyoka."

"You ain't from around here," observed the woman. "Caint place the accent. Where you from, girl?"

"The Congo, ma'am," she replied.

"In Africa?"

"Yes, ma'am."

"Well, if that don't beat all," said the woman. "Travis, you brought home a real African princess." She looked Didi in the eye. "I mean that in a good way, young lady."

"Thank you, ma'am," Didi replied, embarrassed.

"Go get me a folding chair, sweetie," she said to her grandson. "I think I'll set a spell with you young people."

Dutifully, the boy went to a closet and retrieved a padded folding chair, which he placed across the table from their work station. With some effort, the woman transitioned from her walker to the chair and set herself down gently.

"Travis told me about your hip injury," said Didi. "I'm sorry you're in pain."

The woman waved it off. "Don't you go worryin' about me," she said. "I can git around well enough. A neighbor lady takes me shoppin' once a week, and gives me and Travis a ride to church every Sunday."

Didi looked over at the football player, who seemed to be squirming. "That's nice," she told the old lady. "My parents and I attend St. Luke's Catholic church in town."

"We belong to Shiloh Baptist," said the woman. "The Taylors—that's my family's name, and Travis's momma's name—been goin' to Shiloh since they built it right after the Civil War."

"Your family has been here that long?"

"Girl," she said, "my people's been here since the 1700s, or whenever they started the plantation days."

"So, your ancestors were slaves."

"Well, what do you think? 'Course they were." She sighed. "And this"—she swept her hand across the room—"is where we are two centuries later. Lord, Lord." And then she brightened. "But Travis here is gonna change all that. He's goin' to college. Isn't that right, honey?"

"Yes, ma'am," he replied.

"That's why I'm glad you're here, to help him with his books. I want him to realize that his football ain't gonna last forever. I want him to get an education he can fall back on, 'stead of workin' his butt off at the furniture factory for minimum wage."

"I understand."

She sat back in her chair. "So let me ask you a question, African princess," she said. "How do you like goin' to a school named after a man who was fightin' to keep slavery alive in the South?"

"Gramma—" began Bad News.

"Hush, you. I'm asking your friend here."

"The more I find out, the more strange it seems," she said measuredly.

"Strange ain't the word," said Mrs. Taylor. "Ever'body just kinda looks the other way. But you, comin' over here from Africa, you can see how wrong it all is, caint you?"

"What I see is that traditions die slowly here," Didi answered diplomatically.

"Yeah, all the wrong ones," said the woman, who then clucked her tongue while shaking her head. "And what's *your* dream, girl?"

"Me? Well, I'm starting to think I might go into medicine, like my father."

"He a doctor?"

"Yes, at Providence Heart in Columbia, at least for this year. He's in a physician exchange program. That's why we've come from Africa."

"Huh. That's pretty impressive. I'm proud of you, Travis, bringing such a nice girl home."

"We're just doing schoolwork, Gramma," he reminded.

"Hush. Maybe this African princess is just what your school needs. Wake all of 'em up." Her eyes bored into Didi's.

"We should get back to work, Gramma," said Bad News, extremely uncomfortable.

"You do that," the old lady replied, rising to her walker. "Hope to see you again," she said to Didi as she shuffled away.

"Thank you, ma'am," she replied.

Then the woman added, "And Travis, honey, don't forget you have to help me with my bath later."

"Okay, Gramma," he said, wincing with

126

embarrassment. Once the woman was out of earshot he said to Didi, "Sorry about my gramma. She just kind of says anything that comes into her head."

"Well, I think she's wonderful," said Didi. "In fact, I wish she'd stayed longer. There was something I wanted to discuss with her."

"What's that?"

"That Myrtle tree outside. The one with the bottles."

"Oh, yeah. That's Gramma's idea. She likes hanging bottles on it, 'specially blue ones. Some kind of superstition thing."

"Would you like to know the real story?"

Bad News, intrigued, put down his pen. "Okay, so what's it all about?"

"Well," she said, "the Myrtle tree was significant to slaves in the Bible. In the Old Testament, the Myrtle tree represented freedom, and the escape from slavery."

"How...why do you know all this?" he asked.

"Because the idea of bottle trees was brought over here from my country, the Congo, by my ancestors who were slaves, like yours were. The belief is that during the night, evil spirits would find their way into the bottles and become trapped. Since they can't get out, the next day's sunrise destroys them. So, I guess your grandmother is trying to protect your home from evil and lead you to a better life, or something like that."

"For real?"

"Yes. I actually think your grandmother is a very wise woman."

"I guess. I just felt funny, her goin' on about you waking up the school and all that. Sometimes she doesn't realize what she's saying."

"Oh, I think she does," said Didi.

Chapter Eleven

"So, how was your study session at *Chez Bad News*?" asked Heidi on Monday morning.

"It was kind of sad, actually," said Didi. "He lives in a cramped trailer home with his grandmother and seems to be her sole caregiver. I can't say that I blame him for wanting the career of a professional football player. She needs more attention than he alone can provide."

"Interesting. And did you meet this grandmother?"

"Oh, yes. She was actually quite pleasant, though definitely outspoken. I don't think she likes Tanya."

As if on cue, the happy couple strolled by, holding hands. Bad News managed a furtive smile toward the girls, while his girlfriend completely ignored them.

"I'm not surprised," said Heidi. "There's not much to like. Was the lady nice to you, at least?"

"Very much so. I guess she regards me as a positive influence on Travis, at least academically."

"Well, of course. But again, watch your back. Mims probably has spies everywhere."

* * *

That morning in homeroom both Mr. Hufnagel and Pierce rhapsodized about the Friday night exploits of the Stuart Cavaliers in their romp over Ridge View. There was also a buzz in the classroom over the postgame party, which had been held at one of the cheerleaders' homes. Didi was surprised to find out that well over a hundred people had attended, and that although the host's parents were present, beer and other alcoholic beverages had been flowing throughout.

"I don't know how they get away with it," said Heidi, her words tinged with a bit of envy. "The jocks are supposed to be on some kind of honor system during the season—no drinkin' or druggin'. But as you can see, they're kinda above the law. And the parents don't even care! I wonder if our straight-arrow Coach Kurtt would put the hammer down on his boys if he found out. But then again, he's *got* to hear about the partying around school; everybody's talking about it. Did Bad News mention anything about it on Saturday?"

"No," Didi answered, "but he did seem a little worn out. I figured it was just from the game."

"Or from partying with Tanya *after* the game," Heidi wickedly mused.

Didi didn't have much of an answer for that one.

* * *

Though American literature was becoming more enjoyable by the day (the curriculum had now moved to Mark Twain, whom Didi found interesting; and the poet Emily Dickinson, whom she considered strange), and biology offered challenging labs that gave her opportunities for hands-on work, she found that her application to the Civil War course bordered on obsessive. Why this was, she couldn't quite fathom, until one day when she was discussing her research paper with Heidi, whom she felt was taking the easy route by choosing the Pennington-friendly topic of the role of the Confederate cavalry in the conflict.

"You chose *what*?" said the Goth girl when Didi mentioned her interest in the suggestion of blacks fighting for the South. "Are you determined to get a D or something? Jeez, after the reenactment fiasco I figured you'd do something a little less controversial."

"Well," countered Didi, "if anyone should be surprised, it's me. Aren't you the one who told me early on that you were simply taking the course to 'mess with Pennington's head'? And now you've chosen a topic dear to his heart. That's quite a turnaround."

"Maybe so," she conceded. "The more I see what's going on around here, the more I'm convinced that nothing I say or do is gonna make a blessed bit of difference. On the other hand, I think this is becoming personal for you."

"Perhaps it is," admitted Didi. "You know, Bad News also cautioned me about choosing this topic, but once I started researching, it became clear just how much we are being misled in class. All I'm trying to do is find the truth."

Indeed, Didi had begun her fact-finding under the premise that, as Mr. Pennington had intimated, there were many blacks in the Southern states who had willingly taken up arms to fight alongside their masters to help turn back the Northern invaders. What she found was quite the opposite.

As Didi imagined, the advent of the war had

caused those in bondage throughout the South to make extremely difficult decisions. The first thing that had happened, predictably, was that even before the Emancipation Proclamation, which officially took effect on January 1, 1863, slaves had begun running away from their plantations amid the state of chaos the conflict had presented to their masters. Many of these refugees sought out the protection of whatever Union troops were operating in their territory. These numbers grew to where unwieldy numbers of escapees, called "contrabands," simply attached themselves to Union units. Some even served as scouts or spies, as they were familiar with the terrain and the stores of supplies in the areas from which they'd escaped.

Then, after the Emancipation Proclamation went into effect, freed black men from the South, along with their Northern brothers, sought to enlist in the Union army. Pressure from such people as abolitionist Frederick Douglass, himself a former slave and passionate anti-slavery speaker, had led a movement for the formation of colored units. By the time the war ended, blacks made up ten per cent of the Union army and had repeatedly distinguished themselves in battle, suffering more than 10,000 combat casualties.

That much, Pennington had represented in a fairly accurate manner. But from there, the teacher's narrative took a decidedly deceitful turn.

From her half-dozen or so sources that Didi diligently cross-checked, Pennington's "facts" that promoted the idea of Confederate loyalist blacks had crumbled, one by one. First of all, she learned, the concept of enlisting black soldiers for the Confederate army had been debated within the rebel military since the early days of the war. However, this proposal was repeatedly quashed by secessionist government officials in Richmond, who reasoned that the inclusion of blacks into the army would undermine the very foundation of their beliefs: that the institution of slavery was just, and that blacks as a race were inferior. Even when Robert E. Lee, the venerated commander of the Army of Northern Virginia, brought up the possibility of arming blacks in the war's waning days as he faced the crippling depletion of his forces, the Confederate government was unwilling to unconditionally free those men who would serve in their military. Indeed, their secretary of state had said, "...the worst calamity that could befall us would be to gain our independence by the valor of our slaves, instead of our own...the day that the Army of Northern Virginia allows a Negro regiment to enter their lines as soldiers they will be degraded, ruined and disgraced."

Thus, Pennington's narrative, she saw, was actually a myth that appealed to modern day neo-Confederates eager to find "evidence" to defend the principles of their "lost cause." In fact, a deeper dig into the research revealed that claims of as many as 80,000 black soldiers fighting for the Confederacy were utterly baseless, and that those slaves who *did* serve the Confederate army were forced workers who served as cooks, teamsters, and manual laborers, whose tasks included digging trenches and battlefield graves. Further, no documentation was found to exist that any black man was ever paid or pensioned as a Confederate soldier.

So, what was Pennington basing his assertions upon? The only thing Didi could find was that there were two Confederate units—one based in Louisiana and one in Tennessee—that were organized by elite, light-skinned freed men who identified with the white plantation owners. However, the Tennessee troops were never issued arms, and the Louisianans never saw action and even switched sides. Thus, even that "evidence" was without merit.

This didn't mean there were zero black Confederates. As the girl had come to learn, blanket statements about *anything* concerning the Civil War were extremely ill-advised. But she was confident enough in her findings to propose that if the numbers of black Confederates reached even one per cent of their military it was too much, and she was ready to present that claim in her paper.

What bothered Didi, though, even more than her teacher's spouting of misinformation, was its unquestioned acceptance by the vast majority of her classmates, whose own racial bias played into the perpetuation of these Southern myths. It all came down to a simple question for the girl: Was Mr. Pennington, a person who went to great lengths to "immerse" himself in the Civil War, simply incompetent as a teacher? Or was there something more insidious about his actions at work? Because he was, with every passing semester, churning out another group of impressionable teens who accepted as gospel his neo-Confederate teachings, and would thus pass them onto their children someday. To Didi, this was unconscionable.

These possibilities washed over her as she read the first draft of her paper late one night, and so distressed the girl that she went to her bedroom window to listen to the crickets outside for a while and try to clear her head. But the attempt at lifting her spirits failed miserably when yet another possibility entered her mind, the possibility that her father had been right at the football game, and that coming to America had been a huge mistake.

* * *

By the time the second—and final—study session with Bad News rolled around on Saturday afternoon, Didi had finished her own paper, except for some minor editing. That morning she'd seen in the Magnolia newspaper that Stuart had narrowly defeated Pinewood Lake, the visiting team, by the score of 19-14. As she pedaled over to Bad News's residence, Didi wondered if there had been another raucous victory party for the Cavaliers.

However, when the football player answered the door, his demeanor made it clear that he found little joy in the previous night's victory. "C'mon in," he said, again hefting her bicycle as if it were a children's toy.

"Congratulations on last night," she said while unpacking. "I read about it in the paper."

"Yeah, thanks," he grumbled. "We won, but just barely. Some guys' heads are gettin' too big, and it almost cost us. We only scored three points in the whole second half. Coach K. is really pissed off at us. I'm not looking forward to practice on Monday, that's for sure."

"And how is your shoulder injury?"

"Comin' along. I'll be fine."

Sensing that he wanted to close the subject of

football, she turned to the task at hand. "So, where are you with your paper?" she asked cautiously. "They're due on Tuesday."

"Here you go," he replied, handing over a three-page manuscript. "I tried to use all four sources but I could only fit three. Maybe you can help me with that."

"Sure," she smiled, pleased that he had at least made an effort. They sat together this time so Bad News could proofread along with her. When Didi pulled a red pen from her bag, he issued a playful groan. "What's the matter?" she said.

"I hate red pens," he replied, "'cause now you're gonna write all over my paper. I hate when teachers do that."

"You want me to make corrections, don't you?"

"I guess," he said. "I just hope it's not really bad."

"I'm sure it isn't," she said, but even at first glance she spied blatant errors everywhere. "Take out your laptop and find the document," she instructed. "We'll make corrections as we go."

"You're the boss," he sighed.

And so it went. Each paragraph was a tedious slog because of the boy's poor sentence structure and lack of punctuation skills; additionally, the formatting of the quotes he'd pulled from his sources was completely incorrect. But, she reasoned, at least he had an idea of what he was trying to do in the paper, and that was a plus.

"Well, well, it's the return of the African princess!" said Mrs. Taylor, emerging from the bedroom in her customary housecoat and slippers. "How is Travis's paper coming along, dear?"

"We're about halfway through," said Didi. "It's going well."

"Good, good. How about some milk and cookies for you two? I just baked some oatmeal and raisins the other day."

Bad News shrugged, but Didi said, "That would be fine, thank you."

Maneuvering deftly in the cramped kitchen area despite her walker, the old woman set out a plate of moist, crumbly cookies and poured some milk into jelly glasses. "Hope you like 'em, Princess," said Mrs. Taylor. "They're Travis's favorite since he was in diapers."

"Gramma—"

"Hush, boy," she said, and motioned to Bad News for the folding chair. "Travis was tellin' me about the subject of your paper the other day," Mrs. Taylor began as she settled in. "You were able to look up stuff like that about the slaves? I mean, official records and such?"

"Yes, ma'am," Didi replied, chewing the gooey cookie. "The information is there, if one is willing to search for it."

"Uh-huh. And my guess is you found what any idiot should be able to figure out—that the slaves didn't want no part of fightin' for the masters. Am I right?"

"Without a doubt," said the girl before taking a sip of milk. "But, the key is to be able to actually prove it, so that those who claim otherwise would be forced to face the truth."

"And the truth shall set you free," said the woman.

"C'mon, Gramma," moaned Bad News, "don't start gettin' all religious."

"Hush, you. Princess here is making some good points. I hope you ain't too proud to let her help you get a good grade."

"Not at all," he said, forcing a smile.

Then there was a knock at the door, and everything stopped.

"Let me get it," said Bad News, sliding from his seat.

"Uh-oh," whispered his grandmother.

Moving with the same quickness that he displayed on the gridiron, Bad News was at the door in a flash, cracking it open to reveal the presence of none other than Tanya Mims, along with two other teens. "Hey, baby," she cooed, "Darlene was able to borrow her mom's car, and I figured we could all go for a ride to Pinewood Lake—"and then she looked past the boy, who was doing his best to block her view of the kitchen table, but to no avail.

Trying to avoid a scene, Bad News eased out the door and pulled it closed behind him, forcing his girlfriend and her companions down the steps and onto the grass. And though the aluminum door was shut, this sounds of the ensuing confrontation pierced the trailer's walls as if they were constructed of gauze.

"What is *she* doing here?" Tanya shrilled.

"Calm down," said the boy, "we're working on my paper for school—"

"You're *lyin*! Why you doin' me like this?"

"Doin' what?"

"Going behind my back, that's what! How long's this been goin' on?"

"Nothin's going on," he grunted, his tone taking an edgy turn. "I needed help with school, and she's helpin' me."

"I'll bet she is!" answered Tanya sarcastically, her voice rising so she was sure to be heard inside the trailer.

Then, to make things worse, the couple who were with his girlfriend started to chime in, and the group's collective decibel level kept rising until Bad News ended it with a loud "*Enough*! I got no time for this! Y'all go for your ride, and I'll see you at school on Monday."

If Didi could have made herself disappear, she would have—gladly. As it was, she sat there trembling, until Mrs. Taylor reached over and patted the top of her hand, tsk-tsk-tsking all the while as the drama loudly unfolded in the yard.

"You better call me later!" was Tanya's parting shot, obviously offered as a face-saving maneuver. The next sound that came from outdoors was that of a car patching out onto the dirt road.

A few seconds later, Bad News wearily reentered the trailer, quietly clicking the door closed behind him. He trudged to the table and sat down. "Sorry you had to hear that," he muttered.

"It's all right," whispered Didi.

"Oh no, it isn't," said Mrs. Taylor. "But all that mess is for another day. You two have work to do, so I'm goin' back to my room. Time to read my Bible." She rose from her chair and grabbed her walker. "It was nice seeing you again, Princess," she said. "You take care."

"Yes, ma'am."

The woman shuffled off down the hall, trailing a few "Lord-Lord-Lords" under her breath.

"I'm sorry for that," said Bad News. "I'll straighten it all out. She won't bother you."

"I'm sure you're right," replied Didi, though her thudding heart belied her words. And though the girl did her best to concentrate on helping Bad News finish his paper, her thoughts kept going back to Heidi's warning at school, and the fear that what had just occurred was nowhere near over.

Chapter Twelve

That Monday as she prepared for school, Didi couldn't help but notice that she'd put on a few pounds. This, she surmised, was a result of the combination of increasing doses of American food, less walking than she'd done in Kinshasa, and her natural growth process. Her mother, though petite, had a shapely figure, and she seemed to be rounding into that form, albeit slowly. Of course, next to many American girls her age, including the voluptuous Tanya Mims, she would still be termed as "skinny."

These ruminations brought her back to what had occurred at Bad News's trailer home on Saturday. After attending mass with her parents on Sunday, Didi had occupied herself with finishing her Civil War Studies paper and helping her mother with cleaning chores. But she'd spent a restless Sunday night, and now the possible ramifications of what had happened on Saturday made her throat go dry. She decided to find Heidi as soon as possible when she arrived at school on Monday so as not to appear vulnerable. Of course, she also knew she was in for a stern reprimand from her friend, and Heidi didn't disappoint.

"I *told* you so," she hissed, her heavily shadowed eyes darting around. "I don't care *what* Bad News said

140

about calming her down, that witch is gonna be on your butt." She thought for a moment. "Maybe you should mention this to Redwine, or even Mrs. Woodard. You're pals with her, correct?"

"I'd rather not," said Didi. "I think I'm old enough to fight my own battles."

Heidi sighed. "Suit yourself. But don't be too proud to ask me for help if you're under attack, okay?"

"All right. Thanks."

However, to Didi's relief, there were no immediate reprisals, or even hints thereof. On Tuesday, both she and Bad News handed in their research papers with little fanfare (though Mr. Pennington did raise an eyebrow upon the on-time submission of the football player's manuscript), and talk in class turned to Thursday's much anticipated field trip to Charleston. Unfortunately, the class's travel roster would not include Bad News, as the lateness of their return would have caused a conflict with football practice, and there was no way Coach Kurtt would allow him to miss it, especially after the team's precarious victory the week before.

* * *

That Wednesday Didi dropped by Mrs. Woodard's room for lunch, but didn't mention the Tanya Mims drama. She did, however, disclose to the teacher that she'd assisted Bad News with his research paper, for which the woman commended her. "Getting any production out of Travis is a chore," she said while working her way through some leftover fried chicken. "Maybe we should have you run a workshop for the teachers on one of our staff development days. I'm curious, though…what's the situation like at his home?"

"Not great," said the girl. "He takes care of his grandmother, and they live in a trailer. They get by."

Woodard chewed thoughtfully, and then changed the subject. "Do you miss Kinshasa?" she asked.

"Somewhat. I'm rather torn about it, to be truthful."

"Tell me why."

"Well," she said, "as I've mentioned, it's the third largest city in all of Africa. Over twelve million people live there, with more arriving every day. There has been so much unrest in the rural areas, so much poverty and sickness and war, that people flock to Kinshasa for a new beginning. Some travel on incredibly overcrowded trains, even riding on the roofs of the cars. Others float on barges down the Congo River." She paused. "Can I tell you a story?"

"Please do," said Woodard.

Didi got a faraway look in her eyes, as if transporting herself. "Where we lived in Kinshasa— the heart of the commercial district—is somewhat like they say about New York. It never sleeps. There are high-rise buildings with offices and such, and large stores at the street level. The main roads are heavy with traffic and exhaust fumes, the sidewalks full of people going to or from work or school. There are public buses, but these are woefully inadequate in size and number. You have to push your way on, and there is no respect for personal space as here in the States. It's crowded and hot and noisy with all those blaring horns. There are also pale yellow-colored taxis; all of them, it seems, are dented and scratched. Some are even minivan sized. They're always overcrowded and breaking down.

"But despite all that confusion and craziness, I always felt like I never really *went* anywhere in Kinshasa. My life was restricted to a small area which included my home and my school, and not much else.

"Then, one day a couple years ago, my father told us he was going to visit a patient, as a favor to one of his co-workers at the hospital. She was an elderly woman who lived in one of the many slums that have emerged in Kinshasa due to overcrowding and the lack of adequate housing. The woman could not afford to go to hospital, and had no way of getting there anyway. So my father, being the kind of man he is, agreed to look in on her.

"Hearing about his upcoming visit, I begged my parents to let me accompany him. He seemed surprised that I would want to go. 'But why?' he said. 'It will be a shock to you, and such a trip is fraught with danger. We will have to hire a taxi, and there have been kidnappings from these vehicles.'

"But I was adamant. I kept telling him that I was now of an age to find out about the 'real' Kinshasa. Finally, after a lot of nagging, I wore him down, though my mother strongly disapproved. She said, 'What good can come of this, Maurice?' but he answered, 'Perhaps it is time her eyes were opened.' So, my mother reluctantly gave in. I was so excited at the thought of this great adventure."

"What was it like, Didi?" asked Woodard, who was so engrossed that she'd pushed her food away.

"We left early that Sunday morning," the girl said

woodenly, gazing straight ahead as if reliving the event. "It was especially hot, having rained the night before, which only increased the humidity. My father managed to hail a taxi. At first, the driver didn't want to take us to the address, saying it was 'a very bad place, not good for you or the girl.' But my father explained he was a doctor, and that this was more or less a mission of mercy. Then the man looked at me, and for some reason, he relented. 'You are doing a good thing, Doctor,' he said, 'so I will help you.'

"The place where the woman's family lived wasn't all that far away—maybe three miles, a distance we can drive to in ten minutes around here. But that day, it took us what seemed like hours. As we left the city center the roads became unpaved, with large potholes filled with the previous night's rainwater. There were other taxis, buses bursting with people, motorbikes, all of them clogging the road.

"Along the main commercial area the sidewalks, or whatever served as sidewalks, were packed with small stalls or tables with patio umbrellas, selling everything you could imagine, including all kinds of food. The conditions looked nowhere near sanitary, with swarming flies and other insects. In fact, more than once I saw animals—dogs and cats, mostly—that were either dead or diseased, lying among the tables. And the smell was just horrible.

"Finally, we cleared the main part of the thoroughfare and arrived at an area of shanties, lean-tos and tent-like structures. Garbage was everywhere, half-naked children playing amidst the waste. It was obvious these dwellings had no running water or indoor plumbing. The driver agreed to wait for us, as long as we wouldn't be too long. We got out of the taxi, and my father took my hand. In the other he carried his medical bag. 'You must come with me,' he said. 'I cannot leave you here in this taxi.'

"So, we walked through the mud to the woman's shack. It was a distance of only twenty feet or so, but our shoes were covered in mud by the time we got to the entrance, which was a heavy plastic flap of some sort. A young man came to the opening, after my father called out and identified himself, and told us we had come to the right place." At this point, tears started rolling down Didi's cheeks.

"Do you want to stop, honey?" said Mrs. Woodard, her brow furrowed.

"No, let me get this out, please," the girl replied.

"Okay."

"The interior was cramped and smelly. The rains had caused water to come up through the dirt floor, so the rugs they had thrown down to cover it were damp and mushy. There were three mattresses in the room, a couple of chairs, and a table that had been fashioned from vegetable boxes. Roaches crawled on the underside of the corrugated tin roof. And on the wall—I'll never forget this—was a color photo of the Swiss Alps. It was so ironic, I almost laughed to keep from crying.

"The woman lay on one of the mattresses. Her daughter and son-in-law were attending to her. The children, including the young man who'd let us in, stood off to the side. Of course, they were all amazed my father had come. He explained that their relative, a custodian at the hospital, had asked him for help. And they thanked him, over and over. 'Can I get you something?' the daughter asked me. 'Some juice, or fruit?' I was by this time quite hungry, but I couldn't bring myself to take their food.

"My father asked for some space, and then knelt down next to the mattress. He and the woman—whom we learned was fifty years old but looked eighty—spoke quietly in Lingala. Apparently, she had become seriously dehydrated due to some other medical conditions. And so, he tended to her as best he could, and gave her some medicine and bottles of liquid to treat the dehydration. He told her daughter what else they could do to help her, and they thanked him again and bowed to him.

"We were only there for perhaps a half-hour," said Didi, "but it seemed like a lifetime. I'm embarrassed to say that I couldn't wait to get out of that shanty. It felt as if the walls were closing in and would suffocate me.

"My father again took my hand and led me outside, to where the taxi driver was nervously waiting. We climbed into the car, and my father looked so angry. His jaw was clenched to the point where I thought his teeth would break. Finally, after a few minutes, he sighed deeply. 'So, my daughter,' he said, 'what are your thoughts?'

"I started to sob. I said, 'Father, I knew it was bad, but I never imagined this.'

"He nodded. 'Your mother and I argued about this,' he said. 'She wants to protect you from these harsh realities. But I thought it was worth the risk, for a couple of reasons. First, the situation you witnessed today has come about because of years of subjugation. The Belgians, of course, colonized us. Then, in the past twenty years, a civil war erupted that tore the country apart. Refugees streamed in from all over the

D.R.C., seeking anything better than what they had. And now you've seen what they got. This poverty is the handiwork of those who want to hold us down. The fact that I cannot do any more than what I did for that poor woman today pains me deeply. And I can only pray that God will let her live. But you, Dihya, can have a better life, and perhaps live your life in such a way that you'll be able to make a significant difference, where I could not.' Mrs. Woodard, my heart broke for him. He felt so helpless." Didi wiped her eyes and took another deep breath.

"I guess that's why he accepted the position here—to set me on a course to a better life. And so, here I am in the United States, living in a white man's expensive house, and feeling embarrassed for my friend who lives in an area that, while certainly much better than the slums of Kinshasa, is still appalling. I mean, this is *America*, the land of opportunity and wealth that I saw on television back in the D.R.C.

"What saddens me especially is that the things my father told me about the experiences of my people in the Congo—the Belgian oppression, the forced segregation, the civil war and its aftermath—all of these things exist here as well. And when I left Travis's trailer the other day, I couldn't help feeling as powerless as my father did that day in Kinshasa."

Mrs. Woodard reached across the desktop and took Didi's hand. "Thank you for having the courage to share this with me," she said gently. "You know, I think your father is right. Maybe someday you'll be the one who makes a difference. But you have to understand that change comes slowly in these parts."

Didi nodded and said nothing.

147

* * *

"So, are you ready for our big day in Charleston?" said Heidi as Didi climbed into her SUV.

"I guess so," she replied. "It looks like we're going to have great weather."

Heidi had generously offered to borrow her family's car and give Didi a ride to school at the ungodly hour of 6:30 a.m. so they could join the class for their planned departure time a half-hour later. Charleston was at least ninety minutes away; thus, their chartered field trip mini bus would be leaving the campus before the rest of the student body even arrived.

"Have you ever been to Charleston?" asked Didi as they drove along the sleepy streets to Stuart High.

"Yeah, a few times," Heidi replied. "We moved down here around ten years ago, but my folks missed going to the Jersey Shore. So, most summers we spend a couple weeks renting a cottage on Folly Beach, just outside the city. It's actually kind of nice, and the water's a lot better than up North."

"What's Charleston like?"

Heidi thought for a second and said, "Nowadays, Charleston kind of promotes itself as 'Old South.' See, by the time the Civil War ended many of the major Southern cities like Atlanta and Richmond and even Columbia were pretty much trashed. So, when they rebuilt they made an effort to modernize. On the other hand, the fine people of Charleston decided to pretty much put it back together way it was before the war. 'Historic preservation,' they call it.

"You're gonna see all kinds of fancy mansions and stuff, especially close to the harbor. That's where all the plantation owners came during the summer months to sit on the porch and drink mint juleps while their slaves were being worked to death on their land back home in the 'low country.' It's no wonder these plantation owners led the fight for the secession thing—they had it good, and they wanted to keep it that way. Do you know that before the war, Charleston was the largest city in the South? It had the best in everything—theater, restaurants, the whole deal. It even had the country's first public library!

"Anyway, once they decided to make their city a tourist destination, they conveniently played down the Civil War stuff and tried to promote their Colonial era heritage more. You'll see that from just the street names. But there is no denying that Charleston played a big role in the start of the Civil War, and that's why we're going on this trip. I learned a lot of this stuff on my summer vacays with my parents, so for me today is basically just a day off from school. It should be interesting to see how Pennington spins things, though."

* * *

When they arrived in the designated meeting place of the Stuart parking lot, most of the class was there, sleepy and yawning. Mr. Pennington, however, was hyped up, slurping from an oversized *Dunkin Donuts* plastic mug with one hand and holding a clipboard in the other. "Okay, that's Ms. Dorsch and Ms. Diyoka. Check, check," he said as he marked them off with a blue Sharpie. "Take a seat on the bus, ladies. We'll be leaving soon."

They climbed aboard, and Heidi offered Didi the window seat, which she gladly accepted. "I've done this trip so many times I know it by heart," she said. Then she pulled out her cell phone and started checking this and that while munching on a Twizzler.

Didi was a bit envious about the cell phone thing. She'd been begging her parents for one, but her father kept putting it off, claiming she'd become a slave to it, and that kids her age here in the States have lost all sense of good manners by pulling their phones out at the most inappropriate times—even at the dinner table! However, Didi felt she was starting to break through, if only to convince him that she should have a means of communication in the event of an emergency. Unfortunately for her, Dr. Buono had maintained a landline in his house, so Dr. Diyoka saw no great need for either his wife or daughter to have the cell. Since Didi's mom felt she could manage without one, the girl was forced to fight this campaign alone, and she had learned to pick her battles with her strong-willed father.

Finally, the entire class was checked in and the bus pulled out of the parking lot. Mr. Pennington and Ms. Redwine, who had volunteered to help chaperone the trip, sat in the seat behind the driver. She turned and waved to Didi, who waved back.

"So, how are things going with Jonathan?" said Heidi as she stared absently into her cell phone screen. "Have you guys gone out or anything yet?"

"No," said Didi dispiritedly. "He's got the marching band commitment on Friday nights, and most Saturdays he helps his father, who's a carpenter. Besides, his family only has one car. And then, of course, there's my overprotective father."

"Uh-huh," said Heidi, never taking her eyes off the phone. "So why don't you do this? Tell your dad that the three of us are driving up to Columbia to see their Confederate Museum for school. Then, I'll drop you two off and you can go have lunch somewhere."

"But what about the museum?"

Heidi just rolled her eyes.

* * *

The trip down State Highway 26 to Charleston was pretty nondescript, though Didi did find the many roadside billboards intriguing. Mostly they advertised places that sold various kinds of nuts or fireworks. Then, of course, there were the ubiquitous *Cracker Barrel* signs. "What's *Cracker Barrel*?" she asked Heidi.

"It's like a huge commercial restaurant chain that features country-style eats like fried chicken and biscuits and meatloaf," she replied, wrinkling her nose. "The restaurants are all decorated to look like log cabins or something, with rocking chairs on their front porch. It's kinda corny, actually, but people love it—especially the tourists who come down from the North. That's why you'll see a *Cracker Barrel* like every ten miles. It's okay, I guess, if you enjoy that kind of food. Tell you what, though, most of it sure isn't healthy. A lot of it is covered in thick gravy and whatnot—definitely not what you'd be eating back in Africa."

"So…people go there more for the experience?"

"Now you're catching on. Welcome to the South. But it could be worse. If you want 'experiences,' over on Interstate I-95, which goes down the East Coast from

New England to Florida, you'll see a billion signs for this place called *South of the Border*, which is located just over the divide between North and South Carolina. It's this humongous tourist trap that has a Mexican theme, of all things. There are campgrounds, tons of souvenir shops, fireworks places, fast food restaurants, the works. Truth be told, it's really a dump—my parents and I stopped there once—but they literally blanket I-95 with signs for it for like a hundred miles in each direction. I remember I had a burrito there, 'cause it gave me the runs for a week."

Didi found Heidi's musings on American Southern culture interesting; but even more than the advertisements for fireworks outlets and restaurants, she was enthralled with the religious-themed billboards that sometimes shared a marquee with commercial material. *REPENT AND BE SAVED!* cried one. *ARE YOU READY FOR HIS COMING?* blared another.

The most striking highway attraction, however, came about an hour into their trip. Set back a hundred yards or so beyond the tree line that bordered the highway's shoulder, there rose a very tall white flagpole, from which a huge Confederate flag fluttered in the breeze. Didi elbowed Heidi and pointed to the window while they passed it, as someone towards the back of the bus cried, "Wow! Lookit that!"

"Must be on private property," the Goth girl surmised. "Nothing anyone can do about it, in that case. Don't you just love it?" She went back to her phone, but Didi's gaze remained locked on the flag until it was out of sight.

Chapter Thirteen

Fortunately for the high schoolers, their minibus encountered only light traffic on the highway, so they turned into the parking lot of Liberty Square, which fronted Charleston Harbor, just before the first Fort Sumter tour ferry was scheduled to depart. The air was fresh and tinged with salt, and the cool breeze riffling through the city's omnipresent palmetto trees invigorated the teens and their teachers after their confinement on the minibus.

Pennington, always the organized one, had purchased the tickets in advance, so it was just a matter of shepherding his group onto the ferry, with the assistance of Ms. Redwine. Both teachers were attired in bright red Stuart High windbreakers with the garish Cavalier logo on the back.

The kids had been told in advance that their tour of the venerable stronghold in Charleston Harbor would take around two and a half hours, with their actual time inside the fort a sixty-minute window. And so, they boarded and lined up along the ferry's deck railing to enjoy the sights and the breeze, which gave the harbor's waters a slight chop. As she had never been on any kind of boat, Didi was both exhilarated and nervous. Would she get seasick? And if the boat

153

sank, would she drown? Having never learned to swim, this caused the girl more than a little trepidation. Thus, unlike her cohorts, she listened carefully as a tape-recorded message of the location of the boat's life vests was broadcast while they were casting off. This was followed by a rather scratchy recorded monologue about the siege on Fort Sumter, which began, "With the first shot on Fort Sumter, America's greatest moment of conflict, the Civil War, had begun..." Didi's eyes locked on to the fort that sat some three miles offshore. From the ferry terminal it had seemed like a small bump in the water, but as they approached, it came into focus as a low-slung, pentagon-shaped structure of brick that had some kind of dark coating painted on its façade.

The ferry pulled up to the fort's dock, and the passengers, who numbered around fifty including the Stuart High group, disembarked. Didi heaved a sigh of relief that she'd survived the half hour voyage. Although many of the boat's occupants scattered once ashore, the Stuart group headed through the fort's front entrance, to an area where a National Park Ranger awaited them for an official tour. And while Didi's classmates were chatty and playful, she noticed that Mr. Pennington wore a look of reverence, as if he'd entered some medieval cathedral. Even Heidi noticed. "Check out Pennington," she whispered, elbowing her friend gently. "He's really geeking out."

The ranger, who awaited them in the center of the fort's parade ground near an iron Civil War cannon, was notable for two reasons. First, his uniform, which included a khaki shirt and long pants with matching wide-brimmed hat, was impeccably clean and pressed.

Second, he was as black as Didi. As if in recognition of this fact, he shot the girl a quick wink before he began his monologue. "Good morning to all of you, and welcome to the Fort Sumter National Battlefield Park," he said with only the faintest hint of a Southern accent. "My name is Ranger Odarius Bennett. I take it your group is all together. Where are you from?"

"Stuart High in Magnolia," answered one of the boys.

"As in J.E.B. Stuart?"

"Yessir!" the boy replied proudly.

"I see. Well then, I guess all of you are already pretty well-versed in the Civil War."

"This is my Civil War Studies class," volunteered Mr. Pennington. "We're here to see where it all got started."

"Well," said Bennett, "this is as good a place as any. But let's get a few things out of the way first. Please don't climb on any of the battlements or cross any "no admittance" barriers. And please don't sit on the grass of the parade grounds here. There are some nasty fire ant nests, and you wouldn't want to park yourself on one."

The kids chuckled.

"Okay, then," continued Bennett, "let me tell you the story of this place, and you can just stop me if your teacher here has already gone through it with you."

As the students respectfully listened, the ranger told them about the bombardment of the Union-occupied fort on April 12-13, 1861 by the South Carolina militia. At first, the Southern sympathizers cut off all supply ships trying to get to the fort while strengthening their artillery batteries around

Charleston Harbor. When the then-new Confederate government issued an ultimatum to Major Robert Anderson, the Union commander of Fort Sumter, to evacuate, he refused, thus leading to an attack under the command of the elaborately named General Pierre Gustave Toutant Beauregard. The Confederates' two-day bombardment literally reduced the Union fort to rubble, and Anderson was forced to surrender, securing the South's first victory of the war.

At the conclusion of Bennett's recounting of the battle, a few of the boys high-fived and made some pro-Confederate remarks, which the ranger brushed aside. "Are there any questions?" he patiently asked.

Didi raised her hand.

"Yes, miss?"

"Could you please tell me about the attack on Battery Wagner?" she asked. "I believe it's near here." The boys looked confused, but Pennington offered a tight smile, for he knew where this was going.

"I'd be happy to," replied Bennett. "A short distance from this fort across the water, a Confederate installation named Fort Wagner was constructed on Morris Island. It had thirty foot-high earth and sand walls that protected over a dozen heavy artillery pieces that could halt any attackers on warships entering the harbor.

"In 1863, the Union command decided to mount an attack on Wagner, figuring if they captured it, they could both control the harbor and take back Sumter, which was now a Confederate post. However, a bombardment of Wagner by the Union navy was unsuccessful, so they decided to gamble on an infantry assault. After a first attempt failed, the Union commander, General Quincy Gilmore, decided to let the 54th Massachusetts Infantry, an African-American unit, spearhead the attack. And although they stormed and captured the fort's outer defenses in brutal hand-to-hand fighting, their regiment was ultimately driven back, suffering terrible losses, including that of their commander, Colonel Robert Gould Shaw, a white man from an abolitionist family in Boston. And although this battle was a Confederate victory, it changed the attitudes of whites on both sides as to the fighting ability of black soldiers. You might want to check out the movie *Glory* to learn more about the 54th Massachusetts and this engagement, although some of the battle scenes are somewhat graphic. Have I answered your question, miss?"

Didi smiled. "Perfectly, thank you," she said.

After Bennett's talk, the group was free to roam around the grounds of the fort. "Let's go up on the wall," said Heidi. "We'll get some good views of the harbor from there. That is, unless you have some other interesting questions for Ranger Bennett."

"No, I'm fine," Didi answered with a smile. "I just wanted to make sure that both sides of the coin were represented in his presentation."

"Oh, I think you accomplished that," said Heidi. "Pennington looked like he was gonna choke."

Once the girls made it to the top of the wall they were joined by Ms. Redwine, who was busy snapping photos with her phone. After taking one of the girls, she said, "Didi, I had no idea you were so interested in Civil War history. Even I had never heard of Fort Wagner."

"I just happened to come across it while I was

researching my paper," she said innocently. "I figured our class might be interested."

"Sure you did," said Heidi sarcastically.

The three females chatted about this and that, and shortly thereafter Ms. Redwine looked at her watch. "Hey, we've got to get back to the dock. The ferry's leaving soon. Let me go round up some of those boys. They're running around and jumping on the cannons like a bunch of preschoolers."

She took off, leaving the girls on the battlements. Then Heidi leaned over the edge. "Hey, Didi," she hissed, "come look at this!"

Didi leaned over. Down below, Mr. Pennington seemed to be prying a piece of brick from the outer wall of the fort. Heidi elbowed her and called down, "Hey, Mr. Pennington, what'cha doing?"

Knowing he'd been caught red-handed, the embarrassed teacher shrugged and simply said, "Souvenir."

"Don't worry," said the Goth girl with a wry smile. "We won't tell anybody."

* * *

From the ferry terminal it was just a short walk to the City Market on Meeting Street. The market complex, established in the 1790s, was a series of one-story sheds that were rectangular open stalls with center walkways stretching for a few city blocks. In the nineteenth century, this place had provided a convenient venue for the local farms and plantations to sell their meat and produce, as well as for people to gather and socialize. Modern times had seen a changeover in available goods, with vendors hawking everything from souvenirs, handmade jewelry and art, to regional delicacies and hot sauces. There were also local black women, called Gullahs, whose roots went back to the slavery era, selling hand-crafted woven baskets fashioned from palmetto fronds, pine needles and sweet grass, items that had been made the same way for centuries.

Mr. Pennington had set aside an hour for the students to peruse the market and grab some lunch on their own, either from the market's vendors or some of the outdoor eateries on North or South Market Streets that bordered the stalls. It was the perfect day for strolling around the quaint market area; and even though it was a weekday, the place was pretty lively with groups of college kids in cutoffs and tank tops, senior citizens with Nikon cameras slung around their necks, and young couples holding hands. Horse-drawn buggies with tourists aboard clip-clopped around the surrounding streets with livery drivers attired in Colonial era garb giving them the lowdown on "Old Charleston."

After Pennington's release, with the direction to meet out front of the market at one o'clock sharp, the group quickly dispersed, with the teachers sticking together. Heidi and Didi decided to forgo a sitdown lunch for a combination of homemade fudge, kettle corn, and other snacks purchased from various merchants in the market. However, after passing a few stalls featuring the Gullah crafts, Didi persuaded her friend to visit one group of those women who had their wares laid out on blankets and sat on stools weaving their baskets while conversing in their musical dialect.

What was equally fascinating to Didi was the irony of the women's stall being adjacent to a vendor selling all kinds of Confederate-themed memorabilia, including rebel flags of various sizes, bumper stickers, shot glasses, T-shirts and hats.

"I love your baskets," she said to an older woman dressed in African garb similar to hers back in the D.R.C., her head wrapped in a colorful turban. "How much are they?"

"Varies," said the woman, barely looking up from her weaving. "Depends on the style and how big and how much you want to spend."

"I see," said Didi. "They're just so intricate."

The woman stopped what she was doing and looked up. "Where you from, girl?" she asked suspiciously.

"The Congo," she answered.

"Been here long?"

"No."

"Seems like it."

"We're here on a school trip," explained Heidi.

"Do tell. Well then, I would just have to give our visitor here from the Congo a special student discount." For the first time she smiled, revealing a few gaps where teeth had been. After a little back-and-forth negotiating, Didi purchased a small basket for her mother. "I just have to ask you," Didi said to the woman while motioning to the Confederate paraphernalia in the neighboring stall. "What do you think of all that?"

The Gullah lady shook her head with a tsk-tsk-tsk that reminded Didi of Bad News's grandmother. "He sells a lot of that stuff, which by the way is made in

China," she observed with obvious distaste. "Wish he had shirts for sale that said, *'Oh, by the way, WE LOST'!*"

* * *

After their free time the group assembled at the front of the market, where a stone staircase would lead them to a Greek temple-style building that sat atop the open arcade of stalls. It was quite impressive, reminding Didi of ancient ruins she'd seen in books and on television. The front entrance of the brownstone, stucco-covered structure featured four huge columns. This was to be the next stop on the students' tour: the Charleston Confederate Museum.

After taking a headcount, Mr. Pennington explained that the Daughters of the Confederacy had established the museum in 1899 and that it had been opened to the public ever since, except for a period in 1989 after the structure's roof had suffered damage from a hurricane. Then they climbed the steps together and entered the building.

"Well, hello, children!" cooed a pixie-ish, white-haired woman. "Thank you so much for coming! And where are we all from?"

This time Mr. Pennington did the honors. "We're the Civil War Studies class from Stuart High in Magnolia, ma'am," he announced politely.

"Well now, we are *honored* to have y'all as guests!" trilled the woman. "My name is Abigail Worthy, and I am the great, *great* granddaughter of Colonel Jonas Worthy of the 10th South Carolina Regiment, who distinguished themselves in numerous battles and campaigns throughout the War for Southern Independence. Colonel Worthy himself was a respected military commander who later went on to serve admirably in the South Carolina Assembly.

"My role here—which is purely voluntary—is to act as a guide and interpreter for our many visitors, who come from all over the country and the world. As you can see, this is not a large facility, but it is just chock full of historical artifacts, most of which are donations from the families of our brave men who served the South during the war. So, I'll be here to answer any questions you might have. Our only request is that there be no photography or videotaping of the exhibits. Enjoy!"

Indeed, "chock full" was an apt description of the organization of what seemed like thousands of uniforms, weapons, documents, and photographs that were crammed into glass viewing cases which took up almost all of the floor space. The high walls were literally covered with original paintings, flags, and battlefield banners as well.

"Wow," said Ms. Redwine as she and the girls wandered through the maze of artifacts. "The Confederate Museum in Columbia has nothing on this place. I've never seen so much stuff." As could be expected, the boys tended to gravitate towards the more martial pieces, pointing out .44 caliber cavalry pistols, sabers and carbine rifles; meanwhile, the girls spent time reading the original letters of soldiers that had been sent to anxious families and girlfriends back home. "Isn't this incredible?" asked Redwine, taking in some studio-posed daguerrotypes of both bearded men and boys the same age as her students, all of them brandishing arms and looking serious in their uniforms.

"Yeah," said Heidi, "but it would've been cool if Mr. Pennington had listened to Didi's suggestion to also visit the Old Slave Mart here in town. It's also a part of the story, you know."

"Hmm, that actually sounds interesting," she said. "Let me go have a word with him."

The girls kept a casual eye out as the guidance counselor approached the teacher, who was leaning over a display case that housed canteens, eating utensils, and other personal accoutrements from Southern troops. At first he seemed surprised at Redwine's words, and then a bit annoyed—but then she put her hand on his shoulder and seemed to be sweet-talking him. Finally, he nodded his assent.

"Jeez, I think he's gonna do it!" whispered Heidi. "You go, Redwine!"

Some fifteen minutes later, Pennington gathered the group, thanked Mrs. Worthy for her hospitality, and led the class outside and down the stone steps. "Okay, troops," he said, "we're going to make two more stops. I've decided that because we're doing so good on time, we'll take in the Old Slave Mart on Chalmers Street"—he shot a look at Didi and Heidi—"and we'll finish up at the Battery near Charleston Harbor, not far from where we started off. So, let's get cracking!"

There were a few sounds of surprise from the boys, and maybe a few muted grumbles, but Didi and her friend couldn't have been happier as they clipped along the sidewalk towards Chalmers Street. Along the way, she noticed that some of their male companions hadn't waited until they returned home to don the Confederate-themed T-shirts and whatnot they'd picked up at the City Market. "Thanks, Ms. Redwine," Didi said to the counselor.

"Yeah," said Heidi, "I didn't think Mr. Pennington would go for it."

"Oh, it wasn't all that hard to persuade him, actually," said the woman. "Especially because I'm on the committee that has to okay all school trips."

The girls giggled.

A short walk down the spotless, leafy avenues of downtown Charleston led them to Chalmers Street, and their destination, a Romanesque building wedged between two private residences that featured an elliptical brick-and-stucco entrance, bracketed by octagonal pillars. A pair of stately palmetto trees stood guard near the curb. Before they entered, Didi looked up at the horseshoe-shaped sign atop the entrance, which was somewhat faded but gripped her nonetheless, creating a sliver of apprehension about the choice of pressing Pennington to make the visit.

The group was met by a smallish middle-age white man who wore a cardigan sweater over his dress shirt and tie. His nameplate identified him as Simon Bigsby, and he squinted at the teens through wire-rimmed glasses that gave him the appearance of a stodgy old college professor. After Ms. Redwine paid at the front desk for the group's student discount package, Bigsby began his talk. "I see you all are from Magnolia," he began. "Beautiful little town. Thanks so much for visiting us. As you can tell, it's kind of slow today, so you'll pretty much have the place to yourselves.

"You entered the building through an archway. Actually, in the beginning it was the entrance to an alley. That is why you'll notice that the walls on either side of this long room are composed of exposed brick and mortar. Within this simple alleyway came to be a most important site in Charleston. Allow me to explain.

"Before 1856, slaves that were brought to Charleston to be sold at auction were subject to public transactions that could be conducted anywhere on the streets of the city. But then, a city ordinance mandated that these auctions be brought indoors, and in more central locations. Believe it or not, some forty such venues existed within a few blocks' radius of this place. But only this one—purchased in 1859 by a man named Z. B. Oakes and named Ryan's Mart—still exists." The man's monologue was toneless and pedantic, and Didi wondered how he felt about his place of employment. She also noticed an acute awareness of her surroundings, its sights and smells—quite unlike her mostly indifferent classmates.

"Forty percent of all slaves entering the colonies, and then the United States, came through the port of Charleston," continued Bigsby. "This site was originally comprised of the alleyway, which was eventually roofed; a four story holding jail called a barracoon; a two-story kitchen structure; and a 'dead house,' or morgue. You see, when most slaves arrived here after long months at sea, or as runaways from other parts of the South who'd been apprehended and marched here, they were usually gaunt and weak. So, in order to have them bring top dollar, they were held for a while in the barracoon so they could be 'fattened up,' so to speak. There are even stories of the slaves being issued palm oil to spread on their skin to give it a healthy sheen.

"The auction area featured a table which was three feet high by ten feet long, that stood about where we are now. It was also used in livestock auctions." He paused a moment to allow the implication of his words sink in. Indeed, some of Didi's classmates began to shuffle their feet, an obvious sign of discomfort. "Ryan's Mart, as it came to be called, was known far and wide throughout the South, bringing buyers from as far away as Galveston, Texas.

"Inside, you will view a series of exhibits. Some of them might cause you to be sad, or uncomfortable, or maybe even angry. But above all, they should cause you to *think*. So, I'll leave you on your own now, to explore this first floor. There is also a second floor which is accessible by two sets of stairs. Please step carefully going up and down. I'll meet you back here before you leave."

By this time Didi was convinced she and Heidi had made a grave error forcing this visit. She wondered if Pennington had purposely left it off the itinerary in deference to her, because an oppressive feeling of sadness that had come over her made it seem like the walls were closing in. However, she knew she couldn't back out now. And so, with Heidi—who had picked up on her friend's anxiety—at her side, Didi pressed on to view the exhibits. Thankfully, her male classmates, for whatever reason, deemed it wise to put as much space between themselves and her as possible, and had immediately gone upstairs.

The visuals were stunning—auction sale broadsides that had been posted in Charleston and other cities promising specimens of the highest quality; diagrams of the sardine can-like cargo holds of slave ships, along with the ships' manifests; placards offering an explanation of the role of the slave trader, the slave, and the buyer; and other related documents of the era. But what really brought it home for Didi was what she found on the second floor: farming and cooking implements used in the slave quarters led to glass cases filled with shackles, ball-and-chain mechanisms, leather 'cat o' nine tail' whips, and grotesque branding irons—all engineered to retain, restrain, or punish those slaves who stepped out of line.

With each passing minute the weight of what she was seeing heaped itself upon Didi, who learned that a healthy girl her age would bring around $1,300 back then—$40,000 in today's world. "Are you okay?" asked Heidi as Didi stood next to a glass case that featured tattered cloth dolls that had belonged to slave children. "You don't look too good."

"Must have been all that junk food for lunch," she replied quietly, though both girls knew this was not the case. "Let's go back downstairs."

Thankfully, the class was coming back together near the lobby, where Mr. Bigsby awaited them. "Well now, I hope you learned a lot today," the man said evenly. "Any last questions?"

"How did this end up becoming a museum?" asked Ms. Redwine, who had yet to pick up on Didi's distress.

"Well," the man said, "when Union forces occupied Charleston beginning in February 1865, the slaves still imprisoned at Ryan's Mart were freed. After that, the place was converted into a tenement dwelling, and later in the 1920s, a car dealership. Then, in the 1930s a woman named Miriam Wilson bought it and established the Old Slave Mart Museum, which at first primarily displayed African and African-

American art. The actual historical narrative of slavery was kind of played down. But after the museum closed in the 1980s due to budget issues, the South Carolina African-American Heritage Commission restored the building to what you see today. Thanks for coming, and have a safe trip back to Magnolia."

Didi heaved a sigh of relief, and couldn't wait to escape this place of profound sadness. However, she was surprised when Bigsby tapped her on the shoulder and motioned her over. "Young lady," he said quietly, "I couldn't help notice how affected you were by what you heard and saw here. I tried to be as clinical as I could, but believe me, we've had people break into tears and worse within these walls." He handed her a piece of paper with writing on both sides. "Have you ever heard of Denmark Vesey?" he asked.

"No," she said, "though I think I saw his name somewhere in the exhibits."

"Fine. Then I'm giving you a homework assignment. Look him up. He's as important as anyone you've learned about in your class's travels today. I've also written down the name of a film I think you'll relate to. It's hard to find, but you seem to be the sort of person who will be able to do it. I promise you that you won't be disappointed."

"Thank you," she whispered, and hurried outside to join her classmates.

"What was that about?" asked Heidi. "Did you get sick in there or something?"

"No," Didi replied. "I'm feeling much better, actually."

"Let's move out, people!" commanded Pennington, in his best reenactor voice. "We have one more stop to make!" The class trooped down East Bay Street past beautifully restored row houses painted in a variety of colors, and then along the raised seawall that surrounded The Battery, a sprawling park featuring majestic spreading oaks, gazebos and benches. The combination of the nearby shimmering harbor waters and the leafy pathways of the park was pure delight for those who strolled its grounds.

"Man, look at those houses," marveled Heidi as she gazed up at the antebellum mansions bordering the park that had been built on the backs of plantation slaves. "They were living large, Didi." Indeed, the grand palaces that faced the harbor were imposing. Though some featured wrought iron gates out front, there weren't any large front yards to speak of; rather, the owners had them built with wide verandas on each floor equipped with rocking chairs, where they could catch the sea breeze from Charleston Harbor. And despite the structures being set close together, a sharp eye could peer between them into rear courtyards that featured elaborate gardens and marble fountains.

"Undoubtedly," replied Didi some seconds later. "But what's going on over there, at the edge of the park?" Hearing some kind of commotion, the group made its way past Civil War era cannons and howitzers, complete with pyramids of welded-together cannonballs and artillery shells, towards a huge statue at the park's point closest to the seawall. What they came upon stunned them.

Upon a circular brick plaza of intricate design stood an octagonal granite base at least ten feet high, atop which towered a bronze sculpture of at least another dozen feet. A Charleston travel brochure that

Mr. Pennington had circulated on the bus for the students to read described it as "an allegorical depiction of the Confederate defense of Charleston during the Civil War." It consisted of a male figure—the defending warrior—with a sword in his right hand and a shield bearing the South Carolina state seal in his left; and a female figure representing the City of Charleston and holding in one hand a garland of laurel—a symbol of immortality—while pointing with the other out to the harbor, specifically towards Fort Sumter. It was from here that the Confederate artillery had begun the bombardment on Sumter, initiating the War Between the States.

The inscription on the statue's upper pedestal read:

To the Confederate
Defenders of Charleston
Fort Sumter
1861-1865

Another inscription which circled the pedestal bottom read, *Count Them Happy Who For Their Faith And Their Courage Endured A Great Fight.*

However, both of these inscriptions were somewhat difficult to read, as the statue was currently encircled by at least a dozen pro-Confederate demonstrators waving huge rebel flags and yelling, "You won't take us down!" and various other chants; while another group, most of whom were African-Americans, carried picket signs with slogans like *END THE HATE* and *WE WILL OVERCOME.* As the teens approached, the two contingents were practically nose-to-nose, and things were quickly getting contentious.

"Steve, we'd better get the kids back to the bus," said Ms. Redwine. "This doesn't look good."

Incredibly, Pennington seemed to hesitate, fascinated by the whole spectacle. To make things worse, one of the pro-Confederate demonstrators noticed the boys in the school group clad in their rebel-themed acquisitions from the City Market. "Come over here with us!" they screamed to the boys, some of whom (including Seth the landscaper) seemed all too ready to join their ranks, while others were clearly intimidated by their forceful exhortations.

"No! No!" shouted the counter-demonstrators. "Don't feed the hate! Stay with us!"

"Steve, listen to me," pleaded Redwine. "Let's go back to the bus."

Meanwhile, Didi had approached one of the counter-protesters, a black woman in a Martin Luther King T-shirt, who stood on the periphery, checking her cell phone. "Pardon me," she said.

"Yeah, what?" answered the thirty-ish woman testily.

"I just wanted to ask you a question about what's going on here."

"Okay, so what do you want to know?"

"Well, this…demonstration in front of the statue…the people with flags. Did you know this was going to occur today?"

"Yeah," she said, "we got word this morning, so we had to mobilize. Usually they just do this on Sunday mornings. It's something they don't show in the tourist brochures for Charleston, know what I'm sayin'?"

"I see. Well, it seems you've assembled quite a group yourselves."

"Thanks," she said, losing her harsh tone. "I'm Marlene."

"I'm Didi."

"She's from the Congo," said Heidi, who'd been listening in. "Wants to find out all about Southern culture."

Marlene snorted. "I'll tell you what, girl," she said, putting her cell phone away, "if you want to *really* see something, come up to Columbia on Sunday. There's gonna be a big demonstration by those crackers who want to keep flyin' the Confederate flag on the Capital grounds. Should be a lot of folks on both sides. Could get interestin'. Listen, I gotta go." She gave a quick wave and then rejoined her group as they screamed at the rebel flag carriers.

Suddenly, Ms. Redwine was shooing Didi and Heidi, along with the others, back towards the minibus that was parked a hundred yards away. "Sorry you had to witness this," she said as they trotted along, looking back over their shoulder at the escalating standoff near the statue. "I hope this doesn't change your perception of South Carolina."

"Not a bit," replied Didi enigmatically.

Chapter Fourteen

As exhausting and trying as the Charleston trip had been, Didi was pleasantly surprised upon her return home to find her parents joyous over the reception through the mail of her first quarter report card. Despite a B+ in Civil War Studies, she had scored enough A's and A-pluses to be awarded what were called "high honors."

"We're so proud of you, Dihya," said her mother after a great hug. "To come to this new place and excel as you have is wonderful."

"Yes," agreed Dr. Diyoka. "You are certainly to be commended for your hard work. I've seen you staying up late to do your studying, and your commitment to excellence is a reflection on our entire family."

"Thank you, Father," she replied. "I'll try my best to keep it up the rest of the year." And then, an idea hit her. "The one grade I would like to raise, though," she began tentatively, "is the Civil War Studies class. Well, it just so happens that my trip to Charleston today has inspired me to visit a Civil War museum in Columbia. As it turns out, my friend Heidi has volunteered to drive me and another student up there to see it. Would I be permitted to go this Sunday, after we return home from church?"

The request gave her father pause. "And who is this other student?" he asked warily. "Do we know her?"

"Actually, it's a him," she said, trying to mask her nervousness. "His name is Jonathan Harris, and he's a nice boy who is in the marching band. I believe his father has a carpentry shop in town."

"Oh, yes," said Gabrielle, coming to her rescue. "His shop is just a few doors down from my law office. He actually came in a few weeks ago to repair a bookshelf in one of the conference rooms, and he seems like a nice man. I would imagine his son is, as well. I don't see why this should be a problem. Do you, Maurice?"

Still riding the wave of happiness over his daughter's exemplary report card, the taciturn doctor agreed. "Thank you, Father!" said Didi, and gave him a hug and kiss before scurrying up the stairs to her room lest he change his mind.

* * *

"Do you believe Pennington gave us B-pluses?" griped Heidi with a slam of her locker. "It's not like he's that hard a marker; and besides, we have to be the smartest people in that room, *including* him. Guess you have to be a boy to get an A. I'll bet even Bad News got a good grade!"

"Perhaps next time our research papers will lift our grade," reasoned Didi. "He's already told us they were submitted too close to the end of the quarter to be counted on this report card."

"Oh yeah," said Heidi sarcastically, "I'm sure your topic is *really* gonna catapult your average."

Didi waved her off. "Listen, though, I've got good news," she said excitedly. "My parents have approved our trip to Columbia on Sunday. After I go to church, of course."

"Of course, can't miss that," cracked the Goth girl. "There's just one thing: have you asked Jonathan yet?"

"I intend to do so at lunch today," she replied.

"Well, I'll make myself scarce then," said Heidi. "Good luck, but I'm sure he'll say yes." She practically had to scream these last few words because of an uproar that was being caused by a huge entourage of football players, cheerleaders and pep squadders who were marching down the hallway, whooping and chanting about that night's home game versus Camden. By now, Didi was used to the Friday hoopla surrounding each game, but this one had special importance, in that if Stuart was able to defeat Camden, they would be one step closer to securing a spot in the upcoming sectional playoffs, which were scheduled to begin in two weeks. As usual, Troy Winchester led the parade, his corded arms draped across the shoulders of two fawning cheerleaders. "Hope you're coming tonight," he said to Didi and Heidi as he breezed by, causing the Goth girl to dramatically hold the back of her hand to her forehead and remark, "He talked to me! He actually talked to me!" However, in the clamor her snarky humor was lost to all but Didi, who giggled as Bad News, with Tanya firmly attached to his side, brushed past as well. But the cheerleader did manage to fix her with an ominous, dagger-like stare before they moved on.

* * *

Despite the excitement coursing through Stuart High, beginning with both Mr. Hufnagel's and Pierce's passionate PA reminders to turn out that evening for the game, the morning seemed to crawl for Didi, who began having doubts that Jonathan would want to go to Columbia. But she need not have worried; the boy broke into a grin and immediately agreed.

"We get back from church by eleven," he said while demolishing his ham sandwich, "so that shouldn't be a problem. You sure Heidi won't feel funny being with us?"

"I don't think so," said Didi. "We'll at least be able to have lunch by ourselves."

"That's great," said the boy. "Even better, my cousin Keith has a restaurant in Columbia. It's called *Dembo's Down-Home*, and they serve really good barbecue. Do you like that kind of food?"

"Well…I've never had it," confessed Didi.

"*What?* You've never had barbecue? Then you're in for a treat. You're not a vegetarian, are you?"

"No, I'll eat any kind of meat," she assured. "That's what barbecue is?"

"It's like this," he said. "Down here in Carolina the main thing is pork, and Keith makes the best pulled pork and ribs in the state. But he does great chicken, too. See, he's got these big old smokers where the meat cooks for a long time over a low heat. By the time you eat it, it's falling-off-the-bone tender. Then, you put his special Carolina sauce on it, which is made with mustard and vinegar. It's really tasty. He's also got these crazy good side dishes like okra, baked beans and mac n' cheese that'll blow you away."

"It sounds delicious."

176

"Believe me, it is. And if I tell him I'm coming, he'll put out a good spread for us, no doubt."

"Then, it's a date?"

"You know it. Just let me know what time to be ready." He wrote his cell number down on a scrap of paper, which he slid across the lunch table to Didi.

She was in heaven.

* * *

For her big date Didi had decided to wear one of her most colorful Congolese tops, with an understated bead necklace. She didn't want to overdo it, though, so a pair of jeans and sneakers rounded out her ensemble. At 11:30 a.m., Heidi, in her usual Goth garb, pulled up to the house; Didi hugged her parents, who cautioned her to be careful, and skipped out to the SUV, where her friend had the motor running.

"Well, look at you," said Heidi. "Going traditional on us?"

"Do you think it's too much?" asked Didi nervously.

"Nah, not at all. In fact, you should wear that stuff more to school. It looks good on you."

"Thanks," said Didi with relief.

"Relax. He's gonna think you look fine. So, how was church? Uplifting?"

Didi shrugged. "The pastor, Father Robert, is actually rather boring. It's a lot of the same stuff from week to week, unfortunately."

"Listen," said Heidi, "I'm no religious aficionado, but if you want to see people who really get into it, try Shiloh Baptist. Man, you can hear the racket in that place a block away."

"That's where Bad News and his grandmother go. Jonathan, too."

"Speaking of Bad News, did you see that we beat Camden? One more win and it's on to the playoffs for the mighty Cavaliers."

"Well, I'm happy for him," said Didi. "The more they do well, the better chance he'll have for a scholarship. I might even go to the playoff game...if someone will take me there, that is."

Heidi frowned. "I'll think about it. Hey, last year I heard Jeb and his horse showed up to lead the team onto the field for their playoff game. Unfortunately, they got beat. But this year just might be different. I mean, they're *really* good. So, yeah, maybe we'll go— if only to see ol' Jeb ride in."

* * *

Jonathan's modest two-story house was situated in a pleasant enough neighborhood not too far from school. He was sitting on his front steps in a red polo shirt, jeans and sneakers when they pulled into the driveway. With a wave to his parents, who were gently rocking in a bench swing on the front porch, he bounded towards the SUV and hopped into the back seat. "Thanks for driving, Heidi," he said. "Wow, Didi, that's some blouse you're wearing."

The girls stole a look at each other and giggled.

"What kind of music do you guys want to listen to?" asked Heidi as she backed out of the driveway.

"Anything is fine," said Jonathan.

"I was hoping you'd say that," replied their driver, who popped in a heavy metal CD. Soon they were on the highway to Columbia. The air was comfortably cool, and the leaves on some trees were even changing color. Heidi rolled the windows down, leaving a trail of pounding music in their wake.

They made small talk about school, the marching band, and the football team's push towards the playoffs. Jonathan even said he was looking forward to playing before the hyped-up crowds from both schools. "If we get to the state championship game, it'll be played at the University of South Carolina, in their stadium," he said. "That would be really cool." Then, the boy graciously asked Heidi if she'd like to join them for lunch at his cousin's barbecue place.

"No thanks," she replied, "not my favorite kind of food. Besides, there's a coffeehouse a couple blocks from there where I know some people who hang out. You guys want to do something together after you're finished eating?"

"Well," said Didi, "there's the South Carolina State Museum—"

"Which just happens to be next-door to the Confederate Relic Museum," said Heidi. "Jeez, didn't you get enough of that stuff in Charleston?"

"It was just a thought," said Didi.

"I'm okay with it," said Jonathan. "Whatever you two want to do."

"Okay, whatever," sighed Heidi. "I'll pick you up around 1:30. That should give you two enough time to chow down."

* * *

"She's a strange girl," observed Jonathan as Heidi took off from *Dembo's Down-Home*.

179

"At times," replied Didi, "but once you get to know her, she's actually a good person."

They went inside and were immediately greeted by the owner, a rotund man with a large Afro. His white apron was stained with grease and barbecue sauce. "Hi, I'm Keith," he said, extending his hand after wiping it on the apron and hugging his cousin. "And you're Didi. My cuz here says you've never had barbecue. How can that possibly happen?"

"Well, I just got here from Africa a few months ago," she said shyly.

"Okay, I'm down with that," said Keith. "Y'all grab a booth and I'll bring out some stuff."

Dembo's Down-Home wasn't much on ambience; in fact, the place somewhat reminded Didi of the cafeteria at school—minus the Civil War mural, that is. There were about twenty red leatherette booths, and a salad bar serving station in the middle of the room where the side dishes and desserts were laid out. The place was mostly full, a mixed clientele of blacks and whites.

"The way it works is, you order your meat from a waitress, and then you pick your two sides and dessert from the bar," explained Jonathan. Just then, Keith's daughter, whom Jonathan introduced as LaWanda, came and took their drink order (sweet teas) and issued them heavy-duty sectioned cardboard plates for their sides. "My pop's giving y'all a sample platter," she announced. "Hope you're hungry."

They took their plates to the sides bar and made their choices—fried okra and mashed potatoes for Didi, mac n' cheese and baked beans for Jonathan—and a hunk of cornbread for each. Didi was impressed at the selection, and by just how much food the patrons could heap onto their plates without having them cave in. By the time they returned from the bar, a huge platter of ribs, brisket, pulled pork and chicken awaited them. Again, the girl was astounded at the amount of food Keith had set out, and thought of how many people this bounteous meal would feed in Kinshasa.

They dug in, with Jonathan advising her on the proper amount of Carolina sauce to add to each meat selection. The place was noisy, but the teens were still able to chat in a more relaxed manner than at school. Didi learned that Jonathan's goal was to earn a music scholarship; and for the first time, she heard herself say that a career in medicine might be in her future. The time seemed to fly by.

"So, how you liking it?" asked Keith, noticing the sizable dent they'd put in their pile of meats.

"It's delicious," said Didi, wiping some Carolina sauce from her lips. "I don't think I'll be hungry for days."

"Young lady," he replied, "you look like you can stand to hang a few more pounds on that frame. Make sure you try my peach cobbler for dessert. It's heaven on a plate."

They finished up and were issued the bill, which was a fraction of what it should have been for all the food involved. Jonathan gallantly paid the tab, and they said goodbye to his cousin on the way out.

"Eat enough?" asked Heidi, who was waiting at the curb for them.

"I can't move," said Didi.

"I think she likes barbecue," observed Jonathan.

* * *

From Keith's restaurant it was a short drive to the South Carolina State Museum on Gervais Street. The huge, four-story brick structure was fronted by an impressive modern glass entrance. After a little searching, the kids were able to secure a parking space a block or so up the street and went inside, paying the student rate for their tickets. Being a Sunday, attendance was light.

The museum was immense, and pretty much covered the history of South Carolina from the prehistoric era to the present. A dizzying array of exhibits traced the animal inhabitants of the region from dinosaur skeletons to stuffed bears and predatory cats, so lifelike that Didi cringed in fear. Meanwhile, Jonathan was fascinated by exhibits following the evolution of transportation, which began with actual horse-drawn buggies and transitioned to steam locomotives and automobiles; interestingly, Heidi's comments centered on the intricate layers of clothing worn by women in the 1800s and the detailed interior re-creations of a vintage schoolhouse, a log cabin, and a 1950s kitchen. Also spotlighted were the Gullah people, including examples of their artful basket weaving similar to what Didi had seen in the Charleston market.

Overall, though, the African girl couldn't help but be overwhelmed by the incredible strides America had made since her inception. The relentless march of industry and technology in this country had been amazing, and exhibit after exhibit underscored the scope of her power. However, as Didi was learning all too quickly, America's progress and wealth had come at a price.

As far as the Civil War itself, the museum did display some battle flags and armaments, as well as a typical slave quarters re-creation, complete with mannequins of black people in tattered clothing. However, the teens expected that the adjacent Confederate Relic Museum would delve more deeply into this chapter of South Carolina's history. So, while Heidi and Jonathan decided to venture to the fourth floor planetarium, Didi opted to visit the time period that kept pulling her back.

What immediately struck the girl was the decided difference in approach of the adjoining facilities. While the State Museum had many kid-friendly, interactive exhibits, the Confederate Relic and Military Museum was a more traditional collection of glassed-in displays with accompanying explanatory charts that traced the state's military tradition from its settlement through times of modern warfare. Once she reached the Civil War era, Didi walked along the now familiar collections of muskets, pistols and sabers, to full uniforms of common soldiers and officers.

"Excuse me, miss," called a gentle voice from behind. "Is there anything I can help you with?"

Didi turned to find a white man with a handlebar mustache in a too-tight dress shirt and tie. "I'm Peter Benedict, the museum curator. What brings you here today?"

"I'm taking a course in Civil War history at my school, Stuart High in Magnolia," she replied. "Just doing a little research."

"I see," he said. "Well, then you know that this

state pretty much spearheaded the movement to secede from the Union. Are you aware that one in every three South Carolinian men were killed in the war? This state paid dearly for its boldness."

Didi nodded. "And South Carolina's farms and cities were pretty much destroyed," she said. "But, forgive me for saying this, it seems like this museum is fairly accepting of the whole secession thing. Why is that?"

Benedict paused, perhaps sizing up the inquisitive girl. "Well," he said, "the museum was founded in 1896 by the Daughters of the Confederacy. I take it you've heard of them?"

Didi thought back to Mrs. Farnsworth and the D.O.C. meeting she and Heidi had spied upon, as well as the Confederate Museum in Charleston. "Oh, yes," she answered.

"Right. So you must understand that the women who got this museum started were the actual wives and daughters of Confederate soldiers, whose original intention was not to be objective, but to memorialize their dead. That's why everything you'll see in this section of the museum—the uniforms, the regimental flags shot through with holes—are family heirlooms."

"I understand that," said Didi. "My question is, what is the goal of this museum? What are you trying to show visitors like me?"

"As best I can put it," said Benedict, "our mission is to explore the interconnection of people in tough circumstances, making decisions in real time. And to show that, as we have learned, some of those decisions were tragic for our state."

Didi was ready to further her discussion with the

curator when an announcement blared over the museum's communication system: "Ladies and gentlemen," said a woman whose tone seemed quite nervous, "if you have parked anywhere on Gervais Street between here and the Capital Building, we are asking you to please leave the museum and move your car as soon as possible. Again, if you have parked—"

Didi was off and running.

* * *

She made it to the lobby of the State Museum just as Heidi and Jonathan hit the ground floor landing. "Let's get out of here," said Heidi, power walking towards the entrance. "We're parked close to the Capital Building, and I bet something's going on over there."

The Goth girl's words proved prophetic, because as the trio sprinted up the sidewalk towards the SUV, they found themselves engulfed in a sea of people and vehicles that had blocked the car in. Police barriers had also been hurriedly placed to close off Gervais Street. It was then that Didi recalled the invitation of the woman named Marlene during the demonstration at the Confederate Soldiers Memorial in Charleston to attend a major event at the Capital Building on Sunday. She inwardly berated herself for forgetting about this and placing the three of them in this precarious situation.

"Well," said Heidi resignedly, "looks like we're gonna be here for a while. I say we go see what this to-do is all about. What about you guys?"

"I…I don't know," mumbled Jonathan haltingly.

"Then wait here," said Didi. "I'm going with Heidi." The boy, embarrassed, hesitated for a few seconds before trailing behind the girls.

The main thoroughfare of Gervais Street was awash with people, and it quickly became apparent what was going on, and who was involved. On the expansive promenade in front of the capital building stood the stately statue of a Confederate soldier, though not as grand as the one in Charleston. At the statue's side was a modest white flagpole (when compared to the one Didi had seen alongside the state highway, anyway) from atop which flew the Confederate battle flag. "That's the flag they took down from on top of the Capital Building in 2000," huffed the out-of-shape Heidi as they made their way into the crowd. "They moved it to this place, but now there's a big push to have it removed from here, too."

Indeed, the Confederate soldier's plaza, so to speak, was ringed with white men and women holding their own oversized flags aloft; some were identical to the omnipresent battle flag while others were similar to the Confederate regimental flags Didi had seen in the various military museums she'd visited. Still other people held signs that proclaimed YOU CAN'T TAKE OUR HERITAGE, I'M A PROUD REBEL and WE WILL NOT BACK DOWN! There were even some reenactors, in full Confederate dress; Didi was somewhat relieved to see that Mr. Pennington was not among them.

Out in front, a man in a T-shirt with its sleeves cut off, displaying heavily tattooed arms, screamed, "We stand together!" through a mobile microphone; he was surrounded by other men in black short-sleeved shirts, black military fatigue pants, and matching combat boots. They struck a defiant pose with their legs spread shoulder-length apart and chests thrust out. "See the red patch on their chest with the cross on it?" said Heidi. "That's the Klan. Oh, brother. This is not good."

"Shouldn't we go?" said a clearly frightened Jonathan, who'd caught up to them.

"Nobody says you have to stay," snapped Heidi. "But *we* are going over to *those* people." She was pointing to the other side of the hastily installed yellow police barriers where a sizable force of black and white counter protesters, waving their own signs, were chanting "All power to the people!" Some toted flags whose red, black and green colors matched those of Didi's blouse. In addition to the sawhorse barriers, South Carolina state troopers in wide-brimmed hats and aviator sunglasses mixed with local police wearing bulletproof vests embossed with the letters SCDNR. They were obviously there to keep a lid on things, but the fervor on both sides was escalating rapidly.

"I'm going back," said Jonathan.

"See you at the car, then," replied Didi. She watched him turn and go, and realized that with this simple act, something irreparable had happened to their budding friendship. Where there had been a growing fondness, she now felt only disappointment.

And so, the girls stood amid the anti-Confederates, chanting and joining in with their singing of "We Shall Overcome" to drown out every rebel attempt to get a chorus of "Dixie" started. For Didi, this experience, though frightening, was somehow both exciting and empowering. She was able to vent the feelings of frustration and anger that had been building within her for weeks, and wondered how she had been able to stay quiet for so long.

Then, something broke loose in the crowd, and the vanguard of both sides surged past the police barriers and entered into a skirmish reminiscent of the cavalry charges Mr. Pennington had spoken of in class. The girls, who were relatively close to the front, were swept along in the melee. It was at the height of the confusion that Didi noticed her school's principal, Mr. Hufnagel, among the crowd of the Confederate flag wavers, yelling along with the rest of them. But as she turned to tell Heidi about this incredible sight, a rock flew through the air and struck the Goth girl on the side of her face. Down she went; instantly, Didi reacted by throwing herself on top of her friend as a shield, only to find that people started kicking her in the side. She managed to peek up at her attackers to see a girl not much older than her screaming, "Serves you right! Go back to Africa, you black—"

And then a burly state trooper with a blonde crewcut was grabbing both her and Heidi by the arm, hefting them over his shoulders, and carrying them across the street, where he deposited them under a spreading oak. "You okay, miss?" he said to Heidi. "Should I call you an ambulance? Tell me quick, 'cause I gotta get back in there!"

"No, you go," she said with a feeble wave. "I'll be okay, thanks." The trooper pushed his hat firmly down on his head and plunged back into the battle.

"Are you okay to walk?" said Didi, tears rolling down her cheeks, her ribs and too-full stomach aching.

"Yeah," said Heidi. "Help me up, will you?" With Didi's aid the girl unsteadily rose to her feet. Her face wasn't bleeding, but the area near her right eye had begun to swell.

"Maybe we should go to the hospital," suggested Didi as they picked their way through the rear guard of the counter-protesters.

"I'll be fine," her friend insisted. "Now, let's go collect Mr. Gutless and get the hell out of here."

They made it back to the car, but Jonathan wasn't there. He had left a note under one of the SUV's wiper blades, however. It read, *Walking to my cousin's place. I'll get a ride home from him. Hope you're okay.* Didi read the note, crumpled up the paper, and dropped it in the street.

The girls slid into the front seats, and Heidi was able to perform a slow U-turn on Gervais Street, carefully maneuvering through the stragglers around them. Some of them were bleeding. Heidi's face was purpling more with every second, and she noticed Didi staring at her. "Oh well, it kind of goes with my eyeshadow," she said after checking it out for herself in the rearview mirror.

"I'm so sorry," said Didi.

"Don't sweat it," said the Goth girl. "Let's just get home… and God bless America."

Chapter Fifteen

It was a somber Didi Diyoka who entered the portals of Stuart High the next day, stonily passing the cheerleaders who were busy placing decorations around the Jeb Stuart statue's pedestal in anticipation of the football team's upcoming playoff run. Heidi was nowhere to be seen, however; Didi figured she was probably home icing her face. She hoped it wasn't something worse, like a concussion or fracture.

Fortunately, her parents had not put two-and-two together and figured out she'd been near the Capital Building during the afternoon's protest, film footage of which was broadcast on the local network affiliate's news and later picked up by CNN. On the sly, Didi had managed to witness the footage, which had been edited down to a couple minutes. And though the images of the verbal battle that turned physical were harrowing, she was nonetheless relieved to see neither herself nor Heidi. And so, her report to her parents that Sunday afternoon's trip to Columbia had been "a lot of fun, and very educational" was readily accepted. Of course, she later had to sneak into the kitchen, fashion an ice pack from a large Ziploc bag, and hold it to her ribs for an hour, after downing some Tylenol, to dull the pain.

* * *

With the close of the first quarter, it was time for all the teachers to give their students the "blank slate" speech and start anew. Even Mr. Pennington, whose course was only a half-year elective, encouraged Didi's class to "pick it up" for the second quarter. But as she was learning, academic pep talks generally rang hollow with her American classmates. Those who were going to work hard, did so; conversely, those who were just riding out their senior year weren't going to alter their lackadaisical approach.

But although Didi was getting the most out of her classes, and loved learning in general, something had changed in her. She kept harkening back to the previous afternoon and the rush she'd gotten from taking part in the demonstration, and how she felt she was engaging in something worthwhile. Unfortunately, with Heidi absent, she had no one to discuss this with—even Mrs. Woodard was out of the question—and Jonathan was nowhere to be found at lunchtime, though she'd spied him from afar later in the day.

That night as she was taking her clothes out of the dryer (she enjoyed doing the laundry, as the efficiency of the appliances fascinated her, especially the fresh smell her clothes had afterward) she found the scrap of paper the man named Bigsby had given her at the Slave Mart Museum in Charleston. The writing on it was faded from the washer, but legible. So, she set it on the desk in her bedroom and turned on the computer.

The movie that Bigsby had recommended for her viewing, *Brother Future*, was located after a search of YouTube. And although its release date of 1991 made it seem a bit dated to Didi, the film was nonetheless powerful.

In the story, T.J., a teenage hustler in the gritty black section of Detroit, Michigan, who has no interest in his heritage or of furthering his education, is struck by a car while being chased by police, and is somehow transported back to Charleston in 1832, when the South's slave trade is shifting into high gear. Used to having all the privileges and rights of a modern American, T.J. is incredulous when he is captured outside the city, labeled as a "runaway," and brought to a slave market in Charleston, where he suffers the indignation of being auctioned among other Africans who have come right off the boat in Charleston Harbor. He is then purchased by a man named Cooper, who owns a cotton plantation in the area. The plot involves T.J.'s struggle to survive as his ancestors did, and learn that the practice of helping others, instead of thinking of oneself, is the only thing that can advance a society, or any segment thereof.

Didi found herself in tears, or trembling with anger, more than once as she was compelled to share this journey of self-awakening with the film's protagonist. But what was equally gripping for the girl was the blending of the fantasy tale of T.J. with an actual historical event, when the boy comes into contact with the man whom Bigsby mentioned in the museum.

Denmark Vesey was a free black man who lived in Charleston and plied his trade as a carpenter. He had gained his freedom by winning a special lottery; however, his wife and children were still held in bondage on a local plantation. It is during T.J.'s time travel "visit" that Vesey, who could easily have remained passive and enjoyed his freedom, instead secretly attempts to organize a slave revolt by recruiting males from the area plantations when they come to town to sell their masters' produce at the Central Market.

Vesey was playing a dangerous game. The masters were always on the lookout for rebellious slaves, whom they disciplined harshly; thus, Vesey's maintaining secrecy in his plot is of the utmost importance. T.J., as an intelligent, street-smart teen who also has the advantage of being able to read and write, is drawn into the conspiracy, which ultimately fails when one of its key members sells out his brothers to gain favor with his master.

When T.J., by way of providing an act of heroism that saves two of his fellow slaves, is returned to the future, he is crushed to learn that Vesey and his chief cohorts had been hanged for their actions. Nonetheless, his time travel experience prompts him to change his life and embrace the values and heroism of his friend, Denmark Vesey.

As the film ended, Didi wiped her eyes a final time and offered silent thanks to Bigsby for slipping her that piece of paper back in Charleston. At the same time, the germ of an idea came to her, but it was at best hazy. Something would have to happen to bring it into focus and show her the way.

* * *

"So you saw Hufnagel in the crowd on Sunday?" asked Heidi, who'd returned on Tuesday, her cheekbone area somewhat masked with makeup. "You're sure about that?"

"Almost completely," replied Didi as they stood at their lockers. "He wasn't far from the man with the microphone."

"Wow," said the Goth girl. "You think he'd have enough sense not to show up at one of those things, being a school principal and all. But maybe he just doesn't care. I mean, who's gonna come after him? The district superintendent is probably his golfing buddy, and the entire school board is lily-white." She slammed her locker in disgust.

"Are you all right?" asked Didi.

"Not really," said Heidi. "I'm just... so freakin' mad. I wish we could do something about it, but this place is hopeless."

"Maybe not," said Didi. "Let's go to homeroom."

"Okay," said Heidi, "but if I throw up when our esteemed principal comes on the PA, you'll have to excuse me."

* * *

Lunchtime this day was filled with Heidi trying to explain the observance of Halloween to Didi, who had been fascinated by the spooky decorations popping up recently in her neighborhood and around school. According to Heidi, who seemed to be in costume every day, the kids at Stuart didn't dress up as a rule, but Didi was pleased to learn that some teachers would give out Halloween treats. Heidi also advised her to tell her mother to pick up some candy for the ghosts and goblins that would be showing up at their door in a few days. "I don't know who's gonna be more surprised," she mused, "your parents when they see these little kids in their weird costumes, or the parents of those kids when they see who's living in that big old house in their neighborhood."

Later that day during study hall, Didi obtained a pass to visit the girls' restroom. After making sure the room was empty, she went to the sink and quickly lifted the bottom of her T-shirt to check on her ribcage area, which was still somewhat discolored from the kicks she'd received on Sunday. With daily icing, the pain had gradually subsided, and she was grateful she'd seemingly escaped the violence without any breaks.

Just then the door crashed open, and Didi hurriedly lowered her shirt. She turned to go but found her exit blocked by Tanya Mims, accompanied by three of her white cheerleader cohorts. One of the girls leaned on the inside of the door, thus preventing anyone else from entering.

"Well, look who I found," said Tanya, stepping forward so that she was nearly toe-to-toe with her target. "I've been tracking you for a week, girl. So now that I got you, I want you to tell me just what you think you're doing moving in on my man!"

"You're mistaken," Didi answered as calmly as she could, willing her voice not to tremble. "I had no intention—"

"Don't *you* tell me what your *intention* was, Miss Priss!" she yelled, sticking a finger dangerously close to Didi's face. "You've had your eye on Travis since you got here. And then, what happens? I catch you at his house, behind my back! You think you can get away with this?" Tanya's eyes were bulging, and Didi could see a vein pulsing on the side of her neck.

"I'd like to leave, please," said Didi, trying not to bunch her fists at her sides so as to suggest she wanted to fight.

"You're not going anywhere," sneered Tanya. "You apologize to me, right here, right now."

"No," said Didi, her eyes steely.

"*What* did you say?" crowed Tanya theatrically, as her friends' eyes grew wide and gleeful, sensing an altercation.

"I said... *no*." Her eyes remained locked on the cheerleader's.

Now it was Tanya's move. Didi expected the girl to take a swipe at her, and was thus surprised to see her instead remove something from the front pocket of her skin-tight white jeans. "Okay then, Miss Priss," she said, her tone evil and mocking. "I ain't gonna hit that shiny black face of yours. I'm just going to give you a reminder of who you're dealing with." She removed the cap from the tube of lipstick she'd taken from her pocket, and proceeded to inscribe a silvery-pink capital S on Didi's forehead. "Stay still now, wouldn't want to mess this up," she taunted. The process only took seconds, but to Didi it seemed a lifetime. Tanya's buddies howled in the background. Didi stared straight ahead.

Then Tanya Mims stepped back to admire her handiwork. "There you go," she said proudly. "Complements of the Stuart cheerleading squad. You know what? It looks good on you. But you'd best watch your step, 'cause next time it'll be worse, I *guarantee* it." She turned on her heel and walked out, the other girls falling in line behind her. The door hissed as it slowly closed.

Didi turned and regarded her reflection in the mirror, the shiny pink lipstick standing out on her dark skin. Slowly, methodically, she removed some paper towels from the sink dispenser, rubbed off the letter, and dropped the towels into the trashcan. Then, she took a deep breath and returned to study hall.

* * *

"Holy crap," said Heidi after Didi tonelessly related the tale of her bathroom encounter. "How did you not hit her?" she marveled. "I would've clawed her eyes out."

"It was four against one," she replied calmly. "To fight them would have been pointless, and besides, it would mean I was sinking to her level."

"But how...how were you able to just stand there and take it?"

"I made myself go somewhere else," said Didi. "It was odd, though, the things that flashed through my mind."

"Like what?"

"First, I thought of a book we read in American lit, *The Scarlet Letter*, and that woman, Hester Prynne, and how she had the strength to stand up to those who had marked her. But I also thought of other things— like the branding irons for the slaves we saw in Charleston, and how they had to be so strong to endure the pain. And one more thing.

"I recently saw a movie about a boy named T.J. who was thrust into slavery on a plantation near Charleston. The plantation owner had a black man named Zeke, whom he also owned, serve as his slave driver. One of his duties was to whip the slaves who weren't working hard enough, including this boy. While Zeke was whipping him, T.J. said, 'How can you do this to me? I'm just like you!' This incensed Zeke even more, because he felt superior to T.J. based upon his status as the slave driver. He got to live in his own room, and was given the master's hand-me-down clothes, in return for betraying his own people. Heidi, as I stood there looking at Tanya, with her lighter skin and straightened hair, trying so hard to be white in this place, I actually felt *sorry* for her."

"Sorry," repeated the Goth girl, shaking her head. "Ay-yi-yi, Didi. I shouldn't have to tell you that you're crazy to feel *any* empathy for that witch. But on the other hand, I've gotta give you credit for not totally losing it. So anyway, are you gonna report this? 'Cause here in the States they've got this law against bullying—"

"No."

"*No*?" You're just going to let them get away with doing this to you?"

"No, because it's not just those girls in the bathroom today. It's everybody—and everything—that's happened since I've come here. At Pierce's house and the D.O.C. meeting; in Pennington's class and the reenactment; with my parents at the football game; during the class trip to Charleston; and last Sunday, when you and I were attacked. No, Heidi, something's going to be done, but there's just one question: are you 'freakin' mad' enough to help me do it?"

For the first time all day, the Goth girl smiled. "What did you have in mind?" she asked.

Chapter Sixteen

"I must be crazy doing this," said Bad News as he and the girls drove into the blackness of the rear parking lot at the deserted Stuart High.

"Relax, big guy," said Heidi from behind the wheel. "It's a Saturday night, and your game's out of the way for this week—congrats, by the way—so what better things do you have to do?"

He shot her a dirty look from the back seat of the SUV.

"Oh yeah," she said snarkily. "I forgot about Tanya. My bad."

Oddly enough, it was the football player's uncharacteristic gesture that had gotten him involved in tonight's adventure. Apparently, his girlfriend had made the rounds at school bragging about how she'd intimidated "Miss Congo" in the girls' restroom; Bad News had been so mortified that he'd approached Didi at her locker the next morning and said, "I'm really sorry about what happened to you because of me. I owe you one." When she came back at him to collect on his offer a day later he was at first struck speechless by her proposition, but then shrugged and said, "A promise is a promise." So here he was.

"Tell me about the game last night," said Didi,

breaking the stalemate between the athlete and the Goth girl.

"Not much to tell. Dutch Fork was pretty good, but we played better. I had five tackles and a couple quarterback sacks. We won by twenty. So, we clinched a playoff spot by winning our division."

"Congratulations."

"Thanks," he said. "So, what's the plan here? 'Cause the faster this goes, the better."

"Well," said Heidi, "it's common knowledge that Stuart High doesn't have a security system. And on top of that, Didi tells me you know a way in, right?"

"Yeah. A door to the fieldhouse is always left unlocked so the guys on the team can get into the weight room whenever we want. From there, we can just cut through the school to where we want to go."

"Sounds good. It's time to go get Jeb." She snapped off her headlights and they pulled into a dark corner of the parking lot adjacent to the fieldhouse. For a few moments they sat in silence, contemplating what was about to occur.

"Let's do it," said Didi.

They slipped into the building, which was inky black, save for some ambient light coming through the hallway windows. And even that was muted, as the night was cloudy.

"How'd you manage to get out?" Bad News whispered to Didi as they crept through the deserted hallways. "I thought your parents had you on permanent lockdown."

"They were invited to a cocktail party just outside Columbia that one of the other doctors is throwing. Fortunately, it's adults only, though I don't expect them to stay too late."

"Don't worry," said Heidi. "We're gonna be in and out, like a Navy S.E.A.L. operation."

"So, what's the purpose of this again?" asked Bad News, who was clearly nervous.

"Travis," said Didi, "remember when your grandmother said something about 'waking everybody up' at Stuart? That's what I intend to do."

"My gramma's always talking crazy stuff like that," he said. "But you took her *seriously*. You realize we could all go down the tubes for this."

"No," she said. "I'll never breathe a word of your involvement, or Heidi's, to anyone, no matter what. And besides, if it all goes according to plan, nobody will ever find out anyway."

"Suit yourself," he said. "Here we are."

The three teens had reached the rotunda of the main entrance, where a single ray of moonlight cast an ethereal glow on the bronze bust of J.E.B. Stuart as it rested proudly upon its pedestal.

"Jeez, up close it's bigger than I thought," said Heidi. "How are we getting it out of here? You sure you just don't wanna paint a mustache on him or something?"

"He already has one, and a full beard," reminded Didi.

"Good point. So, what do we do?"

"I'll be right back," said Bad News, and took off down the hall.

"You sure he won't squeal?" asked Heidi. "You know that Franklin once said, 'Three may keep a secret if two of them are dead.'"

"Franklin who?"

"Skip it."

Then they heard a rolling sound coming up one of the hallways, and Bad News emerged from the darkness with a large hand truck. "Custodian's room was open," he said. The boy sized up the bronze bust, took a deep breath, and wrapped his muscled arms around the cavalier's head. Huffing and puffing like a power lifter, the defensive lineman hefted the bust from the pedestal and gently lowered it onto the hand truck's platform. "I'm good at squats," he explained to the gaping girls.

They wheeled the bust through the hallways and the fieldhouse, exiting through the same door they'd entered. Heidi opened the SUV's tailgate, and Bad News executed yet another feat of strength, dead lifting the Stuart statue up and into the vehicle's cargo space before Heidi quickly covered it with a blanket. Then, he was off in a flash to return the hand truck to the custodian's office.

Minutes later, they slowly pulled out of the parking lot, and Heidi didn't turn on her lights until they were a block away. "You sure you don't just wanna throw this off the bridge at Pinewood Lake?" she asked.

"No," said Didi firmly. "My intention is not to destroy this statue, just relocate it."

"To where?"

"Somehow, I want to get this thing to the Confederate Relic Museum in Columbia, where it belongs. I just haven't figured out how to do that yet."

"And until then?" asked Bad News, continually swiveling his head to look out the SUV's windows.

"There's a work shed behind my garage that is never used," said Didi. "We'll hide it there until we have the opportunity to move it."

They glided into Didi's driveway and curled around the paved path that encircled the huge detached garage. Sure enough, the six-foot square, roofed storage shed, which was set against the garage's back wall, looked like it hadn't been entered for months. With a little effort, Bad News managed to pry open the rusted door latch; then he lifted the bust from the SUV's tailgate, set it on the dusty floor of the shed among some garden tools, and draped a painting tarp over it. He pulled the door shut and re-set the latch. "Done," he said, returning to the car.

"All right, then," said Heidi. "I'll take Bad News home before he has a heart attack. Didi, you get inside before your folks show up."

"Then what?" asked Bad News.

"We wait," said Didi.

* * *

She exited the school bus on Monday to find the campus in a frenzy. Kids were running up to those newly arrived and yelling, "Somebody stole Jeb!" Ms. Redwine, at her usual post on the front steps, looked out of sorts, surrounded by students asking what had happened. Didi ventured inside to the rotunda, where Mr. Hufnagel, running his hand through his hair, was talking to a Magnolia sheriff's deputy, who diligently wrote down his statement. She got close enough to pick up the words, "just don't know," and "no clue." Her face impassive, she moved on to her locker, where Heidi was waiting.

"Lots of excitement today," said the Goth girl with the faintest trace of a smile. "Wonder what's going on?"

For the first time in a while, the girls eagerly awaited the morning announcements, and they weren't disappointed. To begin, Pierce's recap of the Cavaliers' win and clinching of their division wasn't delivered with its usual flair. But then, Mr. Hufnagel ranged from melancholy to downright angry while delivering his monologue—after praising the team, of course. "Students and staff," he began, "we returned to school today to find that someone, or some people, have taken our beloved Jeb Stuart statue, which has graced our rotunda since the opening of Stuart High, and has been a rallying symbol and source of pride for us ever since. You can believe me when I say that we will get to the bottom of this, and that there will be severe consequences for the perpetrators of this crime. If you have any information leading to the recovery of our statue or the apprehension of the thieves, please come to my office at any time. Your identity will remain anonymous. I will keep you posted if there are any changes in the situation. Thank you." It was the first time he hadn't ended with "Go Cavs!" all year.

Later on, Mr. Pennington doubled down on the principal's anger, wishing he could "get his hands on" whoever engineered the theft. He also put forth the theory that no one person could have stolen the statue, for it would take "superhuman strength" to lift it. Both Heidi and Didi remained impassive throughout his diatribe, and though Bad News assumed his usual snoozing posture, the girls knew he was probably awake.

"How do you think he—uh, they—got in?" asked one of the students.

"I don't know," said the teacher, "but anyone can see this was a well-planned maneuver worthy of a military mind." Again, the girls remained stonefaced, though Didi wondered how Heidi was able to keep from bursting with laughter.

* * *

By the next day, rumors and theories were flying around school, accusing everyone from common criminals who wanted to melt the statue down for the bronze, to liberal left-wingers, and even students from Gilbert High, whose football team Stuart was to face in the first round of the playoffs. Every guess was crazier than the one before it.

Then, at midweek, there came the news that the theft of the bust had made it into the *Magnolia Town Crier*, the town's local paper, and that none other than the regional chapter of the Daughters of the Confederacy had offered a reward of $1,000 to anyone who provided information leading to the statue's recovery. But the hoopla surrounding Jeb's departure, unfortunately, was only beginning.

On Thursday, the story in the *Town Crier* was picked up by the three major newspapers in Columbia, and then the *Associated Press*, topped with the headline CONFEDERATE STATUE STOLEN FROM SCHOOL. By that afternoon, news trucks from the major network affiliates in Columbia and Charleston were in the school's parking lot, interviewing students, teachers and parents for the six p.m. news. The responses the reporters got seemed to fall along racial lines; whites were outraged, whereas blacks were either noncommittal or even mildly amused at the uproar.

By the time Friday rolled around, Mr. Hufnagel

and Sam Haverstraw, the superintendent of the Magnolia schools, were becoming media fixtures, especially after CNN and MSNBC sent crews to cover the story. Stuart High had gone viral.

With every rung on the ladder that the story climbed, Didi became more distressed. While it was true she'd wanted to make a statement with her act, she had no idea it would explode like this. Perhaps it was because her background in Africa rendered her naïve as to the dizzying speed and scope of America's high-tech social media; or, maybe the story had just hit a national raw nerve. Whatever the case, she now feared for herself, her parents, and most of all, her friends. She watched in amazement as political pundits on both sides of the Confederate legacy fence debated the issue on cable news shows, especially after the D.O.C. had offered the reward. (As for her parents, only her father provided any comment, muttering "serves them right." She hoped he'd hold onto that stance if things turned out badly.) She also racked her brain for a way to get the statue off of her property and relocate it somewhere it could be quietly recovered; realistically, the Confederate Relic Museum now seemed an impossible alternative. Anyway, the national spotlight being turned on what she considered the hypocritical culture of Stuart High and Magnolia in general seemed to be more than enough, as far as what she'd hoped to accomplish.

But then, Didi's problem was solved for her, in the most ironic of ways.

On Saturday morning, as the town of Magnolia reveled in the Cavaliers' nail-biting victory over Gilbert in the first round of the playoffs—for which the mounted Jeb Stuart had, indeed, defiantly led the team onto the field, to the delirious delight of the mostly white fans in attendance—the Tomlin Landscaping truck turned into the Diyokas' driveway for its twice-monthly yard maintenance duties.

As usual, the somewhat lethargic Seth Tomlin tended to his chores, which today included the mundane tasks of raking out dead leaves from between the hedges and clearing branches that had fallen during various rainstorms over the past month. However, he had hardly begun when the handle of the old metal rake he was using snapped. Muttering curses to himself, he trudged to the truck for a replacement, only to find that his was the only one they'd brought that day. Hoping this occurrence would lessen his workload, he reported the equipment malfunction to his father, who, after berating him for failing to bring a backup rake, said, "You know what? Try that ol' toolshed next to the garage. Maybe Dr. Buono has one."

"Yessir," the boy said tiredly, and shuffled on back to the shed. After jiggling the rusted latch a little, the door popped open, and he went inside. The interior of the shed was damp and musty, but Seth quickly located a rake in the corner. However, when he pulled it out of its cramped space, the tines caught on a paint tarp. Somewhat miffed, Seth gave the rake a yank, and the tarp fell away, leaving the stunned boy face-to-face with the smiling visage of J.E.B. Stuart.

For a few seconds, he stared at the bust in disbelief; then, a wicked smile slowly curled his lips. "Bingo," he said.

Chapter Seventeen

As is the case with many teachers and administrators in the education profession, Mr. Hufnagel, still riding the wave of satisfaction over his football team's victory during the weekend, was at his school early on Monday; however, when he had arrived carrying his usual takeout coffee and sweet roll, someone was already there awaiting him.

"Principal Hufnagel," said Elmer Tomlin, a hollow-eyed man with unkempt hair and dirty fingernails, "I'm here with my boy Seth 'cause he has somethin' important to tell you. It's about the statue."

The principal ushered them into his cluttered office, snapped on the lights, and shut the door and window blinds. He knew of Seth Tomlin only marginally as a n'er-do-well who was always on the periphery of trouble, though never implicated. "Now, y'all take a seat and let's talk," he said genially. "I'm glad you've decided to come forth, son. I'm sure this took a lot of courage. And you probably thought you had good reason for doing—"

"Doggone it, Hufnagel," exploded Elmer, spittle flying from his mouth, "*he* didn't do it, ya goldang moron! But he sure found out who *did*."

"So tell me, then," said the principal between clenched teeth.

208

* * *

Things moved very quickly after that. Ms. Redwine was dispatched to Didi's homeroom to escort her to Hufnagel's office after the morning announcements. Meanwhile, her mother, who had already arrived for work at the law offices of Leber and Tunney, was requested by phone to come to the principal's office at Stuart High immediately. After being assured her daughter had not been in an accident or fallen ill, Gabrielle asked a co-worker for a ride to the school, but not before she'd put in an emergency call to Providence Heart Hospital and told her husband to come home immediately.

Mrs. Diyoka burst into the main office of Stuart High some twenty minutes later to find her daughter occupying a chair outside the principal's office, her head down. "Dihya, what's the matter?" she whispered fervently. "Are you all right? Has someone done something to you?"

The girl raised her head, her eyes moist. "Oh, Mother," she said sorrowfully.

* * *

As mother and daughter cooled their heels outside the office, a police cruiser was dispatched to the Buono residence to investigate the claim of Seth Tomlin, whose father had suggested the boy wait until Monday to contact the principal. The Tomlins wanted to make sure they moved cautiously so as not to jeopardize in any way Seth's rightful claim to the thousand dollar reward; indeed, all day Sunday the boy had fantasized about the used 2008 Camaro a guy down the street was selling. It had a lot of miles on it and needed new tires, but the bright red paint job was still mint.

By ten a.m. Dr. Diyoka had arrived, and the family, along with Ms. Redwine, who seemed absolutely miserable, were seated in Hufnagel's office.

"Thank you for coming so quickly, folks," the principal began. "It appears we've got us an issue here." Hufnagel then proceeded to tell the stunned parents how the son of their landscaper had discovered the statue of J.E.B. Stuart in the storage shed on their property; how he'd come in bright and early this morning to report the find; and how a sheriff's deputy sent to their address had just confirmed the Stuart bust's presence, taken photographs of the "crime scene," and removed the statue to a storage room at police headquarters for safekeeping.

The entire time Hufnagel was speaking, Gabrielle remained stoic, as did her daughter, who intermittently dabbed at her eyes. And although Dr. Diyoka tried to show no emotion, his shoulders seemed to involuntarily sag with the weight of the principal's words. Ellen Redwine was simply a mess, excusing herself halfway through the narrative to visit the ladies' room.

"You want to tell me who else was involved here, young lady?" gently asked the principal.

"I acted alone," said Didi.

"Aw, c'mon now," he said. "A little bitty thing like you? You're gonna tell me you got that big old statue out of here y'self?"

"That's what I'm telling you," she said evenly.

He leaned forward on his elbows. "Would you mind telling me *why* you felt the need to do this?"

"You wouldn't understand," was her response.

Barely masking his frustration, Hufnagel said, "Dr. and Mrs. Diyoka, I hate to ask, but were you aware of any of this?"

"No, we were not," replied Maurice, who seemed crushed.

By then Ms. Redwine had returned, and apologized for her emotions. "Mr. Hufnagel," she said, "where do we go from here?"

"I don't know," he replied. "As of this moment, the student is suspended from all school activities and will remain at home. It will have to be discussed between the superintendent and the board of education whether this offense constitutes grounds for expulsion."

At these words, Gabrielle let out a choking sob.

"Here's what I want you to do, folks," said Hufnagel. "I want you to go home and sit tight until you hear from us. The next board of ed meeting is in two days, so maybe by that time they'll have it all figured out. I don't know what else to tell you. I'm just sorry this had to happen. Ms. Redwine, please show the Diyokas out."

Quietly, the guidance counselor rose and motioned for the family to accompany her. Didi followed along as if in a trance, somehow managing to put one foot in front of the other and not collapse. Ms. Redwine held the front door open for the Diyokas and joined them on the landing. It was a cool, sunny morning, and birds twittered in the trees. "Do you have a lawyer?" she asked Dr. Diyoka.

"No," he responded.

"I suggest you find one."

* * *

The family drove in silence for a minute or so before Gabrielle said, "Dihya, why?"

"It was something I had to do, Mother," she replied.

"This is a nightmare," her father said, gripping the steering wheel so tightly Didi thought it would break. "Gabrielle, do you think your employers would help us?"

"I'll give Mr. Tunney a call when we get home."

"Good. Dihya, you are to make no calls or have any communication with the outside world without my permission, is that understood?"

"Yes, Father," she said. "I'm sorry I've brought this on you."

"My daughter," he said gravely, "I'm afraid this is only the beginning."

As it would turn out, the doctor's words were prophetic, because by noon Elmer Tomlin had called the NBC affiliate station in Columbia and the *Columbia Post and Courier* newspaper to proudly announce that his son had cracked the case of the missing statue.

* * *

"Thank you so much for coming, Mr. Tunney," said Gabrielle while the red-haired, ruddy-faced Irishman shook hands with her husband. "I didn't know what else to do—"

The man stopped her by raising his hand. "No need to apologize, Mrs. Diyoka. Or may I call you

Gabrielle? You've only been working for me for three months, after all." He managed a smile, and there was a twinkle in his eye that gave her hope the situation might not be as dire as she believed.

"And please call me Maurice," offered Dr. Diyoka.

"Okay then, and I'm Bob. So now that we all know each other, let's sit down and calmly assess the situation." He found a seat in the living room and pulled out a legal pad as the Diyokas settled into Dr. Buono's plush couch. "All right," said the lawyer across the walnut coffee table. "So where are we, then?"

Probably because she knew the man, whom she'd found from their office interactions to be thorough, good-natured and fair, Gabrielle had no reservations about telling him what had transpired that morning in Hufnagel's office. Her husband sat rigidly beside her, holding her hand.

Upon completion of Mrs. Diyoka's account, Tunney let out a low whistle. "Oh, boy," he said. "So this is the statue thing they've been playing up in the media. Well, I wish I could tell you that this will all just blow over and go away, but it won't. I'm sure you're aware of the issues around here regarding how the population views the Confederacy and its legacy. We had the whole State House flag thing some years back, and now it's flared up again. There was even a near riot up in Columbia last weekend that they barely got under control.

"Now, understand that I'm a dyed-in-the-wool Yankee from Boston, which explains this accent of mine," he continued, again with that twinkle. "I came down here to go to school at Furman; met my wife, who's from South Carolina and refused to go live in the North because she hates the cold; and went into business with my partner, Karl Leber, who's also from around here. Let me tell you, I had to make quite an adjustment. The fact is that there's a lot of people down here who still haven't gotten over the loss of a war that occurred a hundred fifty years ago. And they're very protective, and touchy, about their heritage. Of course, I'm talking about whites.

"For a long time, African-Americans down here for the most part kept quiet and stayed to themselves, but this started changing with the new millennium. Now, tension between the races has reached a level bordering on open hostility, and I'm scared to think where it's going. I mean, I have kids who are still attending the schools here, and they see that all the buildings are named after Confederate soldiers, and their hallways are full of these reminders, such as this statue. Of course, they're going to think this is okay, and normal, because no one around here is going to tell them otherwise.

"But your daughter, coming from somewhere as foreign as Africa, probably had no idea what she was getting into. She might as well have been on the moon."

"And now it's come to this," said Maurice.

* * *

Back at school, word had leaked out—thanks, of course, to the attention-craving Seth Tomlin—that Stuart High's transfer student from Africa had been the perpetrator of the statue's theft. For most of the students, this news came as a complete shock. After all, the girl called Didi was small and shy and mostly kept to herself. But others, especially her teachers, were not so surprised. Mr. Pennington, for example, recalled flashes over the past few weeks when the girl had asked questions about his curriculum that bordered on what he considered impertinence. And Mrs. Woodard, thinking back on the heartfelt conversations she and Didi had shared in her classroom, probably wanted to kick herself for underestimating the girl's pain—and her resolve.

As for Heidi, the Goth girl could sense a lot of the kids giving her the side-eye, as she was Didi's only real female friend in the school. Bad News, for his part, just laid low when her name came up, though he did shush his girlfriend when she started to gloat about Didi's situation, suggesting they "just ship her back to Africa." And Jonathan, who had actually shown interest in beginning a relationship with her, quietly distanced himself from the girl in every possible manner.

Of all of Didi's peers, however, the person most affected by the whole affair was Pierce Farnsworth, who felt he had done his part to promote cultural harmony by showing the girl his hospitality in lending her his Civil War class notes and such. But something had triggered a change in her attitude towards him, though he couldn't quite put his finger on what it was. And it seemed ironic to the boy, if not somewhat disconcerting, that his own mother had raised the reward money for a knucklehead like Seth Tomlin to collect by turning the girl in.

* * *

Didi, her stomach roiling with stress, was lying on her bed, trying to concentrate on a book which had been given to her by Mrs. Woodard entitled *To Kill a Mockingbird*, when her father knocked. "Dihya, please come downstairs," he said from outside the door. "There is someone here who would like to speak with you." She crept downstairs to find her mother's boss sitting with her parents, who had put out some tea and biscuits for their guest.

"Hi, Didi," said Mr. Tunney, whose smile immediately put her at ease. "Can we talk for a bit?"

"Sure," she said, taking a seat between her parents.

"Okay," he began, "as you know, I'm a lawyer. But I didn't want you to be frightened by my presence. Your mom called me because she's new in town and just happens to work in my office. Now, I expect that very shortly your phone is going to start ringing off the hook, with calls from legal people—some who are white, and some who are black. And, quite frankly, there might be those among them who will want to make a crusader out of you, or use your notoriety to further their own careers. All of these people, I'm sure, will be gladly offering their services. And you have every right to choose any of them who you'd rather have to represent you—"

"Bob, it is *you* who is representing my daughter," said Dr. Diyoka. "You came here immediately to help us without even being apprised of what was going on. That is important to all of us."

"Fair enough," said Tunney. "What I want you to understand here is that Didi is a minor, a good girl and honor student with no hint of trouble in her past. Now, in the scheme of things, what she has done, in many places, would be considered a harmless schoolkid prank. But Magnolia—especially in its geographical and social context—isn't just another place. So, while there is absolutely no chance, in my opinion, of jail or fines or any of that nonsense for her or her family, there is still the public furor—both local and national—this situation has kicked up. We're going to have to formulate a game plan, and quickly deal with it in order to avoid a negative effect on her future. Understood?"

The three Diyokas nodded.

"Great. Now, all of you listen carefully. I see you have a land line here in the house. Does it have the Caller ID feature?"

"Yes," said Maurice.

"Super. As I said, your phone is about to start ringing off the hook. TV stations, newspapers, and God knows who else. Do *not* answer the phone unless it's someone you know and trust; of course, you can just disconnect it instead. Meanwhile, I'd like to speak to Didi alone for a few minutes, if you don't mind."

Husband and wife looked at each other, then nodded, got up, and exited.

Didi was scared to be left alone with Bob Tunney, but he immediately tried to lighten her anxiety. "Your father called you Dihya," he said. "That's not your common everyday name. Do you know how you got it?"

She nodded. "It's Congolese, and it means 'woman who advances,'" she said.

"Huh. And I guess it's very important to your folks that you live up to your name."

"Yes, sir."

"Okay, then. Now, I want you to understand that

I've been in your school before. My daughter's a junior there, and every time I go into that place I pass Jeb Stuart's statue. There is no possible way that you moved that thing by yourself."

Didi looked down into her lap.

"Listen," he said, "I'm not going to ask you to rat out anyone else who might have been in on this. I just want to know, and tell me the truth: was this your idea?"

She looked up and said, "Completely."

"Fine. Thanks for your candor. Now tell me why you did it."

* * *

Bob Tunney was right; by midafternoon the street and front yard of Didi's house was crawling with news trucks and reporters jockeying for position. Neighbors unfamiliar with such an uproar were either outside on the sidewalk taking it in from a distance, or peering from their windows, lest they be questioned about the seemingly quiet, respectable black family that was occupying Dr. Buono's home. Thinking ahead, the lawyer had phoned in the request for a police cruiser to position itself out front. He hoped that the Magnolia sheriff's deputies—who had no experience whatsoever with a media circus like the one that was shaping up— would be able to at least keep the hordes off the Diyokas' front porch.

But the lawyer also knew that nobody would be willing to leave empty-handed, not with the six p.m. news just a few hours away. So, after he'd spoken to Didi alone, he approached Dr. Diyoka and suggested the two of them address the media. "Let me do the talking," he said. "We want to give them a soundbite they can take with them and get out of here."

"If you think that's best," said the doctor.

And so, at three p.m. sharp, as Didi and her mother peered from behind the curtain of a second floor room, her father, still smartly dressed in the blue suit he'd worn to work that morning; and the lawyer, in his brown suit with matching vest, ventured onto the front porch, to where a battery of microphones awaited them. A sheriff's deputy positioned himself on the stairs that separated the two men from the assembled people and cameras.

"Hello," said the lawyer. "My name is Bob Tunney, and I am representing the Diyoka family here today. With me is Dr. Maurice Diyoka, the father of the student in question.

"Let me begin by telling you that we acknowledge a mistake in judgment has been made here by a young lady who, to this point, has been an exemplary citizen and student at Stuart High. That being said, we are leaving it to Dr. Haverstraw, the superintendent of schools, in concert with the Magnolia Board of Education, to take into consideration the extraordinary set of circumstances surrounding this incident, and come to a resolution that will allow both the Stuart High community and this fine family to resume their normal lives. I'll take a few questions, if you like."

"Where's Didi?" asked a young blonde reporter in a pants suit, signaling that the girl's name was out there in cyberspace.

"She's inside, probably reading," replied Tunney with his most winning smile.

"Is she going to talk to us?" asked a bearded man in a CNN windbreaker.

"I'm afraid not. That's why I'm here."

"Is expulsion from Stuart High a possibility?" questioned another reporter whose cameraman filmed from over her shoulder.

"I'm not aware if that's been officially mentioned by the district," said Tunney.

"Is this matter on the agenda for the board of education meeting on Wednesday?" asked an African-American reporter who resembled a young Whitney Houston.

"You'll have to ask them," said Tunney.

But the Whitney look-alike had another question: "Dr. Diyoka, how is your daughter reacting to all this?" she yelled over the other reporters.

"She's somewhat surprised," he said evenly. "This is all a bit overwhelming."

"Are you going back to Africa?" persisted the woman.

"That remains to be seen," he replied.

Figuring he'd let the interrogation go on long enough, Tunney stepped back into the fray. "That's all we have to tell you, folks," he said. "You'd do better to keep in touch with the superintendent's office. I would just ask that until this matter is resolved, you give the family some space and respect their privacy. Thank you." Gently taking Maurice by the arm, the lawyer retreated into the house. Mercifully, the first drops of a thunderstorm that had been threatening the area began plunking on the remote film cameras and other equipment that had been hastily set up on the lawn. Within seconds, a torrent of rain was unleashed that had the media people scurrying for their trucks. Figuring they had enough to file their story—at least for today—they took off, one by one.

"Did you think it went well?" said Dr. Diyoka, as his wife and daughter came downstairs.

"They're satisfied, for now," said Tunney. "Thank goodness for the rain. But I'm going to ask the sheriff to keep a patrol car out front, at least until the board of ed meeting tomorrow night."

"Do you have any idea how this will go?" asked Gabrielle, holding onto her daughter's hand.

"I have no idea," he said truthfully. "It's up to Sam Haverstraw and the board, and they've got less than thirty hours to think about it."

* * *

As Bob Tunney had said would happen, the phone kept on ringing into the night. Among the callers Maurice did speak to was his counterpart, Dr. Buono, who'd seen the latest report on CNN from the Diyokas' apartment in Kinshasa. Understandably, the American was a bit nervous about some "redneck nutcases," as he called them, trashing his house in retaliation for Didi's actions. He was somewhat relieved to learn that Bob Tunney was on the case, and that a police car was currently parked outside the residence. "How are all of you holding up?" asked Buono through a crackly connection.

"As best we can," answered Maurice. "I'm so sorry to alarm you, Doctor."

"Don't worry about me. My wife and I are doing just fine, although I don't know how you manage working under these conditions over here. I admire you, sir, and I'm sure your daughter had good reason for her actions. You stay safe, and I'll keep watching the news."

By ten p.m. Dr. Diyoka had disconnected the phone. The exhausted man and his wife sat in the kitchen, sipping a cup of tea. "Maurice," said Gabrielle, "you must speak with Dihya. She is distraught, and needs to hear from her father."

The man nodded. He knew his daughter was much closer to her mother, and that at times he could be distant, but it was time for him to "step up" as they said here in America. "I just don't know if I'll be able to find the words," he told his wife.

"You could start by telling her that you love her," she replied. "Then things should fall into place."

* * *

He found his daughter in her pajamas, reading a book. "I'm glad you're not watching television," he said, finding a seat on the corner of her bed.

"Actually, I did, for a couple hours," she confessed. "It's a bigger story around here than on cable news, where they've got global disasters and wars to deal with. But still, it's been in the mix. I thought you did a great job with Mr. Tunney out there. It must have been so difficult for you to stand in front of those people. I know how much you avoid the spotlight."

He waved her off. "It wasn't that bad. Having Bob with me was a big help."

"He seems like a good man," said Didi.

"I think he is," replied her father. He paused for a few moments. "Have I ever told you about my father, back in the Congo?"

"Very little," she replied. "I've picked up bits and pieces over the years, but I've always wanted to know the story."

"Then let me tell you. As you know, our country was a Belgian colony from 1908 until we achieved our independence in 1960. Under Belgian rule, our people were subjected to ruthless violence and economic exploitation. For example, it wasn't until the 1950s that Congolese people were granted the right to buy and sell private property in their names. Our rulers had regarded us as primitive, and tried to mold us in their own image by converting us to Catholicism and promoting Western capitalism. But the entire time, apartheid was the norm. We were regarded as second-rate citizens, to the point where we could not rise above a certain rank in law enforcement, and had to observe a nightly curfew in the major cities.

"Your grandfather, Pierre Diyoka, was a college professor who became involved in politics in the late 1950s. He was a follower of a man named Patrice Lumumba, who was the first democratically elected prime minister of our country. Although an educator, my father made it his life's mission to advance the status of the indigenous Congolese, and felt that Lumumba had the right intentions. But the colonial powers-that-be considered Lumumba too radical, and he was kidnapped and executed in 1961.

"Lumumba's successor, Joseph Mobutu, was an army colonel who seized power in a coup d'état. And although he seemed to push for Congolese self-government and tradition, and even adopted traditional names for the major cities like our home of Kinshasa, he played on his ties with Western countries such as the United States while becoming more radical himself. Your grandfather found himself caught between regimes, and was considered an outsider by Mobutu's government. And so, one night in 1980 some soldiers came to our house and took him away, and my mother and I never heard from him again. Later on, Mobutu would be forced from power, and replaced by another man who himself would be assassinated.

"I believe to this day that my father was eliminated because those in power lost sight of their mission as leaders—to unite all the people and move them forward as one nation. And that is why, Dihya, I am frightened for you. Because I see in you the same spirit that my father exhibited, the same courage. Tell me, then, so I can understand: what made you do this?"

"Father," she said, "when we first came here I was so excited about our opportunity. Here we were, in the greatest country on earth, where those who work hard can achieve success beyond their wildest dreams. But at the same time, I saw the inequities between the races, and the same kind of division that exists within the peoples of the D.R.C. I so wanted this place, and our lives, to be different. But I have encountered a culture, a mindset, that has worked to keep people of color down. Of course, this doesn't apply to everyone, and a lot of what I see isn't blatant, but it is always lurking, everywhere I turn. And that statue is, to me, a symbol of that mindset. So, I figured its removal would make a statement for everyone who felt like me. But now I find myself alone, it seems."

"You're not alone, Dihya. You have your mother and me. And no matter what happens, I can't help thinking how proud your grandfather would be of you, and how proud I am to call you my daughter."

At these words the girl flung her arms around the doctor's neck and cried, great sobs racking her chest and shoulders. "I love you, Father," she said.

"I believe 'Daddy' is more appropriate over here," he replied, in tears himself.

Chapter Eighteen

Dr. Sam Haverstraw had been the superintendent of the Magnolia School District since 1998, and had proven himself to be a politically savvy survivor through the comings and goings of different board of education regimes and school administrators. He managed to keep his job because the community at large considered him a traditionalist who was unlikely to rock the boat. Even in the face of growing public unrest over the flying of Confederate flags and the push to remove rebel statues in major Southern cities, Haverstraw had stayed the course with the Magnolia schools, his folksy, easy-going demeanor the perfect remedy when things got testy. But this statue thing at Stuart High was something else again.

He had begun fielding calls the previous morning, starting with his frantic high school principal and continuing on with his brother-in-law, who just happened to be Magnolia's mayor; dozens of concerned parents; and then the media, who were relentless in obtaining soundbites after Hufnagel had happily passed the baton to him. It became clear to the politically conscious superintendent that the national media wanted to portray Magnolia as a backward bastion of bygone days, and himself as a cornpone clown.

226

But Haverstraw was too smart to cave to the feral media types that were harassing him. He knew who was important—the mostly white parents and completely white BOE who signed his paycheck and allowed him to live in a spacious home near the lake and afford a membership at a nearby country club. And if the calls that were coming in were any indication, the local constituency wanted him to take action and quash this rebellion before it went any farther. If it were simply left to him, the Diyoka girl would have to go; heck, he'd even see to it she got into a local private school where she could quietly finish out her senior year. But first he would have to go through the motions with the board, which included soldiering through tonight's meeting. Of course, nothing would be debated among them in public, nor would a decision be announced. This gathering would simply be an opportunity for any concerned private citizens, student parents, or employees of the district to air their opinions and keep things on the up-and-up. But still, he was uneasy, because he had a sneaking suspicion that the meeting would turn into a media-driven circus. That was why he was now dialing the number of his harried high school principal.

"Tommy, this is Sam," he said. "What's the situation over there?"

"Just getting things ready for tonight," said Hufnagel, who was already on his third cup of coffee that morning. "The kids are buzzing, and there's been some discussion in the faculty lounge over it, too."

"That concerns me," said Haverstraw. "You don't expect any trouble from your people over this, do you?"

"Naw," the principal replied, the faintest waver in his voice. "Maybe you got one or two who are sympathetic to the girl, but overall the staff supports what we're doing here."

"You've met the girl's family," said Haverstraw. "What are these people like? The kind that want to stir the pot?"

"That's what's the dangedest thing," said Hufnagel. "The father's a doctor, very reserved, and the mother is quiet, too. As far as the kid, shoot, she's this little mouse who gets straight A's. I just don't get it."

The superintendent drummed a pencil on his desk. "You're not helpin' me here, Tommy," he said irritably. "I need something to go on. You're telling me that *nobody* saw this coming?"

"Nope. The good thing is, I think once y'all hand down the punishment, these people will fold their tent and quietly go away…maybe all the way to Africa."

"You'd better hope so, son," said Haverstraw, in a decidedly un-folksy tone. "Now, about the location for the meeting. I've been thinking about this, and the school's cafeteria isn't the right place to do it. Not this time."

"You sure, Sam? Heck, we can seat a few hundred in there."

Haverstraw sighed. "Tommy," he said patiently, "first of all, we never have more than a couple dozen people show up for any of these meetings, unless there's a budget crisis. Then, in case you haven't noticed, you got that big ol' Civil War mural hangin' over the room that just might get a few folks around the country agitated, especially once the liberal TV people start keying in on it. 'Cause you'd better believe the media's gonna be out in force tonight. So, to put it bluntly, you're gonna need a bigger room."

* * *

Almost immediately after Gabrielle reconnected the Diyokas' phone that morning, it began to ring. However, the first call she actually accepted was from Ellen Redwine, who was phoning in Didi's assignments, a courtesy extended to all homebound suspension students. After explaining that her husband was working a full day at Providence Heart—which she'd urged him to do so he'd have an opportunity to clear his head—she handed the phone off to her daughter, who dutifully wrote down the assignments.

"Are you okay, dear?" asked the guidance counselor.

"I'm fine, Ms. Redwine," said the girl, though she truly was not.

"Listen," the woman said, "I'm sure all of this will get sorted out after the meeting tonight, and you'll be back with us before you know it."

"I hope so," said Didi.

"I just…why didn't you come to me about this, Didi? I'm talking about before it ever happened. I feel so responsible. We could've talked this out. Was it something you saw in Charleston? Something that happened to you?"

"It's hard to explain," said Didi. "Look, Ms. Redwine, please don't blame yourself for this. It just happened. Thanks for giving me my schoolwork." She gently returned the receiver to its cradle before the distraught guidance counselor could get in another word.

* * *

Later that morning Didi was surprised to find Mrs. Woodard's name on the Caller ID screen. "Just wanted to see how you're holding up," said the art teacher.

"Not too good," she replied. "I'm trying to keep my mind off things by doing my homework, and I'm also reading that book you gave me, which is quite good...but concentrating is difficult. And I'm almost afraid to turn on the television or my computer. Mrs. Woodard, do you realize that Dr. Buono saw me on TV over in Kinshasa? It's hard to believe."

"That's our world today, Didi," she said. "People want a juicy story, and you're giving them one. Which brings me to why I called. Are you and your parents attending the board of ed meeting tonight?"

"That's the last thing we were thinking of doing. My father feels it would be too crazy, and too embarrassing for me." She could hear the teacher breathing steadily on the other end, as if measuring what to say next.

"Didi," she began, "I think it's important that you come, and your parents. I can't say why, but I have a feeling that for you to just sit home and throw yourself upon the mercy of the people who run this district is a mistake."

"You'll have to convince my mother of that," said Didi.

"Then put her on the phone."

* * *

Finally, in the early afternoon when her mother was in the shower, Didi scurried to the kitchen and put in a furtive call of her own. "I was hoping to hear from you," said Heidi, who'd secretly taken the call in the lunchroom and then sneaked off to the nearest restroom for privacy. "How are you doing, now that you're a TV star?"

"Not great," said Didi. "It's been horrible."

"Same here," said the Goth girl. "It's all anyone's talking about. Tell you what, though, your stock has really risen amongst our black schoolmates—except Tanya, that is." This remark managed to get a giggle out of Didi, who desperately needed one. "But listen…" said Heidi, turning serious. "I feel terrible about all this. I know you want to shoulder all of the blame yourself, but I was involved, too. I feel like you're getting hung out to dry."

"I already told you, this is my responsibility," Didi insisted. "If you're really my friend, you'll stay out of it, like we agreed. However, there is something you can do for me, Heidi."

"Name it."

"I'd like you to attend the board of education meeting tonight at school."

"*Me*? Why?"

"For moral support, I guess."

"Wait…you're *going*?"

"Yes," said Didi. "Mrs. Woodard called and spoke to my mom. She thinks it would be for the best if we attend."

"Jeez," said Heidi. "I mean, Woodard's a smart lady and all, but I don't know if she's right on this one. What if it gets ugly?"

"That's why I need a friend there."

For a moment there was silence on the other end of the line, and Didi had a fleeting fear that she had been abandoned. "Well," said the Goth girl, "I might as well. Hey, it's not like I had anything else important to do."

Chapter Nineteen

"Is there a football game tonight or something?" said Bob Tunney, but his feeble attempt at a joke fell flat. Indeed, the Stuart High parking lot was full of cars, mixed in with local and cable network television trucks, which sent Didi's anxiety level skyrocketing. Upon informing Tunney of their desire to attend the meeting, the lawyer had suggested driving the Diyokas in his black Nissan sedan, and the vehicle's nondescript profile was proving to be an asset as they wove their way through the lot, seeking a space.

"If you go around to the back, I know a way in," offered Didi, causing all in the car to turn and give her a look.

"Well, all right then," said Tunney, and steered towards the rear of the building. After Didi's direction, they parked the car and entered through the weight room door. Working from memory, the girl led them across the fieldhouse to the tiled hallway floor. Even from the other side of the building, they could hear the hubbub that seemed to be emanating from the auditorium area. "Figures," said Tunney. "They've moved it to a larger venue. Now, once we get close, just look straight ahead and keep walking right behind me. Don't stop to talk to *anyone*. Got it?"

"Got it," said Didi, her heart pounding. For a moment she second-guessed her decision to wear one of the traditional Congolese dresses she'd brought from Kinshasa. But it was too late to change now.

"Okay, guys," said the lawyer, "here we go." They turned a corner and approached the Stuart auditorium at a lively clip. The hallway outside was choked with people waiting to enter, but Tunney boldly cut through the crowd with the Diyokas in tow, saying, "Pardon me, excuse me, pardon me," as he plowed ahead.

For a few seconds there was confusion among the throng, until someone recognized Didi and cried, "That's her!"

"Pick up the pace, people," instructed Tunney as he led them through the center aisle entrance and down past the tiered rows of the fifteen-hundred seat auditorium. Immediately, the room, which was nearly full, started buzzing. The only seats still open were right up front, so on they went. Didi noticed that there were video cameras set up along both of the outer walls, manned by technicians with headsets and boom microphones. Cables snaked up the side aisles. She tried to look straight ahead as Tunney had ordered, but couldn't help picking out people she knew from school and elsewhere. There were some students, but mostly adults, including a lot of the teachers. Didi tried to read their expressions, but was moving too quickly. It was all a blur.

Tunney guided the three of them to empty seats in the first row of the front left section that faced the stage. The Diyokas settled into their padded theater chairs, with the lawyer standing in front of them lest anyone have the idea to invade their space.

Once Didi sat down she was able to take in the tableau that was forming on stage. There was one long table with a red cloth covering, behind which sat seven people. An older man in the middle, with a shock of snow-white hair, and wearing what was called a seersucker suit and bow tie, seemed to be in charge. To the left of the table was an American flag; the South Carolina state flag bookended the other side. As the stage wasn't too high, she was able to see clearly the faces of the seven, even from her lower angle. All of the faces were white.

A podium with a microphone had been set up facing the stage, out front between the middle seating sections. Didi did a quick turn to find the standing area in the back of the room filling with those late arrivals who couldn't find a seat. She could detect the apprehension on the faces of the board members, who despite wearing dressy clothes in preparation for the event, appeared overwhelmed by the scene unfolding before them. The meeting had been scheduled for seven p.m., but at seven-twenty people were still filing in. It was crazy.

Dr. and Mrs. Diyoka seemed to be in a trance, and Didi's heart broke for them. She was now sorry she'd had her mother talk to Mrs. Woodard.

"Could everybody please be seated?" said the older man on the dais in a syrupy drawl. "We'd like to get started, and we are behind already." In stages, the place calmed down to a constant hum. Figuring this was as quiet as it was going to get, the man said, "Ladies and gentlemen, I'm superintendent of schools Sam Haverstraw, and I'd like to welcome you to this meeting of the Magnolia Board of Education. Would y'all please rise and join us in the Pledge of Allegiance."

Didi and her somewhat confused parents followed the cue and stood as Haverstraw and the board turned and faced the American flag, their right hand over their heart. "I pledge allegiance...to the flag...of the United States of America..."

"Give me strength, God, give me strength," Didi muttered to herself as the pledge went on. At its conclusion, she sat back down with everyone else. The show was about to begin.

* * *

Sam Haverstraw looked out over the vast sea of faces and was able to determine much in a few seconds time. First, the crowd was roughly seventy per cent white, which was a good thing. However, the fact that some of these people were sporting T-shirts with Confederate flags or pro-rebel material was not. He feared that publicity-seeking agitators had infiltrated the gathering of Magnolia district parents, and this could turn out to be a problem if things got tense, especially if those agitators were aware—and how could they not be—of the media cameras lining the auditorium's walls.

Sam also noticed that those blacks who were in attendance had expressions that ranged from sullen to angry, and surmised that there were probably representatives from the regional office of the NAACP and other civil rights organizations in their midst. And finally, he spied the girl named Didi and her parents sitting with Bob Tunney. He wished Tunney's partner, Karl Leber, was there instead, as he was from nearby

Calhoun County, whereas Tunney was a Northerner and most probably felt no allegiance to his adopted state and its heritage. And so, he made some decisions on the fly and got things going.

"Ladies and gentlemen," he began, "again, thanks for coming, and for your interest in the business of our great school district. As you can see, we're packed inside here, so the key to a successful evening will be y'alls consideration and respect for each other and the process which we plan to adhere to. You might want to turn off your cell phones as well. I also want to point out to you the emergency exits that are on the left and right of the stage up front here, and the middle aisle and wings in the back.

"Originally, we had a few items on the agenda for tonight, including ceiling repairs at Hampton Elementary, and the Thanksgiving food drive at Shelby Middle. And, of course, the planning of Stuart High's fall sports award dinner, which will hopefully include the celebration of our football team's district championship." He paused as some parents in the crowd loudly applauded. "But I'm making an executive decision right here and now to table those items until our next meeting, if the board is an agreement." Immediately, the other six people at the table bobbed their heads.

"All right then, fine. So tonight we're going to address a serious situation here in Magnolia specific to Stuart High, and I'd like to begin with a report from its principal, Tom Hufnagel, so we can all be brought up to speed. Tom?"

Mr. Hufnagel, attired in a blue suit with red tie bearing the Stuart High emblem, looked uncomfortable out of the Stuart Athletics golf shirt he usually wore to these meetings. From a seat in the first row opposite Didi's, he strode to the podium and pulled out some notes. "Thank you, Dr. Haverstraw," he began. "Here are the facts. On Monday, November tenth, it was determined that the bronze bust of our school's namesake, General J.E.B Stuart, had been illegally removed from its pedestal in the school's rotunda. With the help of an informant who bravely came forward, sheriff's deputies were sent to the residence of student Diyah Diyoka to search a storage shed, where the bust was recovered, undamaged. The bust is currently being held in safekeeping at the sheriff's office in Magnolia. The student has admitted to the theft, and was issued a homebound suspension beginning that Monday morning. We are awaiting further instruction on how to proceed with any additional disciplinary action. Thank you." He returned to his seat, visibly relieved to be finished. There was a general rustling and grumbling throughout the auditorium as Haverstraw waited for Hufnagel to sit down.

"Thank you, Principal Hufnagel," said the superintendent. "The task for myself and the board is to ascertain what the next step in punishment, which Mr. Hufnagel alluded to, will be. This will not, I repeat, *not* be determined during this meeting. Rather, our gathering tonight will serve as a forum for those concerned attendees to voice their thoughts, should they feel the need to do so. And so, I'll open the floor for any of y'all to speak, one at a time, down at the podium. In consideration to others, please try to keep your comments brief."

For a few seconds there was complete silence,

and people looked around, waiting for someone to take the lead. Then, to the chagrin of those on stage, a beer-bellied man in a black T-shirt with the word HERITAGE stenciled on the front and the battle flag logo on the verso, plodded to the podium. "I just wanna say that stealin' a part of our history and insulting our fine school and our district is a serious offense and should without a doubt result in expulsion of the student!" He spun around on his cowboy-booted heel and returned to his seat amid mild applause, prompting Haverstraw to ask the attendees to please refrain from reacting to the speakers' comments. But the gates had been opened, and now it was *on*.

One by one, pro-Confederate speakers—some well-dressed and eloquent, and some with an obviously rural background—took the microphone to rail against the injustices that had been heaped upon the poor students of Stuart High. The news cameras kept rolling as the intensity level increased with every diatribe aimed at those who would besmirch the legacy of the Confederacy's fallen heroes. But it was going to get better—or worse, depending upon how one looked at it—because Peggy Farnsworth, the director of the local chapter of the Daughters of the Confederacy, felt compelled to add her two cents. From her seat up front next to both Mr. Hufnagel and her son Pierce, who was well-scrubbed and dressed for the occasion, she made her way to the podium, but not before some of the more observant people in the front rows detected a mild sway in her gait.

"Dr. Haverstraw and members of the board," she began, "as a proud member of the Daughters of the Confederacy, I see no other recourse in this matter except to expel the student for her callous show of disrespect to her school and the memory of those brave men who gave their lives for South Carolina and the cause of Southern independence." Despite some audible groans in the audience, Peggy forged ahead, a slight slurring of her words now apparent. But she was on a roll, her eyes sparkling. "I am not ashamed to tell you that I have had this girl as a guest in my home," she said, her voice rising, "and that my son has shown her nothing but kindness...but for her to blatantly turn her back on the very people who have opened their arms to her and her family—"

Suddenly, Pierce was next to her, drawing a gasp from many in the audience. "Mom," he whispered, "that's enough."

She turned, as if shocked at his appearance at her side. "Sit down, young man, and I'll let you know when I'm finished!" she hissed at him, but the microphone caught her words, and there were uncomfortable murmurs in the audience.

"Mom, you've gotta sit down, *now*," he hissed right back at her. "*Please.*" With that, he grabbed her by the arm and steered her back to her seat, where she landed with a thud.

The crowd was still buzzing when the first black speaker approached the podium with measured steps. "Hello," she said in a light drawl, "my name is Althea Woodard, and I am an art instructor at Stuart High School. And, I am proud to say, I am also a friend of my student, Didi Diyoka. I'll be brief, as I'm not used to speaking before assemblies such as this. But what I will tell you is that this girl, who comes from a fine family, had nothing but the best intentions—"

"Send her back to Africa!" yelled someone in the back, causing Woodard to pause momentarily as Haverstraw called for quiet.

"As I was saying," Woodard calmly continued, "she had nothing but the best intentions, I'm sure. However, as I have seen time and again in my years of teaching, our young people's hearts are sometimes ahead of their good sense. And I'm sure there was no malice involved in her thought process here. I'd just like to close by telling you, as someone who has really gotten to know her, that my student Dihya Diyoka is one of the most extraordinary young people I have ever had the privilege of teaching, and I ask you to consider this in making your decision. She has been a valuable addition to our student body, and I would hate to lose her. Thank you for your time." Woodard then turned to go back to her seat, but not before Didi flashed her a quick wave of gratitude.

However, the art teacher wasn't yet back to her seat when an old black woman with a walker labored to the podium, put the walker aside, and grabbed onto the podium's top, leaning on her elbows so that the microphone was almost touching her lips. "Evening, Dr. Haverstraw," she began. "My name's Lettie Taylor, and my grandson goes to Stuart High. I been sittin' in this room for quite a while, and I've got to tell you, it's gettin' hot in this place. You should tell someone to open a couple doors." There were a few chuckles in the audience. But then the woman added, "'Cause it's about to get hotter." Some muffled clapping rose from a section of dark faces on the right.

"Now, I've lived my whole life in Richland County. My daddy was a sharecropper, and his daddy was a slave, maybe on one of y'all's plantations 'round here. You might not know me because my place of residence, if you want to call it that, is just outside of town. But that doesn't mean I don't know what-all's goin' on here.

"Anyway, believe it or not, I actually got something in common with Mrs. Farnsworth over there. That's right. Just like her, I've had that girl Didi as a guest in my home. She rode her bicycle all the way out to my place so she could help my grandson with his schoolwork. And in the time she spent with us, I could see what a *fine* young lady she is."

Now there were a few uttered "tell its" and such from the black attendees that punctuated the old woman's words and gave them a sermon-like flavor.

"So," she continued, warming to her task, "here you got three schools and all of 'em have a Confederate soldier's name slapped on the side. How do you think that makes me feel? How do you think that makes *any* of us black folks feel?"

"Yeah!" shouted someone in the back.

"Anyway, what happened was, this girl from Africa comes over here and sees your nice little town for what it really is, and tries to do something about it. So, what are you threatening to do? Throw her out, of course. I'll tell you what, Haverstraw, instead of punishing her, you should be *thanking* her!"

Now there was sporadic applause, and the superintendent had to restore order. "Is there anything else, Ms. Taylor?" he asked, hoping there wasn't.

"Nope, I'm done talking," she said. "But you mark my words, Sam Haverstraw, and all you sittin' up there at that table. Things are changing. You just ain't figured that out yet!" She grabbed her walker and shuffled back to her seat, the crowd in an uproar.

"Thank you, Ms. Taylor, for your insights," said the superintendent, trying to draw things to a close before they got out of hand. "Is there anyone else who would like to—"

The girl they called Didi meekly raised her hand, and Haverstraw's eyes widened. Quickly recovering, and hoping the TV cameras hadn't caught his expression, he said, "You have the floor, miss."

Didi left her seat, her parents and Tunney looking at each other with surprise. The plan had been for all of them to keep a low profile this night. Apparently, that was not going to happen. "Might as well go down swinging," muttered the lawyer to himself.

As she adjusted the podium's microphone, Didi caught a glimpse of Heidi, sitting way to the side, giving her a thumbs-up. Then she took a deep breath and began. "Good evening, Dr. Haverstraw, members of the board of education, and everyone else here. My name is Dihya Diyoka, and I suppose I am the reason for all of this tonight. I'm sorry if coming here inconvenienced any of you.

"In August, my family moved here from the Congo, so that my father could participate in a physician exchange program. He works at Providence Heart in Columbia, helping children with heart conditions. Meanwhile, I became a senior transfer student at Stuart High.

"I've learned so much during my brief time here, about America, and about life. The education I've received in the classroom is only a small part of my experiences, but teachers such as Mrs. Woodard, Mr.

O'Toole, Dr. Zavorskas, and Mr. Pennington, my Civil War Studies instructor, have made learning both interesting and rewarding. More importantly, they have prompted me to seek information on my own, beyond the classroom. And so that's what I've done. But some of the lessons I've learned haven't been pleasant.

"I want to tell you that, from the viewpoint of someone who has come from far away, America is an extraordinary place. Here the opportunities are great, if one is willing to work hard and be persistent. But there are also negative aspects to this great country of yours. Whether you choose to acknowledge it or not, there is a distinct inequality here between the races which, I have learned, goes back to the nation's beginnings, and helped fuel the institution of slavery, which as you know led us to a great war that tore the United States apart, and whose effects are still felt in South Carolina today. I have seen traces of the past everywhere, from the hurtful words people thoughtlessly use to the racist slogans on their clothing. I've seen symbols, whether they be flags or statues, which reflect a time when my people were regarded as less than animals. And it hurts me that a country so great as America could not see this for themselves. You know, a few weeks ago on a class trip in Charleston, at the Slave Mart Museum, a man—a white man—passed me a slip of paper. On it he had written, 'A society's greatest madness seems normal to itself.' And he gave me the name of a man named Denmark Vesey, whom I researched. As it turns out, he's one of the two greatest men I've ever learned about.

"Denmark Vesey was a free black man in Charleston who put his life on the line to try to organize a slave rebellion that would release his fellow Africans from their bondage on the plantations of South Carolina, a rebellion that ultimately never occurred. And for that, he was hanged in 1832, his heroic efforts a footnote in history."

She took another deep breath. "And then, there was my own grandfather, Pierre Diyoka. He was an educator who decided that our country in Africa, which had been under Belgian colonial rule for centuries, should be free, and its indigenous citizens treated as equals by the European ruling class. But, like Denmark Vesey, he was labeled an instigator, and was taken from us in the dead of night, never to be heard from again. And so, I came to consider it my responsibility, and my destiny, to follow in the footsteps of people such as these, though I understood, as they did, that the stakes were high.

"J.E.B. Stuart, whom I've also researched carefully, was a great soldier. He was a brilliant tactician and very brave under fire, a natural leader of men. Some consider him the equivalent of a medieval knight, with his bold, dashing appearance and chivalrous persona.

"The problem is that this gifted military mind fought to defend a cause that was unjust and morally wrong. And every day when I walked into that school that bears his name, I was faced with this truth, in the form of General Stuart's statue. That gave me the idea to remove it—not so that it could be destroyed, but instead relocated to a museum where those who saw it could be presented an even-handed account of the man's life, and not worship him as some kind of false idol. Unfortunately, my plan never got that far.

"I do not regret what I did. For if it has caused *anyone* in this audience to at least rethink their beliefs, then I have succeeded where people who sacrificed far more have failed. Thank you for listening to me."

She returned to her seat where her father, tears in his eyes, patted her knee. Then someone in the audience yelled, "Nice try, but you're *still* goin' down!" and chaos ensued, with the pro-Confederate faction beginning to chant, "Send her back! Send her back!"

"Ladies and gentlemen, *please*," implored Haverstraw as the back-and-forth in the crowd escalated. He stared out at the mess, hoping that somehow, some way, he could restore order.

That's when the door at the top of the middle aisle banged open, and the people in the crowd turned to see what had caused the explosion.

Two rather large boys stood in the doorway, framed by the hallway light behind them. One was white, the other black. The white boy, who was taller, was strikingly handsome, with wavy black hair and blue eyes; while the other boy appeared to have been chiseled from stone, with long brown dreadlocks cascading to his shoulders. Both wore scarlet football jerseys with black numerals trimmed in gray. Together they walked down the middle aisle of the auditorium, followed in single file by sixty or so other young men in similar jerseys. Bringing up the rear were six coaches in red golf shirts and khaki pants.

At the bottom of the aisle the players broke off to the right and left until they formed a line facing the stage that extended from one side of the auditorium to the other. The tall white boy and his stocky partner stepped to the podium. "Good evening, Dr. Haverstraw," said the dreadlocked boy. "I'm Travis Braxton, and I am here with my brothers of the Stuart High varsity football team to visit with you." At those words a good deal of the assemblage rose to their feet and cheered.

Haverstraw smiled as the crowd's adulation washed over the young athletes. Thank God for the football team; it was something everyone in Magnolia could agree on. It was going to be all right. "We're glad to have you, boys," he said, now returned to his usual folksy manner. "And you can be sure we're all gonna be there when you whip Greenwood in the championship game!" The crowd whooped, and there were even some Rebel Yells mixed in.

"Thank y'all," said Travis, after the cheering subsided. "But the main reason we're here is, we talked amongst ourselves, and the fact is, if our friend and classmate Didi Diyoka is expelled, we're not playing."

An audible gasp rose from the crowd.

"You what?" said Haverstraw.

"We…are…not…playing the championship game. We quit."

At these words the superintendent's eyes slitted, and he looked at Hufnagel, who appeared on the verge of a coronary. Then he glanced over at the coaches, who stood with their arms folded across their chest. "Coach Kurtt," he said, "are you and your staff in support of this decision?"

Kurtt came to the podium and his captains stepped aside. "I have to go with the hearts of my boys, sir," he said. "If the young lady's expelled, the season's over." He turned and marched back to join his assistant coaches, his jaw muscles flexed as if what he'd just had to do had taken a Herculean effort.

Haverstraw drew a deep breath. It appeared that the hordes of media who'd shown up at a board of ed meeting in this tiny Southern town were getting a lot more than they ever bargained for. Somehow, he had to save face and put a halt to the stare-down with these resolute, upstart jocks. "And if the student in question is *not* expelled, gentlemen? Are you averse to the statue being returned to its place in the Stuart High School rotunda?" he asked.

Troy Winchester flashed the smile that had broken a dozen hearts and replied, "Dr. Haverstraw, I don't play for the honor of Jeb Stuart, I play for my coaches and teammates—doesn't matter if they're white, black, or purple. So as far as that statue's concerned, *you can just stick it*...anywhere you want."

Epilogue

And so, that's the story of how I stole Jeb Stuart. But that big school board meeting—which they're still talking about in Magnolia to this day—wasn't the end of things.

After they decided late that same night not to further discipline me—whether the words of myself and my supporters or the varsity football team's threat turned the tide is for you to decide—we were all able to breathe a sigh of relief.

The next day was a whirlwind. Early on, we got a call from Ms. Redwine telling us I could return to school on Friday, which she seemed genuinely happy about. And then, predictably, the TV stations and newspapers started calling, requesting my reaction to the brief statement the district put out to the media saying I'd been reinstated. I just told them I was happy to be back, and left it at that. After a couple days, the phone calls stopped. As Heidi said, "You're yesterday's news, honey. On to the next crisis!"

However, there was one call that stands out. Thursday night as we were eating dinner the phone rang yet again, which of course caused us all to groan. My mother got up and checked the Caller ID. "I'd better take this one," she said cautiously. We watched as she said,

"Yes, sir…yes, sir," a few times, followed by, "Thank you." Then she looked at me. "It's for you," she said.

"Hello?" I said.

"Hello, Dihya. I just wanted to call and congratulate you," the man said in his familiar rich baritone.

"Th…thank you, sir," I responded, almost unable to speak.

"I won't keep you long," he said. "But I want you to know that I have two daughters, and I can only hope that in their lives they will show the same courage, conviction and grace that you've demonstrated."

"Thank you," I said.

"You know," he continued, "we have a great country. But as you've learned, we're not without our problems. Sometimes it's people like you, who come to us from other places, that can give some perspective to those who just take our democracy for granted. I'm hoping that you'll stay way longer than your senior year of high school."

"I hope so, too," I said.

"Let's keep this conversation between us," he said. "But if you're ever considering stealing another statue, call me first. You know where to find me."

"Thank you, Mr. President," I said, and hung up the phone, still in shock.

I've never told anyone about this.

Until now.

* * *

Pretty quickly, things at Stuart High got back to normal, or rather, *their* normal. Jeb Stuart's bust was put back, the football team went on to win the sectional championship game (which I attended), and I uneventfully finished out the year, making the honor roll the last three quarters. The funny thing was, after the statue affair a lot of the black students who had pretty much ignored me now invited me to sit with them at lunch. And my teachers, for the most part, acknowledged my act as admirable. Even Mr. Pennington told me, "You've got guts, young lady," when we had a moment alone (he gave me an A for the course, by the way). Unfortunately, the one person who kind of faded from the scene after the board meeting was Jonathan. I guess he considered me a little too unpredictable, or maybe even dangerous. But as Heidi said, "That's his loss."

So here we are at the beginning of 2019, and though Confederate statues have started coming down in the South—they finally removed the battle flag from the grounds of the South Carolina State Capital—and some schools are even dropping their Confederate names, not much has changed in Magnolia, or at Stuart High. The football team is still king, although they have a new coach: none other than Travis "Bad News" Braxton! You see, he did fulfill his dream of earning a full scholarship to Clemson, where he was a member of their national championship team. But the shoulder problem which had begun in high school steadily worsened throughout his college career, so by the time he graduated, the National Football League passed on drafting him. Fortunately for Travis, he made the most of his scholarship, majoring in physical education and graduating on time with a teaching degree. So, when Coach Kurtt moved on to a college position at Mississippi State, Travis was hired to replace him. Of course, by this time Tanya was long gone. The last I heard she was waiting tables at the *T.G.I. Friday's* in Columbia. And, oh yes, Travis's grandmother got her hip replacement, which was arranged by my father as a thank you for her inspiring speech in my defense at the school board meeting. She and Travis still live together, but in a tidy house closer to school. I'm told he even has a serious girlfriend, whom he met at church. I wish him well.

As for Heidi, my "partner in crime," she ended up attending college at the University of California at Berkeley, which has always had the reputation of being an extremely liberal school. The last we spoke, she had graduated and was backpacking across Europe. We keep in touch through Facebook (and yes, I did eventually get a cell phone!) so she'll turn up every few months to tell me she is safe and sound. But if you saw her today you'd be shocked. Gone are her black choppy hair and vampire eyeshadow—though she does have a nose ring.

I'll bet you're wondering what happened to Pierce. His story might be the most interesting of all. You see, after the statue incident, I think he realized the hypocrisy of the beliefs his mother and her people were promoting. Much to her dismay, he quit the Children of the Confederacy and swung the other way. In fact, it was Pierce who called me to report that Seth Tomlin, who had spent his reward money on a flashy car, had shortly thereafter driven it down an embankment and into the water while out drinking with his friends one night at Pinewood Lake (he survived but the car didn't). Pierce went on to take part in anti-hate demonstrations after the Charleston church shooting, and became involved in community affairs while attending the College of Charleston. We do stay in contact, and he recently told me that he's going to use his degree in political science to go into law with the ultimate goal of becoming a state senator, which is fitting. We always did think he was a politician at heart.

And me? Well, I went on to earn my undergraduate degree from Howard University, one of the most respected black colleges in the United States, and I'm now at Duke University Medical College, for which my parents are very proud. Sadly, they returned to Kinshasa after my father's one-year exchange position at Providence Heart, because they both missed their homeland, which is understandable. I'll continue to visit them whenever my schedule permits, and maybe someday I'll persuade them to return and live with me. Because I've decided that, despite the negatives I've encountered during my time in the United States, including all the current turmoil regarding the ongoing issue of race that we have here, America is the place for me. And though I don't see myself doing anything as dramatic as the night I stole Jeb Stuart, the fact that I'll be helping others as a doctor, and hopefully instilling the correct values in my children, will have a far more lasting effect.

Because statues and flags are only objects. It's what is in our hearts that's important.

-Dihya (Didi) Diyoka, 2019

From the Author

I never thought I would write this book, but perhaps it was meant to be all along. Allow me to explain.

Ever since I was a kid growing up in Pelham, New York, I've been a Civil War geek. It all began when I paid a visit to an elderly neighbor whose grandfather had been the first doctor to assist the stricken Abraham Lincoln as he lay mortally wounded in Ford's Theater on April 14, 1865. Her stories ignited in me a passion for history that has never waned.

As I grew older there were Boy Scouts and family trips to battlefields and museums, and my devouring of all the Civil War books in my local library and at school. Later, as a young teacher, I sat with rapt attention through Ken Burns's groundbreaking documentary series, and proceeded to hunt down every Civil War documentary program that followed in its wake. But although the scope of my battlefield visits was to spread throughout the South, there was also the nagging thought that I wasn't delving deeply enough into the war's causes, focusing instead on military tactics.

By the 1990s I was teaching in an urban school district in New York that was ninety-five per cent African-American. Although I was an English instructor, I felt that my students were being shortchanged as far as black history and literature. Sure, they knew that slavery had occurred, and that a war had been fought over it until the slaves had been freed. But I wanted to go deeper. To this end, for years I taught the book *The Autobiography of Miss Jane Pittman* by Ernest Gaines and showed the companion film with Cicely Tyson. *Roots* by Alex Haley was also a valuable resource. But the piece that seemed to hit home the most with my kids was the made-for-TV film that I mention in the book, *Brother Future*, starring Phill Lewis. For some reason—maybe because my students felt a connection to the protagonist—the movie struck a chord with them. Of course, when I left the district after twelve years and moved to an affluent white community in Connecticut, I tried my best to incorporate as much black and Latino material as I could, but it was difficult and frustrating due to tight curriculum restrictions, and a sometimes lukewarm commitment in our district to become more culturally diverse.

Anyway, the Civil War was never far away from my thoughts, so when I saw my first young adult novel in the **T.J. Jackson Mysteries** series published in 2013, its setting was, predictably, Gettysburg. And in all the subsequent books of the series, the subject of race and the themes of acceptance and compassion among different groups would provide a steady thread.

Nine books later, and with my retirement from teaching after some forty-two years, my wife and I decided to drive down to our vacation residence in Vero Beach, Florida, during the summer of 2020 to avoid the risk of contracting the Covid-19 virus on an airplane. The trek down I-95, which we decided to pull off in two days, was not my first. In 1966, when my parents packed their three kids and luggage into the station wagon for our only Florida excursion (in August, no less, and without air-conditioning in the car), I had noticed remnants of the Jim Crow era everywhere, including WHITE ONLY signs that had yet to be removed—two years after the Civil Rights Act had been passed—from public facilities throughout the Southern states we crossed. These vestiges of the past were not discussed in the car, as I recall. My parents' attitude was, "That's just the way it is down here." So we pushed on to the Sunshine State, but an impression had been made. As a ten year-old, these kinds of things stay with you.

Fast-forward to 2020. Our family (including my daughter Caroline, who is now married) had done the Florida road trip once before, vowing never again to put ourselves through the drudgery of the ride. However, the pandemic had left me little choice but to do it again. That being said, this excursion for my wife and I would be the most memorable—and eye-opening—for me since that initial trip in '66.

Our plan was to stop midway in Rocky Mount, North Carolina. Well, it was not far from there on the much-traveled I-95 that my wife and I came upon an incredibly huge roadside Confederate flag, an event which was "borrowed" for Didi's class trip to Charleston. Even though the country was in the midst of the George Floyd murder's aftermath of demonstrations and rioting, so blatant a display of pro-Confederate loyalty was nonetheless disturbing. Then, on our trip home some six weeks later, further events led to the decision to write this book.

We had planned to break up the twenty-hour trip

home with stops in Charleston and Spotsylvania Courthouse, Virginia. (It is no coincidence that both of these places had Civil War ties; thus, my historical appetite would be satisfied). My wife and I had been to Charleston before, and enjoyed its genteel Southern charm. So we made the usual excursions to the City Market shops in the historical district, as well as a visit to the museum housing the Confederate submarine Hunley, which had been raised intact from Charleston Harbor in the early 2000s, and was in the process of being conserved. But then, an innocent Sunday morning stroll in the Battery Park led to a similar experience that Didi had in the book.

To our surprise, pro-Confederate and Black Lives Matter groups were heatedly clashing across the narrow roadway separating the Confederate Memorial Monument from the seawall, as the Charleston police stayed vigilant to keep things calm. The outright hatred and vitriol exchanged between the flag-waving Confederates and the mostly African-American counter- protesters was palpable. Much like Didi had done, I sidled up to a lady with a Black Lives Matter T-shirt and asked about the demonstration. "They do this *every* Sunday," she said with a sigh. We left soon after, with my wife (who had immigrated to the United States as a nine year-old) stunned that a scene like this could occur in such an upscale, touristy destination.

Then, on our second stopover, in the Civil War battlefield town of Spotsylvania Courthouse, we stayed in an Air B&B run by an African-American couple. Their setup was not typical for Air B&B, in that our bedroom and bath were smack in the middle of their house, and we would have to traipse through their kitchen and living room to get there. But any trepidation we might have felt was quickly dispelled when they invited us to join them for cocktails and dinner (it was delicious) with their extended family that first night, and suggested we stay another, as tropical storm Isaias was bearing down on the area. We gladly accepted.

This remarkable family featured three military members. The mother was a retired captain in the Army Nursing Corps; the daughter had been an Army first lieutenant who flew Blackhawk helicopters; and her husband, who was white, was a retired Marine captain and graduate of the United States Naval Academy. It was during after-dinner coffee that I related the story of what my wife and I had experienced in Charleston, which didn't surprise them. I then asked their opinion on the call for unilateral removal of Confederate monuments from public places, some of which had already occurred. Their responses were interesting. In sum, they felt that although the military skill, heroism and sacrifice of these men merited some kind of recognition, a disclaimer of some sort most definitely had to be attached to *any* Confederate memorial, so that people who visited them were made fully aware that the cause these men fought for was unjust, and their efforts misguided. In other words, pretty much what Didi said in her speech.

The issue of removing/renaming Confederate monuments, schools, et cetera, is ongoing. There are still many institutions of learning across the South that bear Confederate names. In fact, at this writing one can find *two* high schools in South Carolina named for the dashing Confederate cavalier Wade Hampton, whose statue still resides on the South Carolina capital grounds (the flag present during the protest surrounding Didi's visit was moved to the Columbia Confederate Relic and Military Museum in 2016). But things may be changing.

In the Wade Hampton High School of Greenville, South Carolina, a sixteen year-old African-American student named Asha Marie started a petition in 2017 to change the school's name, and received moderate support; one year later, a junior at the actual J.E.B Stuart High School in Fall's Church, Virginia named Julia Clark—again, a young African-American student—helped lead the fight to successfully change the school's name. These two brave girls were the inspiration for my character Didi Diyoka. But as I have learned from the Charleston church shootings, the George Floyd tragedy, and my own Southern travels of 2020, there is still a long way to go, and the Confederate legacy issue remains unresolved and contentious. One only has to look at the horrible events in our nation's capital on January 6, 2021, when rioters who stormed the Capitol Building were proudly brandishing Confederate flags.

Although Didi is a fictional character, I hope her words at the board of education hearing will resonate with those who read the book; and that we as Americans can find some kind of common ground where acceptance and understanding will ultimately win the day.

The Girl Who Stole J.E.B. Stuart
Book Club Discussion Questions

1. Which characters turned out to be different than what you first thought, and why?

2. What events foreshadowed Pierce's turnaround, and the football team's role in the story's end?

3. Discuss the similarities Didi encountered between the Democratic Republic of the Congo and the United States.

4. Have you encountered teachers like Mrs. Woodard or Mr. Pennington in your life?

5. This story takes place in 2013, but how are its events and themes relevant in America today?

6. If you had to predict Didi's future (after the epilogue) what would it include?

7. Do you have an opinion on whether reminders of the Confederacy (statues, flags, school names, etc.) should be removed from 21st Century America?

8. Why was/is the Civil War so important to American history?

About the Author

Paul Ferrante is originally from the Bronx and grew up in the town of Pelham, NY. He received his undergraduate and Master's degrees in English from Iona College, where he was also a halfback on the Gaels' undefeated 1977 football team.

Paul was an award-winning secondary school English teacher and coach for over forty years, and the first recipient of the Team Westport Community Leadership Award for promoting cultural diversity within the school district.

He has also been a columnist for *Sports Collectors Digest* since 1993 on the subject of baseball ballpark history. Many of his works can be found in the archives of the National Baseball Hall of Fame in Cooperstown, NY. His writings have led to numerous radio, television, and podcast appearances related to baseball history.

The young adult **T.J. Jackson Mysteries** series has led Paul to speak at the 150th Anniversary Battlefield Commemoration in Gettysburg, PA, and the National Baseball Hall of Fame during their 75th Anniversary celebration. He has also been a guest speaker at many secondary schools, and served as a presenter at the Westchester (NY) Young Writers High School Conference.

Paul's novel *30 Minutes in Memphis: A Beatles Story* has seen him interviewed on numerous podcasts around the world and favorably reviewed in various Rock & Roll publications.

He lives in Stratford, Connecticut and Vero Beach, Florida with his wife Maria.

Please visit Paul's website www.paulferrante author.com for information on the **T.J. Jackson Mysteries** and his other writings; also visit the **T.J. Jackson Mysteries** page on Facebook.

Books by Paul Ferrante

The T.J. Jackson Mysteries Series (Fire & Ice Young Adult Books)
Last Ghost at Gettysburg
Spirits of the Pirate House
Roberto's Return
Curse of the Fairfield Witch
The Voodoo Cult's Treasure
Terror in the Tower

Other Titles:
The Rovers: A Tale of Fenway (Melange Books-adult)
A Bermuda Triangle Love Story (The Ionian Press-adult)
30 Minutes in Memphis: A Beatles Story (The Ionian Press-teen/adult)

Rita
Trudy
Candace
Marilyn L.
Karin
Steve
Kathy Lea
D 2
Phil
Pertrinea
Vanessa

Carol Young - Graphic Artist

Made in the USA
Middletown, DE
31 August 2021